"I'M NOT LEAVING TIMBERLAKE, SO FORGET IT!"

Cliff couldn't believe what he was hearing.

"I need a place to crash for a while," Liza continued. "I'm not here because of you, Forrester, so stop thinking I'm hot for your body or something, because I'm not—even if you're hot for mine!"

"You are the most exasperating woman—"

"Oh, cool down," Liza said with an impish grin. "I think you could use some exasperation. You've gotten too comfortable up here all by yourself." She tossed her head pertly. "I've heard about you, Forrester."

"Exactly what have you heard?"

"You've got quite a reputation around town. You're a hermit or a lone wolf. Some people even think you're dangerous."

A few things began to clear up in Cliff's mind. "That's why you've come dancing in here this way, isn't it, you get your kicks out of dangerous men."

"Where I get my kicks is none of your business," she replied. "I'm curious about you, that's all. You're a mystery man, Forrester, and I love a mystery."

Special thanks and acknowledgment to Nancy Martin
for her contribution to this work.

Special thanks and acknowledgment to Joanna Kosloff
for her contribution to the concept for the Tyler series.

Published March 1992

ISBN 0-373-82501-3

WHIRLWIND

WHIRLWIND
NANCY MARTIN

Harlequin Books

TORONTO • NEW YORK • LONDON
AMSTERDAM • PARIS • SYDNEY • HAMBURG
STOCKHOLM • ATHENS • TOKYO • MILAN
MADRID • WARSAW • BUDAPEST • AUCKLAND

TYLER

American women have always used the art quilt as a means of expressing their views on life and as a commentary on events in the world around them. And in Tyler, quilting has always been a popular communal activity. So what could be a more appropriate theme for our book covers and titles?

WHIRLWIND

This pattern, which resembles a child's whirlagig toy, captures the unceasing prairie wind that was the bane of many frontier women's existence. The vivid triangles and squares dancing against a contrasting background are reminiscent of the dust devils that whipped across the untamed plains.

Dear Reader,

Welcome to Harlequin's Tyler, a small Wisconsin town whose citizens we hope you'll soon come to know and love. Like many of the innovative publishing concepts Harlequin has launched over the years, the idea for the Tyler series originated in response to our readers' preferences. Your enthusiasm for sequels and continuing characters within many of the Harlequin lines has prompted us to create a twelve-book series of individual romances whose characters' lives inevitably intertwine.

Tyler faces many challenges typical of small towns, but the fabric of this fictional community will be torn by the revelation of a long-ago murder, the details of which will evolve right through the series. This intriguing crime will profoundly affect the lives of the Ingallses, the Barons, the Forresters and the Wochecks.

Renovations have begun on the old Timberlake resort lodge as the series opens, and the lodge will also attract the attention of a prominent Chicago hotelier, a man with a personal interest in showing Tyler folks his financial clout.

Marge is waiting with some home-baked pie at her diner, and policeman Brick Bauer might direct you down Elm Street if it's patriarch Judson Ingalls you're after. The Kelseys run the loveliest boardinghouse in town, and you'll find everything you need at Gates Department Store. When spitfire Liza Baron returns to town, the fireworks begin. So join us in Tyler, once a month, for the next twelve months, for a slice of small-town life that's not as innocent or as quiet as you might expect, and for a sense of community that will capture your mind and your heart.

Marsha Zinberg
Editorial Coordinator, Tyler

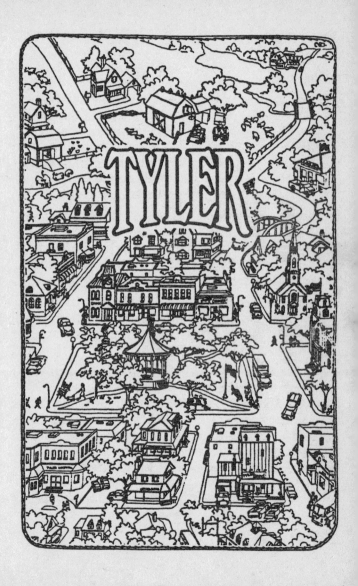

CHAPTER ONE

FAILURE DROVE Liza Baron home.

She went one cool summer night in a vintage Thunderbird convertible, the last personal possession she still owned free and clear. She started out in a rage in Chicago about midnight and drove toward no particular destination at first. It just felt good to *go,* with her hair whipping in the wind and the radio blasting rock and roll.

But around four in the morning, after aimless driving along highways she'd never known existed, Liza found herself in Wisconsin just ten miles from Tyler. After that, it was like automatic pilot. In the dark, she drove the white car up to the lake and her grandfather's lodge, which she figured would be empty. Liza didn't want to see anybody. The last thing she needed was a damned heart-to-heart with some well-meaning family member. Or worst of all, her mother.

Liza just wanted to be alone.

The sky began to lighten as she turned into the lane marked by two brick columns and started up the hillside under the canopy of century-old trees. The air was hushed. Magical, really. A dreamy white mist eddied upward from the lake and engulfed the car in a kind of swirling cloud. Someone who didn't know the road might have plunged off into the trees or blundered into the rocks, but Liza drove confidently, her heart suddenly beating fast with anticipation. The Thunderbird's tires crunched and spun in the gravel at the turns, until at last the car burst out of the mist, and the rooftops of the lodge appeared through the trees.

Timberlake, it had been called in its heyday. A grand name for a grand place—a summer house, a hunting lodge, the site of lavish prewar entertainments—and a few romantic intrigues, if the family tales could be believed. At night they used to turn on the tiny lights they'd strung through the oak trees and barbecue whatever game had been killed that day. Once there'd been a wedding on the veranda, and a swing band of ten played in the grand hall long into the night.

Liza caught her first glimpse of the lodge's twin chimneys and her throat constricted queerly. They were crumbling now, and loose shingles hung crookedly on the steep-pitched roof and five gables. She saw the sagging shutters and dozens of ghostly black windows, some with broken panes. Seeing it all for the first time in many lonely years caused a great swell of sadness to sweep up from inside Liza Baron, blinding her for a split second.

Which was when the T-bird slammed into a fallen tree.

Liza fought for control, crying out as the car thumped over a branch and crashed straight into the tree trunk that lay across the drive. The impact threw Liza against the steering wheel, knocking the breath from her body.

"Dammit!"

She killed the Thunderbird's rumbling engine with a shaky hand, and suddenly there was no sound—just the majestic, eerie silence of the forest and the forgotten lodge. The cool, soundless air enveloped Liza. The crisp scent of pine surrounded her, washing her with memories. She sat for a minute, wondering if her heart had stopped, if the whole world had ceased and she'd been transported to a magic place between heaven and earth. A place for ghosts.

But then Liza tasted blood, and she checked the rearview mirror to see how badly she'd cut her lip. The moment snapped, and she felt normal again.

"Not bad," she said to her reflection. Reaching for the door handle, she muttered wryly, "As usual, you do everything in a big way, Liza."

She got out of the car to have a look at the damage. The convertible's nose was a mess, badly dented and half-embedded in the fragrant branches of the fallen tree. Liza tottered a few steps in her high-heeled suede shoes and climbed onto the trunk of the car despite a very short skirt. Perched there, leaning one elbow against a white tail fin, she crossed her long legs, lit her last cigarette and contemplated the ruin of the lodge. And her own life.

"You're fired," Sara Lillienstein had said, rather helplessly it seemed, as she sat behind her antique desk in Chicago. "I'm sorry, Liza, but you just don't fit in here."

"But I've been doing my best work!"

"We're losing money on your projects, dear. You're just too slow when it comes to the details."

"But the details are everything!"

Sara sighed. It was an argument they'd had a dozen times before. "Take my advice, Liza, will you? Stop fighting your own personality. Take your skills to a smaller place. Try opening your own firm. Why not? You're very talented. I'm sure you'll be a success someday. But not here. At heart, you're still a small-town girl."

A small-town girl? Liza should have laughed at such a suggestion, except the whole situation wasn't funny at all. Nobody knew how desperately she wanted to escape Tyler—the town, the attitudes, the life-style and, yes, her own family. Oh, she'd cut those ties with a very sharp knife indeed, made her own way through school, scraped by in one lousy job after another until landing the right spot at the top interior design firm in Chicago. Once there, she'd fought her way into some of the best assignments.

And blown it.

Now, it seemed, her subconscious mind had brought her home. Close, anyway. The old lodge was easier to handle than the staidly elegant Victorian house in town where the whole clan was ensconced now. Yes, the abandoned lodge suited Liza's state of mind. It was big enough and empty enough to throw a first-class breakdown in, and nobody needed to know.

As the dawn grew lighter, Liza smoked her ciga-rette down to the filter and threw it into the tall grass by the edge of the lane.

"Careless, aren't you?"

His voice shattered the moment, a low growl less than three yards away, behind her. Liza whirled around and cursed, scrambling off the car to meet her assailant head-on.

"Who the hell are you?"

A dark figure stepped out of the dappled shadows. He had materialized soundlessly from the forest and stood larger than life on the drive. Having bent into the dewy grass, he'd come up with her still-smoldering cigarette, which he held out to Liza as if it were Exhibit A. "You want to start a forest fire?"

"Damn," Liza said, still instinctively clutching her fist to her chest as if to start her breathing again. "I didn't hear you coming. What did you do? Beam down from a spaceship?"

He was tall and toughly built, wearing a shabby, unzipped mountain parka over a faded black T-shirt and jeans. In one large, capable hand he carried a fishing rod and a string of slick bass, the latter dangling from his grip. With the other hand he extended the cigarette, but he might as well have been pointing a lethal weapon at her. His menacing body language said as much.

His face was arresting—sharply cut around the jaw and cheekbones, with the rest of his features blunt. A few steely-gray hairs to the left of his widow's peak blended into the remainder of his thick, somewhat shaggy dark hair, combining with the lines in his face to allow Liza to guess his age somewhere just shy of forty. He was probably ten or twelve years her senior.

It was his voice rather than his appearance that most commanded Liza's attention, however. It began as a powerful rumble deep in his chest and finished in a controlled, deceptively quiet growl. It was the voice of a man who'd never need to shout to make his point.

He said "I don't like your cigarettes in my grass, honey. In fact, I don't like you here at all, so turn your fancy car around and get the hell out, all right?"

"*Your* grass?"

"I'm in no mood for conversation this morning, so—"

"Neither am I, honey," Liza snapped. "But I'd like an explanation just the same. Who are you? Does my grandfather know you're trespassing up here?"

"Grandfather," he repeated, and something dawned in his hooded, black eyes—something akin to recognition as he looked into her face for the first time. His eyes were very dark and full of shadows, quirking at the corners as he studied her standing there in the first break of sunlight.

"I see," he said, dropping the cigarette onto the gravel and grinding it out with the heel of his boot. "I suppose you're Liza."

That surprised the heck out of her, but Liza put up a brave front just the same. "How do you know my name?"

"Educated guess," he replied, meeting her gaze again with a penetrating, sidelong look. "Your grandfather talks about you. Liza's the reckless one. The black sheep. The pain in the ass with the smart mouth."

"Well," she said tartly, "it's nice to know I'm remembered kindly in my old hometown. What else do you know about me?"

He seemed for a moment on the verge of telling her, but something held him back. He leaned his fishing rod against the passenger door of the T-bird and dug into his jeans pocket for a handkerchief. Handing it to her, he said instead, "Your lip's bleeding."

He was very tall, Liza realized in that instant. Several inches more than six feet, and his body was whip thin beneath his loose jacket. His clothes were worn, and his boots were caked with trail mud. His hands, she noticed as she accepted the frayed handkerchief, were also dirty. From fishing, probably.

Watching her dab her lip, he said, "I also know you've made a lot of people miserable in this town."

"Me? Do I look like the kind of girl who would make anyone miserable?"

He took the question as an invitation to examine Liza more carefully. With a glance that wasn't especially flattering, he studied her stretchy minidress—skintight and black, her bare legs and the fuchsia-colored spike heels she wore just to make a statement. It was the kind of outfit that made Liza feel good in the city—sexy and exciting. She was a young woman on her way up—a woman with style and ambition. At the moment, though, she was damn cold. She could feel goose bumps on her arms, and if that weren't enough to cast her in a vulnerable state, she realized her nipples were rock hard.

"You look like a tramp," he said when he'd finished his inspection.

"What are you? The local fashion expert?"

He shrugged. "It looks like you're going to a costume party, that's all."

"At this time of day?"

He gave her a thin, unamused grin. "From what I hear, you'd go to a party at the drop of a hat. That getup is sure to win first prize, if you ask me."

"Well, I didn't ask, buster. Just who the hell are you, anyway? What gives you the right to—"

"I'm Cliff Forrester," he said. "The lodge caretaker."

"Obviously, you've been doing a great job," she cracked, indicating the time-damaged facade of the lodge with an exasperated wave of his handkerchief. "Besides the fish, exactly what are you supposed to be taking care of?"

"That's between me and your grandfather," he retorted, dropping his voice into the rumbling register again. "Are you hurt?" he asked then. "Besides the lip, I mean?"

Liza examined his handkerchief and saw a dime-sized splotch of dark blood staining the frayed linen. "I'm okay, I guess. Except for this. Am I going to need stitches, do you think?"

With one hand, he reached out and roughly grasped Liza's chin. As if catching himself, he was gentler as he slid his fingertips along her jaw and tilted her head higher, stepping close to have a look.

At that instant, a feeble ray of sunshine pierced the tree branches overhead, and Liza closed her eyes against the sharpness of the light. In a heartbeat, a funny feeling stole over her. Standing there with his callused hand cupping her face, she realized she could hear Cliff Forrester breathing, and the warmth of his lithe body seemed to pull her like a magnet. Though a whole world pulsed around them, Liza felt as if the universe had narrowed to only two people.

She peeped one eye open to look at him again. For an older guy, he wasn't bad to look at. Just too damn serious. In her mind's eye, she tried to conjure up a mental image of how he might appear with a genuine smile on his face. Or how his laugh might sound. But Cliff Forrester didn't seem the kind of man who did a lot of laughing. A tightness in his face told Liza he hadn't lived an amusing life. The years had been hard on him. Maybe harder than Liza could imagine.

He could dish out abuse, though, and Liza almost smiled at the thought. She wasn't afraid of him, of course. Liza Baron wasn't afraid of anything. But she felt uneasy in his presence just the same. As if unworthy.

"Nope," he said, releasing her as casually as he'd touched her. "No stitches. At least, I don't think so. What's wrong? Are you cold?"

She had begun to shiver. Liza told herself it was her abbreviated dress that wasn't up to the challenge of a Wisconsin morning, but another thought flitted through her mind: perhaps Cliff Forrester had the power to make her shiver, too.

Abruptly, she said, "Nothing's the matter. I'm leaving, anyway, and the car heater's still working. Could I trouble you to help me with the car? Or must you hurry back to your caretaking duties?"

"I have a few minutes," he said, ignoring the taunt in her question.

"What's this tree doing here in the first place? Isn't it your job to clear it away? Somebody could get hurt running into it."

"Nobody ever comes up here."

"What am I? Chopped liver?"

He tied his string of fish on a nearby branch and sauntered back to the car, stripping off his jacket as he came. "You could have been chopped liver if you'd been driving any faster. What was the rush, anyway? I heard the car from the lake and got to the boathouse in time to see you ram this tree like you wanted to push it into the next county."

"I always drive like that."

"Like an idiot, you mean?"

"Look, Forrester, why don't you go jump—"

"Put this on," he commanded, dropping his jacket across her shoulders, "before you freeze. Why a grown woman would wear a dress like that—"

"There's nothing wrong with my dress!"

"You must have left half of it at home, that's all."

"If you don't like it," Liza said, fed up at last, "I'll take it off."

Cliff had heard a lot about Liza Baron in the ten years he'd lived in Tyler. She'd hightailed it out of town after high school and returned only a couple of times before a conflict with her mother drove her away, leaving behind a long litany of stories that celebrated her wild ways.

She was as beautiful as everyone said, he'd admit. As beautiful as her legendary grandmother. Nearly six feet tall in her heels and lean as a greyhound, she had the look of a cover girl right down to the damn-you gleam in her eye. Her platinum hair was an astonishing tangle, and her face had an oddly asymmetrical quality he couldn't seem to take his eyes off. Her cold blue gaze challenged his, her patrician nose seemed perpetually upturned in a cocksure attitude and her slightly off-center mouth, a flaw that was accentuated by the ragged little cut on her lower lip, was...well, mesmerizing. She moved constantly, too— tapping her toe, swinging the mane of her hair over her shoulders or flipping it back from her forehead with an impatient hand.

Her earrings caught the morning light and glittered. From one ear dangled a golden angel with a glinting glass eye, but from the other ear swung a larger figure—that of a devil carved out of onyx. Oh, Liza was devilish, all right. But she seemed to be trying awfully hard to keep that bad-girl facade in place.

So Cliff wasn't surprised when she let his jacket slip off her shoulders and started to peel off her dress.

He stopped her by grabbing one slender wrist just as she began to yank the dress. She looked up, feigning surprise.

"Take it easy," he said, determined not to let the vixen ruffle him. "If you die of exposure, it'll be me who has to answer a bunch of questions."

Her gaze burned into him with the power of a hot laser. "I'd hate to trouble you."

"Then keep your clothes on." He released her wrist and turned away. "Let's see what's wrong with the car."

A moment later she followed him around the convertible, quite composed and haughty. "You must be a pretty handy fellow to have around, if my grandfather hired you."

"I do what I can." He kicked some branches away from the hood of the convertible and bent over the mess to check on damage.

"Do you see him often? Granddad, I mean?"

"Now and then." Cliff examined the damage to the car's grille and headlights.

"Does he come out here?" she asked, standing behind him on the gravel. Her voice sounded casual. Maybe too casual.

Cliff glanced up at her. "Nope."

She quickly mastered her expression, endeavoring to look unconcerned. "Does he look well? I mean...is he healthy?"

"What is this? Twenty questions? He's your family, not mine."

She flushed. "I haven't seen him for a while, that's all."

"Three years, right?"

Her pouty mouth popped open, then snapped shut quickly as she covered her surprise. Her glacial eyes narrowed. "Exactly how do you know so much about me, Forrester?"

"I wish I could say that I get around a lot, but stories about the infamous Liza Baron are repeated all the time." Cliff crouched by the front tire and pushed back the tree branches to get a better look under the car. "Even I've heard the one about how you spiked the punch at the homecoming dance. People still can't figure out how you did it—and got crowned homecoming queen in the same hour."

She shrugged. "I hid the bottle in my underpants until the time was right."

"Hmm," said Cliff, guessing that she'd said that just to see his reaction. He chose to ignore the lie and said, "The fender's bent pretty badly. It'll cut the tire if you try to move the car."

She leaned over his shoulder. "Can't you yank the fender out a little? I've got a tire iron in the trunk, I think."

"It'll ruin the fender."

"Do it anyway," she said blithely, bending over the closed door to tug the keys out of the ignition. Cliff couldn't stop a glance down the amazing length of her bare legs, but she pretended to be unaware of his scrutiny. She straightened and led the way to the trunk with a taunting sashay, saying, "It's good to know people still think of me now and then. My mother hasn't poisoned everyone against me."

Suddenly on guard, Cliff said, "Why would your mother do that?"

"We're estranged. That's a polite word for hating each other."

"I know what it means."

"We don't communicate. Haven't spoken for years."

"And you're proud of that?"

Liza snapped open the convertible's trunk. "It's a fact of life in our family. My mother despises me."

"Alyssa Baron couldn't despise anybody."

Liza looked up from rummaging in the trunk and skewered him with those clear blue eyes of hers. "You know my mother?"

"We're acquainted."

"You talk about me with her?"

"Any mention of your name," Cliff said, "causes her pain." He took the tire iron from her hand, and with care added, "And I wouldn't hurt Alyssa for anything."

"Alyssa, is it?" Liza asked, her beautiful face suddenly stiffening with a frozen sort of smile. "My, my. You're a little young, aren't you?"

"For what?"

"For squiring her around town these days. I mean, she's almost fifty—"

"My relationship with Alyssa is completely pure, I assure you, Miss Baron. We're friends, that's all."

Cliff didn't owe anyone an explanation for his tie to Alyssa Baron, the one person in the world he could stand to spend any time with these days. Alyssa's quiet acceptance, her unspoken support, her— Well, there were many qualities in Alyssa Baron that Cliff appreciated deeply. Qualities he didn't see in Liza at all.

Liza eyed him with one brow raised coldly. "You don't strike me as the Garden Club type. And I bet you don't sit on her precious hospital board, either. Which one of her bleeding-heart causes do you have in common, I wonder?"

"We're friends," he repeated.

"Oh, that doesn't surprise me. She's been very friendly with all kinds of men since my father died."

"I don't think I like your implication, Miss Baron."

"Truth hurts?"

He laughed shortly and turned away. "I can see that everything I've heard about you is true. You find a weak spot and attack, don't you?"

"Have I found your weak spot, Forrester?"

He chose not to answer that and returned to the front fender. "'Liza's always looking to make people uncomfortable'—that's what your mother says, at least. Is that your way of getting attention, I wonder?"

She gave an unladylike snort. "In my family you have to practically die to get some attention. You must know my brother and sister, right? Both bright, shining examples of wonderfulness?"

"They're well respected, I hear. And you're not. So? Do you get your share of the family limelight by acting like a spoiled starlet?"

"Boy, who put the chip on your shoulder?"

He yanked the twisted fender with the tire iron. "Just don't try muscling me the way you muscle the rest of your family, okay? I don't give a damn if you go away and never come back—unlike your mother."

"What's that supposed to mean?"

"Nothing. Expect maybe you'll find she's glad you've come home."

"I haven't come home," she said quickly. "I'm just passing through. I may not even stop at the house. I don't want to see them."

He heard a new note in her voice and glanced up to see Liza frowning. "Scared?"

"No!"

Cliff laughed at the swiftness of her exclamation. "Yeah," he said. "You're scared, all right."

"Who died and made you the Seer of All Things?"

Cliff didn't care to talk about himself. Why had he managed to find a pleasant isolation at this forgotten lodge if he wanted to spill his guts all the time? He didn't. His past was his own business, and he could take as much time as he liked forgetting it. So he kept his mouth shut, which infuriated the pretty Miss Liza Baron.

As he worked on the fender, she said, "You're really annoying, you know."

"Because I won't play your game?"

"I don't play games!"

"Oh, yes, you do."

"I'm completely up-front with everyone. I—"

"Like hell. You make everyone jump through hoops to prove how much they love you." Cliff stood up and looked her straight in the eye. "Well, you can needle me all you like, Miss Baron. I'm not going to jump."

She leaned her backside against the car and crossed her long legs at the ankles, returning his glare with a measuring gaze. She raked her blond hair back with the manicured fingers of her right hand. "You like calling the shots, don't you, Forrester?"

"I like being my own boss, yeah."

"You like being in control."

He wiped his hands on his jeans and said, "I don't like surprises, that's all."

"Oh, really?" She began to smile wickedly. "Sometimes surprises can be nice."

"Most of the time, surprises can be damned annoying."

"Tsk tsk. What a boring attitude about life."

"How I live my life is none of your business."

"Want to know what I think?" she asked.

"Not really."

"I think you could use a few surprises now and then, Cliff Forrester."

With that, she came away from the car with a fluid motion and caught the front of Cliff's shirt in her hand. Her grip tightened, and she tugged, pulling him close enough to kiss. Her face was almost level with his, and her laughing blue eyes teased him boldly. Suddenly Cliff could smell the sweet fragrance of her perfumed hair and feel the lithe strength of her legs against his.

She said, "How about one right now?"

She didn't wait to be kissed, but lifted her mouth up to his and caught his lips swiftly. She tasted crisp and warm, and when she slanted her mouth across his, Cliff felt his senses quicken. His blood was suddenly tingling everywhere, a tide of heat beating hard in all his nerve endings. Liza's tongue found his and played a mischievous game for a moment. Sensations Cliff had thought were long gone came bubbling up from a secret place deep inside, and surprised the hell out of him, all right. Standing there in a shaft of sunlight with the vibrant young body of Liza Baron pressed provocatively against him, Cliff felt his mind go blank. And his body come alive.

Then it was over. She loosened her grip on his shirt, leaned back and tilted her head to look him saucily in the eye. The lazy pleasure that shone in her gaze exactly matched the expression on the face of the little devil that swung from her earlobe.

"See?" she breathed. "A surprise can be very nice."

Sometime in the past ten seconds, Cliff's hands had found their way to her arms, and he held her very tightly. From between clenched teeth, he said, "You take a lot of chances, don't you?"

"I like to feel good."

"You like playing with fire, I think. I wonder if you've ever been burned?"

He couldn't stop himself. Her cocky smile, the tease in her eyes, the supple contour of her body—yes, all those things combined to trigger an inexplicable anger in Cliff. He found himself gripping Liza hard, pulling her close and kissing her with every ounce of pent-up energy inside himself.

With a sigh, she gave herself to him, abruptly relaxing in his arms. One of her knees eased between his two, and her hands crept slowly around Cliff's neck as the kiss deepened into a hot and savory contact.

But Cliff didn't want her relaxed. He knew her game and intended to change the rules. Swiftly, he tightened his grip on Liza and forced her back against the car. She squirmed and choked on a protest. She clutched his shoulders for balance and then fought the kiss like a wildcat. Roughly, Cliff pushed her mouth open and ravaged her tongue with his own. He could feel her breast quiver against his chest, and her breath came in gasps.

Then he tasted blood.

At once, Cliff let her go. His stomach churned, and he found he was trembling as he stepped back.

Liza sat up on the car, hastily straightening her tiny dress where it had slipped low on one of her breasts. There was blood on her lip again, a bright droplet where he'd been kissing her a moment before.

"What was that for?" she asked shakily, lifting her hand to her lip and staring at the blood that came away on her fingertips.

"I don't like being manipulated, Miss Baron."

She looked up, blue eyes widening. "I wasn't manipulating you. I just thought—"

"You couldn't get under my skin verbally, so you tried the next best way to get a reaction out of me." Cliff half turned away, angry with her and disgusted with himself. "That was a stupid trick," he snapped. "It could have gotten you into a lot of trouble."

"I don't think so," she said, studying him with an unnerving solemnity. "You're not as tough as you pretend to be."

He cursed under his breath—half at himself for reacting to her ploy. He was shaking inside.

"In fact," Liza said quietly, watching as Cliff worked at pulling himself together, "I'm beginning to think we're a little alike."

He laughed shortly and shook his head. "There's a fundamental difference between you and me, Miss Baron."

"Which is?"

"You're a born fighter. You like to get a rise out of people and make them angry. You feed on conflict. Hell, you're at war with the whole world!"

"And you?"

Cliff turned away, suddenly wishing he was alone again. "Me," he said, "I've given up."

CHAPTER TWO

IF SHE'D HAD enough nerve, Liza would have asked him a dozen questions then. But the memory of his ferocious grip and a kiss that had been clearly born of anger, not attraction, along with the shuttered expression on Cliff Forrester's taut face, told Liza she'd better keep her mouth shut. For once, she listened to the voice of common sense in her head.

He didn't give her a chance to work up more courage, either. Curtly asking for her car keys, he got behind the wheel and tried the Thunderbird's engine. It started, but the rattling sound that immediately rose from under the hood prompted him to shut off the ignition at once.

Still behind the wheel, he considered the problem for a long moment, during which he appeared to fight with his own feelings. "I'll drive you into town," he said eventually, looking as if he'd rather subject himself to the Spanish Inquisition than prolong his time with Liza. "You can hire a tow truck at the garage."

Liza quailed at the thought of going into Tyler. Now that she was so close, she suddenly wanted to put a lot of distance between herself and her old hometown. Trying to conceal her anxiety, she said, "Can't you fix my car?"

Forrester got out of the car. "From the sound of that engine, the damage is beyond my skills. You'll need a real mechanic. I'll go get the truck and take you to a garage."

Liza noticed how tight his jaw was. But there were other signs that he wasn't quite in control of himself. His hand might have shown a tremor when he closed the car door. And the set of his shoulders gave away something Liza couldn't quite pinpoint.

The man was peculiar, all right. One kiss had clicked an emotional switch in him. One minute he'd let passion overwhelm him. Then he'd looked positively shaken by what had transpired. Now, the prospect of driving her to town seemed to fill him with loathing.

Insulted, Liza said, "Don't do me any favors, Forrester. I'll hitchhike to the nearest garage."

"In that getup?" he said as the color began to return to his face. "The only drivers on the road this morning will be farmers, and none of them will risk picking up a hot number like you."

"A hot number?" Liza repeated, amused. "Now, that's a blast from the past. We're called women today, Forrester."

"The gossips around town would call you a hot number," he retorted, turning to grab his fish and leave.

"I don't know which is worse," Liza called after him, "showing myself to the gossips of Tyler or spending the next twenty minutes with you."

"We don't have to talk," Forrester said over his shoulder. "You could take a nap instead. Looks like you could use it."

Liza considered throwing something at him as he walked away, but nothing was handy.

When he was out of sight, she snatched his jacket off the ground and said, "It was just a kiss, for crying out loud. There's no need to get all bent out of shape!"

Liza wasn't quite sure why she'd done it. The man had looked like he needed shaking up, that was all. She hadn't meant to manipulate him with the kiss. Not exactly. Kicking the T-bird's tires, Liza frowned, wondering for an instant if he was right. Did she like conflict all the time? Had she kissed Cliff Forrester just to stir up trouble? And why did she feel so damned stirred up herself around him? His rumbling voice gave her goose bumps.

Or maybe it was just the cool morning air. Shivering suddenly, Liza put the jacket back on.

He reappeared a few minutes later, materializing like a ghost out of the shadows.

"Damn!" Liza jumped. "Do you have to do that?"

"Do what?"

"Sneak up on a person like that!"

Forrester didn't answer, but tossed a thick sweater at her. "Here," he said. "Put this on before you go into shock."

"I'm fine."

"Yeah, right. You want me to run you to the hospital so somebody can take a look at that cut on your lip?"

"It's just a scratch, for heaven's sake." She handed him his jacket.

He seemed on the verge of saying something else, but hesitated. A moment later, he shrugged. "Have it your way. The truck's out back."

Liza followed him around the lodge, simultaneously pulling on the long sweater and trying to stay on her feet as her narrow heels sank into the soft earth. The sweater reached her midthigh, two inches higher than the hem of her miniskirt, but it was wonderfully warm.

The truck turned out to be the same rusty old pickup Liza remembered from her youth—the vehicle her grandfather had used for hauling yard trimmings away. The idea of getting into it with an unknown quantity like Cliff Forrester made Liza a little nervous, but she decided to brazen it out.

"This old thing is still running?" she asked, yanking open the passenger door.

"I don't use it much."

"Oh, you have a car of your own?"

"No, I just don't drive often." He got in and slammed his door.

Liza did likewise. "Are you some kind of hermit, Forrester?"

"What's wrong with being a hermit?"

"Not a thing," she replied tartly, "if you like living alongside birds and skunks and chipmunks—"

"In the peace and quiet, you mean?"

"Is that a hint for me to shut up?"

"If I wanted you to shut up, I'd have told you," he said, turning the key in the ignition. The engine spluttered and caught with an unmuffled roar. "Hang on tight," he advised over the noise of the truck.

There were no seat belts in the old pickup, so Liza did as she was told.

Forrester drove carefully down the narrow road that wound through the trees from the lodge, the truck bouncing roughly in the potholes despite his caution. When he hit the highway at the bottom of the long driveway, he didn't pick up speed but continued to drive the noisy truck very slowly. His prudent driving might have annoyed Liza under most circumstances, because she liked to get where she was going without dillydallying. But this morning she was in no rush to get to the town where she'd grown up. The thought of setting foot in Tyler made her very nervous. Unconsciously, she started chewing her thumbnail—an old habit she'd never broken completely.

"Look," she said when they headed west on the highway with the sunlight streaming after them, "maybe there's a better garage in Bonneville. Why don't you turn around and go the other way?"

"Don't worry so much," said Forrester, not taking his eyes from the road. "Maybe you won't see anybody you know."

"I'm not worried about that! It's my car, that's all. It's a delicate machine. It needs expert care."

"Like the kind of care you were giving it when you ran over that tree? Don't try to snow me, please. It's obvious you're scared to death about going home again."

"I am not!"

"Why did you come back to Tyler if you didn't really want to see your family?"

"It was a mistake," Liza said, turning sulky. She looked out the window at the passing scenery—the lush pastures punctuated by stands of tall, Wisconsin trees. Sunlight was just starting to sparkle on the dew, turning the landscape into a dazzling green carpet.

Half to herself, Liza said, "I—I didn't mean to end up here. It just happened. I was driving around."

"What for?"

"I was mad! I was—oh, what do you care?"

"Mad about what?"

Liza sighed and leaned against the window, propping her fist against her chin. Despite her instinct to keep the facts secret, she said, "I quit my job."

"Quit?" Forrester shot a look across at her.

"All right, I was fired. Satisfied?"

"How come you got fired?"

"It's a long story, and the ending isn't very interesting. I'm broke, to tell you the truth. The lease on my apartment expired last week, and the landlord changed the lock. Can you believe it! The old coot won't give me my clothes until I pay the rent!"

"That explains the outfit, then," Forrester said wryly. "It was the only thing you could get from the Salvation Army, right?"

"Who asked you for an opinion?"

He didn't react to her anger, but continued to drive along the pasture fences. "Why don't you just pay your rent?"

"I told you. I'm broke."

"A grown woman like you can't balance a checkbook?"

"It's not that simple," Liza said. "I'm an interior designer, see? I really wanted my last job to turn out great, so I...well, I kicked in a few bucks of my own. It messed up my cash flow."

"What did you do that for?"

"Because I wanted the job to be wonderful! You see, it was this great executive office—overlooking Lake Michigan, marvelous sunlight all day, this beautiful view from a dozen floor-to-ceiling windows—everything! I made the place look terrific. Everybody said so. It needed a sculpture, though, to finish the concept. An artist friend of mine had the perfect piece—this mother and child thing that's great—emotional, you know? Erotic, too, in a way that was very sophisticated. It was perfect for the office, and my friend needed the money very badly. So I—"

"So you spent your rent money on a sculpture that you're never going to see again."

"It's not like that!"

Liza remembered the whole scenario in detail, but doubted she could make Forrester understand. Her artist friend, Julio Jakkar, had needed the money to finance a trip to a drug rehab clinic. Julio was ready to make it work this time, he said, but he'd refused Liza's offer to pay for the treatment outright. Buying one of Julio's pieces had seemed like the perfect solution to his problem. Except Liza hadn't counted on losing her job a few days later.

She couldn't make a tough loner like Cliff Forrester understand the complexities of a friendship with a sensitive, vulnerable guy like Julio, though.

On another sigh, she said, "I just had to do it, that's all."

"So now you've got no apartment and no job."

"I'm not running home to my mother, if that's what you're thinking! I've been in scrapes before. I can get myself out of this one."

"Sure," said Forrester.

"I'd never run to my mother for help, anyway. She's got troubles of her own, in case you haven't noticed."

"She's stronger than you think."

"*I'm* stronger than everybody thinks!"

Forrester didn't say a word at that, and Liza pretended to be interested in the passing scenery. Things hadn't changed much, she noticed sourly. People still treated her like a rambunctious child.

Other things hadn't changed, either. The same farms still stood along the road to Tyler, with even the same names painted on the mailboxes. German names and Swedish names, mostly. Old families that could trace their family trees back to the first settlers.

The history of Tyler was much like the history of other small towns in Wisconsin. Founded 140 years ago by German immigrants who fled autocratic rulers in their native land, the original town was called Tilgher, after one of the founding families. Years later, the name was anglicized to Tyler by an impatient official from the land office who couldn't pronounce the German word. Swedish immigrants followed the Germans, each family paying ten dollars to receive 160 acres of farmland.

One such Swedish immigrant had been Gunther Ingalls, who took his family by wagon train to his parcel. On the rugged trail, he stopped to help an Irish immigrant mend a broken wagon wheel. Jackie Kelsey and Gunther Ingalls became friends over that wheel and proceeded to Tyler together, where they split Gunther's acreage into two small farms. In the century that followed, the Kelsey family and the Ingalls family flourished side by side. And sometimes feuded, too.

Now Liza's grandfather, Judson Ingalls, was hailed as the town's most prominent citizen. Known by most of the citizenry as the venerable, though sometimes crotchety owner of Ingalls Farm and Machinery Company, Judson Ingalls commanded respect in Tyler. As his granddaughter, Liza had felt watched all her life—like a bug under a microscope. Every twitch she made was news to the townspeople of Tyler.

As the truck rumbled past the elementary school playground and inside the boundaries of Tyler, Liza found herself automatically watching the streets for her grandfather. Judson's tall frame, his distinctive long-legged, slope-shouldered walk and shock of white hair—Liza expected to see him on the next street corner. He was as much a part of Tyler as the picturesque Victorian houses on Elm Street or the stately central square lined with the town hall, the old post office, the Fellowship Lutheran Church with its pretty facade and Gates Department Store. Even Marge's Diner—tucked on a side street just off the town square—didn't seem as much of a landmark as Judson Ingalls himself.

Liza realized she was holding her breath as Cliff Forrester drove through the intersection of Main and Elm Streets. She couldn't stop a cautious peek up the tree-lined boulevard where she had grown up. The huge Victorian home where she'd played as a child was obscured by a pair of giant elm trees, and Liza was glad she couldn't see the house. It might be too painful. And she didn't want to alert her mother that she'd come home. No use giving up her advantage.

As if guessing what was on her mind, Cliff Forrester said, "Want me to drive by the old place?"

"Heavens, no!" Liza collected herself, not wanting to reveal how stirred up she felt, arriving in Tyler
for the first time since her last monumental blowup
with her family. She said crisply, "Just take me to the
nearest garage, please."

Forrester leaned out the window to check the clock
in the tower on the bank. "It's only seven o'clock," he
noted. "I'll bet Carl's garage is still closed."

Exasperated, Liza snapped. "Small towns! Haven't
all-night business hours reached the provinces yet?"

"We're not used to wild girls driving their convert-
ibles around in the wee hours, I guess."

"What about some breakfast?" Liza proposed,
sitting up straight in the seat as the thought struck her.
Anything to avoid stopping at her mother's house!
Manufacturing some eagerness, she said, "Does
Marge still make those yummy blueberry pancakes?
We could go to the diner and have something to eat—
coffee, sausage, the works! Do you know how long it's
been since I had real Wisconsin sausage? Let's go. My
treat. I'm starved."

Obediently, Forrester whipped the wheel over and
made a slow U-turn on Main Street, aiming for a lucky
parking space right in front of Marge's Diner. He
slipped into the spot and put the truck in park. But he
didn't shut off the engine or make a move to get out.

"You go ahead," he said, keeping both hands on
the wheel.

"What?"

"Go get some breakfast. You can walk over to Carl's when you're finished. You know where his garage is?"

"What is this?" Liza demanded on a laugh. "A brush-off?"

"Go eat," he said stubbornly.

"Look, Forrester, I'm sorry." Firmly she said, "I'm sorry about that little scene back at the lodge. Maybe I *was* trying to manipulate you. I can't help it sometimes. It's a habit, I guess. I can be pretty brassy, and I shouldn't have pushed you—even if it was a pretty good kiss. But I'm willing to put the whole business behind me if that's what you want. What do you say? If you were going to eat those fish, here's a chance for something better. I'll buy you a real breakfast and we'll forget it happened."

"I thought you were broke," he said, looking out the window to avoid meeting her eye.

Liza laughed. "Well, I've got twenty dollars left, I think. Plenty for a couple of orders of pancakes. Come on."

He shook his head mulishly. "I have work to do."

"Like what? More fishing? Look, I'm trying to make it up to you! Come on."

"No, thanks."

"For Pete's sake, Forrester, what's the big deal?"

He turned to Liza and put his hand out, but didn't meet her eye. "It's been an education meeting you, Miss Baron."

"You could call me Liza, at least," she said dryly, not accepting his handshake, but impudently folding her arms over her chest instead. "I think we got to know each other well enough for that, don't you? I mean, that was one hell of a kiss you gave me."

"I'm sorry about that," he said, turning back to determinedly stare out the windshield. "I was annoyed and took it out on you. Let's forget it."

Liza couldn't believe her ears. "That's it? You're throwing me out of the truck and saying goodbye?"

"It's nothing personal—"

"Nothing personal! I like that! Fifteen minutes ago you were kissing the stuffing out of me, and I've caught you looking at my legs—don't deny it! So you can't just say goodbye like this."

"Miss Baron—"

"Liza!"

"All right, Liza!" he said, temper snapping. "I'm not hungry, get it? And I've got things to do, dammit!"

"Like what?"

"Just get the hell out of my truck, will you?"

"It's not *your* truck—"

"I've got more right to it than you do, so *get out!*"

Furious, Liza shoved open the passenger door. "You can't get rid of me so easily, you know! I've got to go back to the lodge to get my car. And don't try hiding in the trees when I come, Forrester! You won't get away with that!"

"Goodbye!" he barked as she got out of the truck.

"Good riddance!"

Liza slammed the door of the truck and stood breathing hard on the sidewalk while he pulled out and and drove back down Main Street without even waving in the rearview mirror.

"Jerk!" Liza shouted after him.

The door of Marge's Diner opened behind her, and
a man stepped out onto the sidewalk. He was tall and
white-haired, and he squinted in the bright sunlight.
"Mary Elizabeth?" he demanded.

She spun around. "Granddad!"

Judson Ingalls stood under the canvas awning of the
diner, fingering a toothpick and glaring up the street
after the departing truck. Without further greeting, he
said, "Was that Cliff Forrester?"

"Yes." Liza strode to his side, absurdly happy to see
her grandfather in the same old jeans and flannel shirt
he had always worn despite his position of respect in
the community. He looked just the same as ever—a
gnarled but strong oak of a man with a sun-bronzed
face, commanding Ingalls eyes and the firm Swedish
jaw of his ancestors. "Oh, Granddad, I can't believe
how wonderful it is to see you!"

Judson said, "You shouldn't be hanging around
with a man like that, Mary Elizabeth."

She laughed and reached for her grandfather with
both hands. "I'm back in town for the first time in
three years and already you're criticizing the men I
see? Granddad, how about a hug?"

Avoiding the hug with a firm grip on Liza's shoul-
der, Judson met her eye at last and said abruptly,
"That Forrester fellow is dangerous, Mary Elizabeth.
You shouldn't be with him."

Liza faltered. "Dangerous?"

Judson's brow was thunderous. "The man's violent—a crazy Vietnam vet who's still screwed up. Why,
I'm surprised he even spoke to you. Usually he avoids
people completely."

"He was in Vietnam?"

"Vietnam or Cambodia or some such place. You stay away from him, my girl. I don't want you getting hurt by some fanatic! Keep away from Cliff Forrester, you understand?"

Liza blinked in confusion, hardly able to digest the information. But in the next second her grandfather gave Liza a big bear hug and turned hearty.

"What are you doing in town?" he demanded, laughing as he kissed her cheek and tweaked her chin. "You're looking prettier than ever."

Liza gave him a shaky smile and allowed herself to be drawn into the diner for some breakfast. All hopes of slipping out of town without meeting anyone from her past evaporated as Liza was greeted by half a dozen of her grandfather's cronies. She should have known they'd all be having breakfast in the diner. Some things never changed.

Liza also recognized several familiar faces from her youth. Rose Atkins, the elderly lady known for riding her oversize blue tricycle all over town when Liza was still in high school, gave a cheery wave from a corner booth where she sat having breakfast with Tisha Olsen, the longtime owner of her own beauty salon, the Hair Affair.

"Why, it's Liza!" cried several voices.

"Judson, who's that darling little girl with you?" demanded one old gentleman. "That's not Alyssa's youngest, is it?"

"Sure is," Judson called back, casting his arm across Liza's shoulder. "She's grown up taller than her daddy, don't you think? Take a seat here, Mary Elizabeth. We'll get Marge to get you some fresh orange juice."

Quiet herself, Liza let everyone make a fuss over her. She was glad nobody forced her to talk just yet. She found she couldn't clear Cliff Forrester out of her mind right away. His peculiar refusal of breakfast made sense now, if her grandfather's words were to be believed.

But Cliff a wild-eyed maniac? It hardly seemed likely. He appeared completely sane to her—saner than most of the men she met these days, in fact. Just a little erratic. Angry one minute, and kind of shaken up the next. His temper had exploded in the truck, but Liza had provoked that. Why did he have such a reputation around town?

Judson guided Liza to the most central table in the diner and made a show of pulling out her chair. When he'd sat down opposite her and ordered a large breakfast for her without benefit of a menu, he finally looked at her with a growing, indulgent smile and said, "All right, you can tell me what this is all about now. How come you just waltzed into town without warning?"

"Do I need to warn my family when I come to visit?"

He cocked a grandfatherly eye at her and said, "You know what I mean. Are you in trouble?"

"Of course not!"

He laughed expansively at that, not caring if his friends turned to look up from their own conversations. "You haven't learned to lie yet, have you, my girl? What's going on? Boyfriend problems?"

Liza sighed. "Nothing that easy."

"Need money?"

"Granddad," she said slowly, "would you mind if we didn't talk about me just yet? I'm ... well, coming back to town will take some adjusting."

"So," he said, "you're going to stay this time?"

"No," Liza replied quickly. "Well, I'm not sure. I'm at loose ends, I guess."

He nodded, understanding. "Tyler is a good place to come when you're at loose ends. I don't suppose the town has changed much since you left. What can I do to help this time?"

"Nothing. Just be yourself, I guess. Boy, it's great to see you!"

The waitress returned with steaming coffee cups at that moment. Marge's Diner was famous for its coffee, and the waitress said, "Here you go, folks! This'll unclog your arteries, Mr. Ingalls."

"Thanks, Betty."

It was half a minute before she left, then Judson turned back to Liza and asked casually, "Have you seen your mother yet?"

"No, and I don't care to talk about that yet, either. Give me a chance to catch my breath, okay?"

He grinned and reached for his cup of coffee. "So far you've shot down every topic of conversation I can suggest. What's left?"

"Well," said Liza, leaning forward and bracing her elbows on the table, "you could tell me about Cliff Forrester. Were you serious about him?"

Judson put his cup down, splashing coffee on the tabletop and frowning sternly. "He's bad news, Mary Elizabeth. I wish you hadn't met him."

"What's so bad about him?"

"He's screwed up. Some business overseas. He must have been in the war, I guess, and when he returned— well, he came back abnormal."

"But you hired him to take care of the lodge, right?"

"He was one of your mother's ideas," Judson grumbled. "She's always looking for some poor soul to save. Well, she met Forrester when she was working for some charity—saving the boat people or whatever. You know how she is—always trying to help. She said he looked like a walking ghost, so she invited him to Tyler and he came."

"Why? Doesn't he have any family?"

"Don't ask me questions like that," Judson snapped. "How am I supposed to know? Once he was here, he stayed at the Kelsey boardinghouse for a while, but he gave people the creeps. The boy never slept, I hear, and he hardly said a word to anybody, just walked the streets at all hours. Is that normal? Anyway, Alyssa jabbered at me until I gave him a job, so he moved out to the lodge. He's been there ever since—five or six years, maybe more."

"Why did you hire him if he's unstable?"

"He can't hurt anybody up at Timberlake. He can be as crazy as he likes up there and nobody will mind."

Liza drank some hot coffee and said softly, "The lodge looks terrible, Granddad. If he's supposed to be taking care of the place, he's doing a miserable job."

"He's not supposed to be looking after the lodge," Judson said gruffly. "Just the land and the lake. He's the gamekeeper and takes care of the guys from the Fish Commission for. . . things like that. We're trying to restock the bass population after a virus killed off most of 'em, so he's supposed to be keeping an eye on the fish. I didn't give Forrester permission to do a thing to the building."

"Why not? Granddad, it's a mess! The whole place will come crashing down if you neglect it much longer."

"I don't care," Judson said with finality, reaching for his coffee once more.

"Don't—!" Amazed, Liza cried, "Granddad! How can you say such a thing! Your own father built Timberlake, and you—why, you and my grandmother added all those wonderful—"

"I don't give a damn about that lodge," Judson said sharply. "The place holds a lot of bad memories for me. If it burned to the ground tomorrow, I wouldn't care."

Liza was shocked into a brief silence. Then she said, "Good grief, why don't you sell it, then?"

"I've had offers," he admitted, toying with the knife at his place. "One from a fellow your mother used to know way back when. He's in the hotel business now, I understand."

"Well, rather than letting the building go to pot—"

"How bad is it?"

"You mean you haven't seen it?"

"I don't want to see the place. Not without your grandmother," Judson declared, glaring at Liza as if daring her to argue further.

"Granddad, she's been gone forty years or more! You haven't ever been up to the lodge since then?"

"I have no reason to go," Judson growled. "And you can just forget—"

"Sell it," Liza commanded, cutting off his threat. "It was a beautiful place once and somebody should enjoy it."

"Let Cliff Forrester enjoy it. He deserves something."

"I thought you didn't like him."

"I didn't say that! I just don't want him hanging around my granddaughter, that's all. He's done his duty for his country, and I know what that's like, so he can have the lodge to himself if he wants his life that way. I don't associate with him more than once or twice a year, and that's all you ought to do. He deserves a place to live out the rest of his days in peace."

Liza couldn't help laughing. "You talk like he's an old plow horse who needs a pasture. He's a young man!"

Judson gave her a frosty glare. "What are you thinking, Mary Elizabeth? You haven't fallen in love with that boy, have you?"

"Don't be silly! I just met him an hour ago! It's just—well, he's not crazy. He seemed perfectly nice to me. A little peculiar, maybe. And he's not a boy! He's a grown man, and a very attractive one, if you ask me."

"He's ten years older than you, at least!"

"So what?" Liza countered angrily. "When are you going to stop interfering in my life? I have a right to make friends with whoever—"

"Simmer down," Judson said, finally allowing a weary grin. "I thought a few years in the city might tone down that temper of yours, but I can see it didn't. Your grandmother could fly off the handle faster than anyone I knew—until you came along!"

"I'm sorry," Liza said, wishing she hadn't flown off the handle quite so fast.

"No, you're not sorry. You like putting me in my place once in a while, don't you?" He laughed ruefully. "Are you going to stay in Tyler or not?"

"For a day or two maybe," she said cautiously.

"All right, what do you want from me?"

Liza smiled. "How about loaning me twenty dollars so I can go buy some jeans at the dime store?"

"Done", said Judson, reaching for his hip pocket. "That's a damn peculiar outfit you're wearing, I must say. Some jeans would be an improvement."

"Shut up, Granddad."

"Don't tell me to shut up when I've got twenty dollars in my hand. Here, take fifty." Judson threw the bills on the table between them. "There's more where that came from. I've got charge accounts in every store in town, so you buy what you need."

"But—"

"No buts about it! It's the least I can do for my favorite granddaughter. Now, what are you going to do once you buy your jeans?"

"I'm going back up to Timberlake."

His face flushed at once. "Who gave you permission to go back to the lodge?"

Liza grinned. "You will."

"Like hell! Tangling with Cliff Forrester is too dangerous—"

"Tangling with *me* has been known to be hazardous, too, you know!"

"Oh, for crying out loud!" Judson exploded. "What would you do with yourself up there, anyway? Make that boy's life more miserable than it is already?''

She shrugged airily. "I don't know what I'll do. I'll see what happens, I guess.''

"Mary Elizabeth . . .''

"I can take care of myself, Granddad.''

He glared at her. "You have a plan, don't you?''

"I've got some ideas," Liza admitted, laughing at the pained expression that grew on her grandfather's face.

"You're just like your grandmother," he said with a sigh. "Headstrong and reckless. There's no talking sense to you. And no use warning you about Forrester, right?''

"No use at all.''

Marge arrived then with a plate loaded with blueberry pancakes, and made a fuss over Liza. In a few minutes she brought a side order of sausage and hash brown potatoes, too. Marge had been a part of Tyler since Liza's childhood. Her diner was the local meeting place and Marge made it her business to be friendly with everyone. She welcomed Liza back to town and traded jokes with Judson before heading over to another table to refill some coffee cups.

Liza ate her pancakes voraciously, listening to her grandfather tell her all the local gossip. The biggest news was that the school had hired a new football coach, which had set the town on its ear since the coach was a woman. Someone at the next table heard Judson mention the issue, and a friendly argument broke out.

"Hiring a woman football coach is like electing a monkey to the Senate," one man bellowed. "Sure, he can do the same job as all the other senators, but he sure looks silly doing it!''

Liza listened to the townsfolk argue, feeling suddenly quite invigorated as she was swept up in Tyler's latest controversy. It felt a lot better than being swept downstream by her own troubles. Life wasn't so terrible after all.

An hour later at the dime store, she bought some jeans, a couple of T-shirts, a few pairs of panties and some cheap sneakers. The clerk was one of her high school classmates, and they chatted for twenty minutes before Liza left the store.

She added cigarettes from the market and then walked across the street to cajole Carl into driving her up to the lodge to look at her disabled Thunderbird. The mechanic agreed, and while riding in the tow truck, Liza planned what she was going to say to Cliff Forrester when she moved into the lodge.

CHAPTER THREE

CLIFF HAD BEEN under siege before. In Cambodia, he'd experienced some of the most frightening barrages of gunfire known to man. He'd been scared then.

When Liza Baron descended on Timberlake, she did it with just as much noise as incoming artillery. But Cliff wasn't scared this time. He was furious.

"Just what the hell do you think you're doing?" he demanded, confronting her in the kitchen while the mechanic from town tinkered with her convertible outside.

She dumped a huge plastic bag full of clothing on the stainless steel kitchen counter, bestowing on Cliff a wide, self-satisfied smile. "What does it look like I'm doing?"

"Like you're moving in."

"Give the man a cigar!" Liza crowed, prancing happily around the counter and ripping open the plastic bag. "That's exactly what I'm up to!"

Cliff throttled back the surge of anger that rose from inside him. "You're *not* moving into the lodge."

"Oh, yes, I am. In fact, Granddad gave me permission to do whatever I please while I'm here." She rummaged around in the plastic bag and came up with a new package of cigarettes.

Cliff struggled to keep his temper and growled, "That wasn't the arrangement he made with me. I'm supposed to be the sole tenant."

Nonchalantly, Liza leaned against the counter and proceeded to unwrap the cellophane from her cigarettes. Looking very pleased with herself, she said, "I guess he changed his mind. I have been known to have that effect on people, you know. Have you got a match?"

Seething, Cliff said, "I'm not sharing this place with you, Miss Baron."

"Heavens, Forrester, my great-grandfather used to hold hunting parties up here and invite a hundred guests. It's a big lodge." She blinked prettily, then gave him a taunting smile. "I'm sure we'll manage to stay out of each other's beds if we try, don't you?"

"Dammit, you can't barge in here like this!"

"I already have," she replied, cool and amused as she flipped a cigarette out of the pack and expertly waved it between two fingers. "Are you scared of me, Forrester?"

There were limits to human suffering, Cliff thought savagely. Without warning, he snatched the cigarette from Liza's grasp and managed to grab the pack out of her other hand before she could react.

"Hey!" she cried, affronted.

"I may be forced to tolerate you," he snapped, "but I won't have you stinking up the place with cigarette smoke!" He squashed the pack in one hand and threw the crumpled remains on the counter between them.

Liza glared at him as she stood squarely in the middle of the lodge kitchen, still wearing his sweater over that ridiculously short skirt. Her high-heeled shoes were gone, however, and in their place was a pair of brand-new sneakers. She looked young and fit and breathtakingly lovely.

And very angry, too. Her eyes were throwing blue sparks as she glared at Cliff.

"I don't take orders from anyone," she said. "I'll smoke if I want to smoke."

"It's a stupid habit. You probably do it only because you think it makes you look sophisticated."

"That's not it at all. I—"

"You're a silly, shallow, spoiled girl, Miss Baron, and you're probably used to inflicting yourself on people all the time. Well, I won't put up with it. If you want to smoke, go back to Chicago."

Her expression turned shrewd. "That's what you want, isn't it? You want to get rid of me."

"Damn right!"

"Well, you can't chase me out of here that easily, Forrester. You want me to give up smoking? Fine, I will. But I'm not leaving Timberlake, so forget it!"

Cliff couldn't believe what he was hearing. "A couple of hours ago you said you were passing through, and now suddenly you're the prodigal daughter! Why in heaven's name have you taken it into your head to barge in here—"

"I need a place to crash for a while," she cut in. "To revitalize my creativity. To open my consciousness to new experiences. To—"

"Oh, for crying out loud!"

"I'm *not* here because of you, Forrester, so stop thinking I'm hot for your body or something, because I'm not—even if you're hot for mine!"

"I am *not* hot for your body!"

"I've seen how you look at me, Forrester."

"Miss Baron—"

"My name is Liza."

"I know your damned name! My God, you're the most exasperating woman—"

"Oh, cool down," she said with am impish laugh, folding her arms over her chest and clearly enjoying his pique. "I think you could use some exasperation. You've gotten too comfortable up here all by yourself." She tossed her head pertly. "I've heard about you, Forrester."

He quelled the urge to strangle her and ground out, "Exactly what have you heard?"

"You have quite a reputation around town. You're a hermit or a lone wolf—one or the other. Some people even think you're dangerous."

A few things began to clear up in Cliff's mind. "That's why you've come dancing in here this way, isn't it?"

"Huh?"

"You get your kicks out of dangerous men."

"Where I get my kicks is none of your business," she replied, standing straight again and repacking the items in her plastic bag. "I'm curious about you, that's all. You're a mystery man, Forrester, and I just love a mystery."

"I'll tell you all my secrets," Cliff said at once, "if you'll pack up and leave in the next ten minutes."

She laughed and gathered up her bag. "I'm here to stay, Forrester—at least until I feel like leaving. Which bedroom is mine?"

Cliff felt perilously close to boiling over and found himself clenching his fists. "Damn you—"

"I'll take the little pink room at the back of the second floor, okay? You haven't set up housekeeping in that one, I'll bet. Pink isn't your color. I'll use the bathroom near the back stairs, okay? It's working?"

"If you don't take showers by the hour."

She grinned. "Don't get your hopes up. Were you planning to watch me through the peephole while I'm in the shower?"

"*What* peephole?"

"The one my cousin drilled so he could watch me in the bathroom. He was very immature, but I didn't mind. I kind of liked the idea, you know?"

She was outrageous. At least, she tried to be outrageous. Cliff doubted such a peephole had ever existed. He knew exactly what she was doing. Liza Baron liked to make up lies just to watch people's reactions.

"Oh, one more thing," she said, turning on the bottom stair. "Will you check with Carl about my car? Tell him I'd like to have it fixed by tomorrow morning, okay? And maybe you'd get some of my stuff out of the trunk? It's all the junk from my office. Thanks."

She trotted up the stairs then, humming a cheery tune and laughing aloud when she reached the second floor.

Cliff balled up his fists and struggled with the urge to shout after her. He wasn't going to play the butler to her lady of the manor!

"Get your own junk," he muttered, and went out the back door of the lodge to the terrace.

He plunged into the woods, growling to himself. To have his privacy plundered this way was unacceptable. Enraging, even! Who did she think she was? And what was her plan, for God's sake? The tigress came barging in and started ordering him around like he was her hired hand!

"What does she think she's going to do?"

A girl like Liza got her kicks out of disrupting people, making them miserable. It was her entertainment, a sport.

"Damn her!"

Suddenly Cliff stopped short under the oaks, struck by a thought. For the first time in recent memory, he was fuming over the actions of another person.

It was weird.

Of course, he'd been alone for years. He'd wanted it that way. Staying out of the mainstream had been a distinct choice for him—a way of avoiding the kind of emotional turmoil he hated. Life at Timberlake had been peaceful, and he'd needed peace. The silence of the forest and the tranquil lake had worked together to mend his spirit. He hadn't needed other people. He'd avoided them for lots of reasons.

Now that bewitching Baron girl came bursting into the lodge as if she owned the place! It was a cataclysmic event, Cliff realized. She was the first to break in on his private world. The only person who'd dared.

Grimly, he set off into the forest again. "I can't live under the same roof with her. It's impossible."

She was a troublemaker. A naughty youngster bent on wreaking havoc wherever she went. She was the last thing Cliff needed. Already she'd gotten him all churned up inside. Heaven only knew what might happen if she stayed.

He walked for a couple of miles, but it did no good. Still muttering under his breath, he found himself heading for the hilltop that overlooked Tyler—a sparsely treed vantage point that had once been part of the Gerhardt farm. The Gerhardts, he knew, had been forced out of the dairy business by the crunch in farm prices, and their land had not yet been taken over by the conglomerates that were moving into the area. The top field was overgrown now, the lush grass congested by tangles of wildflowers.

Cliff stopped at the break in the trees, resting his hands on the weathered fence post, his gaze drawn by the panorama that spread out before him. It was a scene that had often calmed him. The green pastures of neighboring farms, dotted with cattle, were bordered by darker fields of alfalfa, corn and the pale green-yellow of new oats. It would have made a pretty postcard—picturesque and serene.

But he didn't feel serene as he glared at the wide landscape that spread out majestically before him. The warm breeze that rustled in the leaves of the trees at his back did not ease Cliff's mind. Nor did the warmth of the sun relieve the tension that tightened the muscles of his neck and shoulders.

"Cliff!"

A gentle voice called to him from the field below, and a fragile woman stood up from where she'd been plucking wildflowers. She lifted a slender hand to the brim of her straw hat and called, "Is that you?"

It was Alyssa Baron, perhaps his only friend in Tyler.

Cliff waved weakly, not sure he wanted to see even Alyssa this morning. But he vaulted over the fence a moment later and went down the hillside to meet her.

She had brought her basket and was filling it with cornflowers and daisies. To ward off the morning chill, she had pulled a pair of casual but clearly expensive slacks and scalloped sweater over her slim frame. Her pruning shears swung from the worn ribbon on her belt, and bits of earth clung to her manicured hands.

Alyssa's fair skin was flushed with sunlight and she wore no makeup to conceal her age. With her light hair pulled back into a clip under the hat, she looked ten years younger than she should have. Her blue eyes were large and expressive.

For a queer second, Cliff noted how much she looked like Liza. But Alyssa's was a fragile kind of femininity counterbalanced by the strength in her expression. Liza was more vibrant, in personality as well as appearance. Her features were like her mother's, but exaggerated—not quite so delicate. And her voice wasn't gentle.

Alyssa's was as soothing as the soft sound of the morning breeze. On a self-deprecating laugh, she said, "I can't get used to the way you just appear out of the forest. It's like magic. How can you move so quietly? A man your size?"

He didn't answer, and she thrust her basket into his hands, chatting as if he'd made a clever riposte.

"Don't tell anyone," she went on blithely, "but I'm stealing flowers. Do you think someone will arrest me? I'm in charge of arranging centerpieces for the senior citizen dinner tonight, and of course I left it to the last minute! Aren't I awful?"

Alyssa Baron wasn't awful. She was beautiful, and she possessed one of the purest hearts in the world.

She was also very perceptive.

Looking up at him, she said suddenly, "What's wrong, Cliff?"

"Nothing."

Alyssa smiled with understanding. "Not sleeping again?"

He shook his head. "It's not that. I just...it's been a long day."

She laughed. "My dear, it's not even noon yet! What's going on?"

He couldn't tell her about Liza's arrival in Tyler, Cliff realized. That was Liza's business, not his. He knew how Alyssa was going to react to that news, and he didn't want to be around to watch. Alyssa might cry. She wore her emotions quite close to the surface when it came to her children—Liza especially. How many times had she expressed her feelings about her wayward youngest daughter? Cliff didn't think that he could stand breaking the news of Liza's return and watching Alyssa's eyes fill with pain as she soaked in the information.

So he said, "I'm not used to being around people."

"Ah," Alyssa said wisely. "Did you go into town this morning?"

"Just for a minute."

"That always upsets you," she said, shaking her head. "I wish it didn't. People don't hate you. They don't know you, that's all. You make them nervous, I suppose. You don't know how to chat."

Cliff laughed shortly. "No, chatting isn't my strong suit."

"It's all right," Alyssa replied, bending into the flowers again and snipping stems with her shears. "I know you're perfectly nice. Someday everyone else will figure that out, too."

As Alyssa cut more flowers for her centerpieces, Cliff held her basket and considered her words. He didn't disagree. Not aloud, anyway. But Cliff knew in his heart that he wasn't perfectly nice. He could be perfectly awful—that was the problem. And if he wasn't careful, somebody could get hurt by his awfulness.

He hated the thought of hurting anyone. Perhaps that was why he'd come to live at Timberlake in the first place. To be alone. To stay away from people in case he went truly crazy.

That was his biggest fear, he supposed. Going really nuts. It could happen, he knew. He'd read about other guys who'd come home from Southeast Asia and lived normal lives for a few years before snapping out completely. Posttraumatic stress disorder, it was called. Funny how something so terrible could be made to sound easy to cure.

Staying at the lodge was safe, though. Cliff saw Alyssa Baron once every couple of weeks—that was it. Oh, a clerk at the grocery store or at Murphy's Hardware might say a word or two when he made his monthly foray into town, but he forged no real connections. Cliff preferred life that way.

Now Liza had steamrolled into the lodge and it scared the hell out of him. Cliff realized he was trembling again as he held Alyssa's basket. It was being around people that frightened him. He knew he was capable of doing terrible things to his fellow man.

And Liza. She had the power to push him over the edge, Cliff decided. Not knowing the kind of horror she would unleash, she'd taunt and torment and goad him until he exploded. What might he do to her if he went crazy? The thought terrified him.

Alyssa straightened and read his expression. Alarmed, she put her hand on his arm and said, "Cliff?"

He shook off her touch. "I'm sorry. I'm—I'm not..."

"What can I do to help?"

Nothing, of course. *Just stay away,* he wanted to tell her. *Get your headstrong daughter out of the lodge before I do something insane.*

But he didn't say that. He wasn't capable of expressing those feelings, not even to Alyssa, who'd been a kind of therapist for him over the years, whether she knew it or not. Alyssa had accepted Cliff from the beginning without making demands on him. She had not insisted that he talk. Nor had she forced him to spill his guts and explain himself to her. She'd simply taken him into her life the way he was—broken and frightened of the world. And of himself, maybe.

She said, "Don't be upset."

A lot of responses boiled in his head, fighting to get out. But he said on a tight sigh, "Sometimes I just want to forget everything."

"You will. You'll get over it, Cliff."

"Should I?" he asked, half to himself. "Should I keep trying to put it in my past?"

Alyssa sighed, too, sounding troubled. "I don't know what to tell you. Some people think it's best to confront the worst, but I...well, I'm not an expert. I just hate seeing you so distressed, Cliff. Every time you start thinking about what happened over there..."

"I did some bad things," he said, closing his eyes and letting the sunlight warm his face. "I don't want to be that way again."

"You won't!" In a rush, Alyssa said, "Cliff, that was a terrible time. You did what you had to do to protect people you cared about."

Alyssa said more, but Cliff had stopped listening. She didn't know everything. Not the worst, anyway. She knew why he'd gone into the hills and befriended the people of that mountain village. She knew how he'd found himself trapped with them when the enemy struck. He'd learned from the Hmongs and taught them his own skills, and they'd fought together. They'd managed to find escape routes for women and children.

But after that...well, he'd been unable to tell Alyssa the rest of his story. Perhaps she could guess the kinds of atrocities he'd seen. Maybe she imagined what he'd done to survive and to shepherd the innocents to safety. But Cliff couldn't bring himself to tell gentle Alyssa Baron about the nightmare he'd lived in Cambodia.

Nor could he tell her how terrified he was that it might happen all over again—that the bonds of reason might snap inside him and trigger something horrible.

Alyssa's hand was on his arm again, and she shook him. "Cliff," she said severely, "stop thinking like that! Stop it! You're only making it worse for yourself!"

Maybe she was right. With an effort, Cliff pulled his mind back from the quagmire of his past.

"I'll be okay," he said.

She smiled up at him, kindhearted and beautiful. "I know you will."

Cliff left her on the hillside picking flowers. He didn't tell her about Liza.

He returned to the lodge a couple of hours later. He didn't keep track of time, but his stomach started growling, so he headed back through the woods, not sure what lay ahead.

He found Liza on the wide front porch. She'd dragged one of the old wicker chairs outside and sat in it with her bare feet propped up on the railing, long bare legs stretched out and a sketchbook propped in her lap. A huge pair of sunglasses obscured her eyes and reinforced her spoiled-starlet look.

Cliff stopped at the bottom of the steps, half afraid to get any closer. She looked beautiful and unstoppable—a predatory female looking for trouble. He hesitated in the trees, not ready for another volatile confrontation.

"Good news," Liza called, catching sight of him and smiling broadly as he warily approached. "My car can be fixed."

"Good news indeed," Cliff replied sourly, mounting the porch steps. "You can leave."

"Not yet. Carl had to take it to his garage to make the repairs."

"That means you're stranded here."

"You got it. We're all alone together, Forrester."

She laughed and peeled off her sunglasses, to pin him with an observant gaze. Her dangly earrings caught the sunlight, and the black devil winked at him. "You ran off," she said. "Just when things were heating up."

"I tend to stay away from heat."

"That's a mistake," Liza pronounced with a cat-like smile. "A little fire's good for the soul."

"My soul's just fine," he retorted.

She eyed him again, but didn't go so far as to accuse him of lying. Instead, she pulled her feet off the railing, crossed her legs, tapped her sketchbook and said airily, "I've made a few decisions while you were out."

"Oh?"

"I'm going to stay here awhile."

Cliff nearly choked. He wanted to explain, to warn her. There was danger here, didn't she see that? He struggled to put the right words together. "Miss Baron—"

"And I'm going to fix up the lodge. I'm going to make it into a resort."

"*What?*"

She grinned at his reaction, twirling her colorful sunglasses. "It's a good idea, don't you think? This place could be fabulous. It was really special years ago, and it could be great again. All it needs is a little TLC, and fortunately, I find myself with a little free time on my hands."

"Hold it—"

"So I've been making lists and drawing some ideas. I thought I'd start with the common areas first—the dining room, then the bar and lounge."

"Wait just a—"

Liza didn't listen, but began to outline her plans with blithe enthusiasm. "The kitchen's a real wreck and will need a major overhaul if it's going to serve many guests, but I like the rustic flavor of everything else, don't you? If you ask me, rustic is making a comeback."

"Will you please—"

"I'll need some fabric books, of course. The place really cries out for chintz, right? And wall coverings will have to be chosen with caution, since—"

"Will you shut up for one minute?"

She blinked. "Sure. Something on your mind, Forrester?"

He was filled with dread and anger. Throttling both emotions, Cliff managed to grind out, "Just what the hell are you doing?"

"Aren't I making myself clear? I'm going to refurbish—"

"Why?"

"Why? Why *not,* for heaven's sake? It's beautiful up here!"

"The only way it's going to stay beautiful is if people leave it alone! You can't fix this place up. People will start coming here and tramping through the woods, running powerboats on the lake—"

"Of course they will! It'll be lovely!"

"It'll be horrible!"

She laughed at him. "You can't keep the lodge a secret, Forrester. It's been your private playground long enough. We're going to make it look wonderful, and people from all over will come and—"

"We?" he snapped. "Who's we?"

"You and me, of course. You could use some real work to do, I think, to snap you out of this hermit phase. With my creative ideas and your strong back—"

"Go to hell, Miss Baron!"

"What's the matter?"

He threw himself into pacing up and down the porch, trying not to think about breaking her neck on the spot. "For one thing, I have not been placed on this earth to do your bidding, Miss High and Mighty! And secondly, I hate the whole idea and refuse to have any part of it! I have a deal with your grandfather, which says I can stay here *alone* in exchange for the job of taking care of—"

"We can discuss the quality of your fishy work some other time," Liza said dryly. "Meanwhile, I think we should concentrate on the future and—"

"*My* future has nothing to do with your future," Cliff snapped, standing over her. "So you can forget about me fixing up the lodge for any reason whatsoever."

She began to tap her pencil, calmly and deliberately. "I'm sorry to hear you say that, Forrester," she said. "It's a good thing that blood is thicker than water, I guess."

"What's that supposed to mean?"

"That my granddad has the final say. And I know he's going to tell me I can do whatever I like."

Cliff balled up his fists and choked down a shout of complete fury.

Liza smiled demurely up at him from her chair. "Let me be honest, okay? I need a project, Forrester. I've arrived at a crossroads in my life, and this is the perfect thing for me. I'm going to do it."

Seeing the gleam in her eye, Cliff had no doubt she was going to get exactly what she wanted. A project—that was what she called what would turn out to be a multimillion-dollar construction job involving hundreds of skilled professionals and months if not years of painstaking work. And Liza talked about it as if she could throw up a few new curtains and end up with a finished landmark.

Worst of all, she clearly had no idea how impossible the whole idea was.

With enormous difficulty, Cliff said, "You don't understand."

"About what?"

"About me. And this place." He tried to dig into his brain to find the words, but it was hard. He'd never been able to verbalize his trouble—never had to. That was why he'd come here in the first place. So he wouldn't have to talk. He said, "It's... I need to be here."

She waited expectantly, and when he couldn't say more, she prompted, "Okay, so what's the big deal?"

"I have to be alone."

"Oh, nonsense!" She laughed again—beautiful and innocent and naive.

"It's true," Cliff argued, aware that he had started to sweat. "I can't... I can't be around people."

"Why not? It's not like you're pug ugly or something. I mean, women would fall all over themselves in Chicago if you walked into town. Listen, Forrester—"

"No, *you* listen," he retorted, his voice rising unevenly. "I can't do it. You can't bring more people. You can't—"

"Oh, yes, I can," said Liza, smiling like a naughty angel. "And you're going to help me, Forrester."

"Like hell!"

"Oh, come on. You're not going to let a little inconvenient sexual attraction get in the way, are you?"

"*What* sexual attraction?"

She grinned. "Do you deny it?"

"My God—"

"'Fess up, Forrester! You think I'm the sexiest little tidbit who ever knocked your socks off, right? Take it easy. We'll have a good time and still get the work done. You'll see."

Cliff escaped before he caved in and did some real damage. He stormed into the lodge and left the silly little bitch humming happily on the porch.

CHAPTER FOUR

THOUGHTFULLY, Liza watched Cliff stride off the porch. What was he so churned up about? She couldn't imagine.

But she found herself smiling. He was good-looking for an older man, after all. And there was something under that surly facade he tried to keep in place. Something very attractive and . . . well, vulnerable.

She liked seeing his face change when she crossed him. His expression seemed so dead most of the time. Cliff looked like a man who was functioning underwater. Every reaction was slow and seemed filtered through a screen or something. But when she managed to make a remark that irritated him, Cliff looked like a completely different man. His eyes grew fiery, his mouth hardened and his careful speech—that modulated voice and slightly New England accent—became a direct link to his brain.

Liza liked Cliff best when he got steamed enough to yell back at her. He was more alive. More human.

Something was bugging him, though.

"I think I'd better find out what it is," Liza murmured to herself. "After all, it's not healthy for a guy to keep secrets bottled up inside. It's for his own good."

She stayed out of his way for the rest of the afternoon, but planned to get back to him later. In the meantime, there was work to do, after all. Busy with her sketch pad, Liza made more drawings, deciding on color palettes and curtain designs and what kinds of furniture she should coax her grandfather to buy to really make Timberlake look fabulous. Some of those Adirondack chairs, for instance. And a wrought iron table from Italy. And maybe an antique canoe suspended from the trusses—that was what the porch needed to give it style! Liza licked her pencil and made more notes.

At sunset, however, the darkness drove her indoors again. In the kitchen, she found Cliff.

"No," he snapped as he fixed a sandwich for himself. "You may not have anything to eat."

"How about those fish you caught this morning?"

"I ate them for lunch."

"I hope they gave you indigestion."

"I burned them, as a matter of fact."

She laughed at him and boosted herself up to sit on the counter so they could be eye to eye. With a quick tug, she pulled her skirt down over her thighs, then crossed her legs provocatively.

She asked, "Are you going to try starving me out of the place? I'm *hungry*, Forrester. You can either share what you've got or drive me into town for a decent meal."

He glared at her for ten long seconds, then averted his gaze before she had a chance to read anything in his expression. He gave an infuriated sigh and shoved the sandwich plate across the kitchen counter at her, growling, "I hope your plans for renovating the lodge are better organized than your living arrangements."

"Oh, don't be a fuddy-duddy," she said, settling down cross-legged to munch on the sandwich he'd prepared. "I'll go to the store tomorrow and get us something really good. Do you like spaghetti with hot peppers? That's my specialty."

"Why? Because you can't cook anything else?"

She grinned, mouth full of delicious ham and Wisconsin cheese that had been liberally slathered with hot mustard. "I'm a lousy cook, as a matter of fact. How'd you guess?"

"Shot in the dark," he said shortly, setting about making another sandwich. He worked without haste, putting two slices of whole wheat bread on a new plate and carefully arranging lettuce on both pieces. It was amazing how careful he was, his large hands surprisingly agile and quick, but precise. He said, "Cooking takes care and patience, two qualities you don't seem to have in abundance."

Liza shrugged amiably, not taking offense. "I hate following other people's directions, even in recipes. I'd rather toss in a little extra spice and see what happens, you know? And I lean toward very hot things. I like zip in my food. Are you too old for that yet? Hot food, I mean?"

Cliff stopped working and simply looked at her for a moment. "Can I ask you a question?"

Liza swallowed an enormous mouthful. "As long as I can have something to drink before I answer. Got any wine? Or a cold cola, maybe?"

Cliff closed his eyes as though asking a higher power to give him enough strength to keep going. Liza hid her grin as he crossed to the ancient refrigerator, opened it and took inventory. "I have milk or orange juice. Or water."

"No booze? Not even beer?"

"Yes, there's beer."

"Light, I hope?"

"Just plain beer. Nothing fancy or imported, just ordinary American beer."

"I'll have one anyway."

He brought two to the counter and twisted the cap off one bottle before passing it to Liza. "You're old enough to drink this, right?"

She took the beer and gave him a sardonic look, absurdly pleased that he could still razz her despite his anger. "Is that the question you were going to ask me?"

"No. I was going to ask how you managed to grow up in the Baron family and turn out to be so unlike the rest of the clan."

She took a swig of beer and asked, "Who says you have to be like everybody else?"

"But you're practically from another planet compared to the rest of them."

Slamming the bottle down on the counter, Liza exploded, "Why is everybody so obsessed about that? I'm my own person, for God's sake! I don't have to be as prissy as my mother or as smart as my sister or as brilliant as my noble brother or—or... Why are you smiling?"

He was! Cliff bent over his sandwich to cut it into two, but his slight grin was unmistakable. It made him look much younger, too, a detail that pleased Liza. She hadn't realized until that moment how pale he looked, but twin splotches of color began to darken his cheekbones—another good sign.

Accusingly, she said, "You just said that to get me going, didn't you? Just to make me mad."

He managed to control his smile again and said mildly, "I'd rather have you on the defensive than hammering at me all the time, I guess. See you later."

"Where are you going?"

He'd picked up his sandwich and bottle of beer and was heading for the door. "To eat my dinner."

"Let me come, too," Liza cried, hopping off the counter, grabbing her meal and tailing Cliff into the hallway. Now that she had his attention, she wanted to keep it. Exploring Cliff Forrester's personality was even more fun than planning the redecoration of the lodge. "Wait for me!"

"There's no need to keep me company," he said over his shoulder.

"I'm lonesome! Besides, a stimulating dinner conversation is good for the digestion. It's a proven fact. Where are you going? The old dining room? The lounge? Or how about a picnic by the boathouse?"

"Really, Miss Baron, this lodge is a very big place. You said so yourself. There's no reason why two people can't stay here for a short while without bumping into each other all the time."

"What's the matter? Don't you like my company?"

"I don't like *anybody's* company, as a matter of fact. That's why I came here in the first place."

"Why are you so dead set on being alone?"

"That's the way I like it."

"My granddad says you were in Vietnam. What's the matter? You have a rough time over there or something?"

Cliff turned in the hallway then, and for a sizzling moment, he said nothing. Liza couldn't see his face, for evening had fallen and the light wasn't on. But she could feel her heartbeat skip, and she realized she had gone too far.

Coldly quiet, Cliff said, "What do you think you know about me?"

Liza took a pace backward. "N-nothing."

There was something menacing in the way his voice dropped and his body went utterly still. Tension crackled in the air.

Quietly he said, "I have not gone prying into your private life, Miss Baron."

She swallowed hard. "I know."

"Nor have I demanded that you leave."

"Okay, okay—"

"But I think it would be best for both of us if we agree right now to give each other some space. I want to be left alone."

That command was intended as an exit line, Liza realized, because Cliff turned and went into the lounge with his meal in hand. He put the bottle and plate on one of the small tables by the hearth, then hunkered down to wrestle with some logs and tinder. Liza couldn't stop herself. She eased into the room and watched Cliff work. She admired the tight stretch of his shirt across the muscle of his shoulders and the narrow curve of his back. His body was spare and functional—very male, she decided.

She wondered how it would feel to smooth her hands across those broad shoulders, to ease away the tension that was so obvious to her eye and perhaps coax something other than commands out of Cliff.

In a minute or so, he'd built a fire and struck a wooden match from the box kept on top of the log pile. At once, a small flame leaped up, casting a warm light across the floor of the lounge. The soft crackles of the flame were the only sound in the room.

Cliff stood up and turned. Surprise flashed across his face, then irritation at finding Liza still present.

Snapping out of her momentary daydream, and feigning a cocky swagger, Liza sauntered the rest of the way into the room. She took another swig of beer. "You really want me to leave you alone?"

"Completely," Cliff said, remaining on his feet.

Liza curled up in the old cushioned chair across from the one he'd obviously chosen. Her heart was beating very fast, but she attempted to appear utterly calm. "It's not healthy for a guy your age to stay all by himself all the time, you know."

"What does my age have to do with it?"

"Nothing, really. Nobody should be a complete hermit, if you ask me. It's not natural." She began to eat her sandwich again and said, "I mean, your sex life alone must have suffered enormously."

Cliff's hands immediately tightened into fists. "My sex life is none of your business."

"That was just an example." Liza waved her hand dismissively. "Think about it for a second. If you're alone all the time, *everything* must get rusty. Why, even your vocabulary must suffer. If you don't use it, pretty soon you'll be talking like a toddler, you know?

And social graces must be exercised regularly or else—"

Cliff burst out, "Why are you doing this to me?"

"Doing what?"

"Chattering about completely ridiculous subjects when all I want to do is eat my meal!"

"Who's stopping you?" Liza demanded. "Sit down and eat, for crying out loud!"

Cliff threw himself into his chair, but didn't reach for his sandwich. He snatched up his beer, however, and glaring at Liza, took a healthy swig.

She chose to ignore the rage in his expression and continued to nibble her sandwich. She wanted to know more about Cliff. And since he wasn't very forthcoming on his own, she was being forced to drag the information out of him. Trouble was, how hard could she push before he blew up?

Faking a disarming smile, she said, "Being alone has a lot of disadvantages. I mean, what happens if you accidentally lock yourself in the bathroom? Or if you get dressed in the morning and forget to zip your pants? Or—"

"I don't care if my pants are zipped or not. There's nobody here to see me."

Liza grinned lasciviously. "Does that mean you run around naked sometimes? Golly, Forrester, I didn't think about that! I'll bet you have more fun than I first figured. Do you ever play pretend games when nobody's watching? Or make love to inflatable dolls or something?"

"You're a pistol," Cliff said wearily, reaching for his sandwich at last.

She wolfed down the last bite of her meal and licked her fingers happily, glad that he hadn't exploded in the face of her needling. "I don't think you're the inflatable doll type, actually. But weird magazines, maybe? I mean, what do you *do* for sex, Forrester? You're still young enough to think about it, right?"

"Of course I . . . Oh, hell, why can't you leave me alone?"

Liza sat forward. "What do you think about sex, Forrester? I'd like to know, really. Do you drive that old pickup into town on Friday nights and hang out at a bar looking for available women?"

"No," he said shortly.

"Go to church on Sundays so you can make polite conversation with the girls in the choir?"

"No!"

"Hide in the bushes to watch some nice lady undress every Saturday night?"

"Has anybody ever slapped you for having such a smart mouth?"

"Do you want to?"

"No," Cliff said. He cast his sandwich back onto the plate and added, "But you've certainly spoiled my appetite."

"In that case, do you mind if I finish that for you? I'm starved!"

He glowered at her as Liza popped out of her chair and snatched his sandwich. She devoured it quickly, strolling around the familiar old room to absorb some of the details she remembered from her youth. The family hadn't lived at Timberlake after she was born, of course, but Liza and her siblings had often entered the lodge without permission and had considered the place their private playground. How many long, warm afternoons had she indulged in girlish games in these old rooms?

After finishing Cliff's sandwich, Liza toyed with the keys of the old piano and found the instrument woefully out of tune. A lump of sadness rose in her throat.

"My dad used to be a great piano player."

"Oh?"

"He was a big hit at parties. I took lessons for a while, but I didn't like the practicing."

"I'm not surprised."

As the memories threatened to overwhelm her, Liza quickly turned to the tall windows that looked out over the lake and saw the gleam of water through the trees as the last daylight faded over the horizon.

She forced herself to sound cheery. "Boy, I have a lot of memories of this place!"

"Good or bad?"

Afraid Cliff was more observant than she'd first thought, Liza said quickly, "Good, of course. Amanda and Jeff—my brother and sister—and I used to play up here by the hour. Some of my cousins, too, until they started worrying about ghosts. Mother never knew we got in here, of course—"

"Would she have objected?"

Liza shrugged. "It was our secret place, and we wanted to keep it that way. Nobody else came here. Mother hated the lodge."

Cliff shifted forward in his chair, as if his interest had been piqued. "I've noticed Alyssa never comes near. Why is that?"

"I'm not sure exactly. She lived here when she was a little girl. Maybe she associates it with my grandmother."

"What's so bad about your grandmother?"

Liza smiled indulgently. "You mean you don't know the story of Margaret Ingalls, my wicked grandmama?"

"Why should I?"

Liza laughed. "Because she was the most exciting person to ever live in Tyler! Compared to her, the rest of this damn town has been *asleep!* She disappeared, you know."

"What?" Cliff looked genuinely surprised. "I thought she died young."

"Oh, no. Maybe my family likes to pretend that's what happened, but it wasn't that way at all. She ran away."

"We're talking about Judson's wife? Alyssa's mother?"

"Right. My grandmother. Margaret was the original party girl. A true free spirit. She came from Chicago and hated the small-town life. She spent a few years turning the lodge into a palace, but she must have gotten bored with that after a while. There are some who think she ran off with one of her lovers."

"One of her—"

"Does that shock you?" Liza asked, amused.

"Women didn't do that sort of thing in those days."

"Margaret did. She did whatever she pleased."

"Ah," said Cliff.

Liza frowned, suddenly not liking his tone. "What does that mean?"

He eyed her steadily and said nothing.

"You think I'm like her, don't you?"

"Aren't you?"

"In some ways, maybe. But not all! I'd never do what she did—abandon the people I love."

Very quietly, Cliff said, "Isn't that what you've done?"

"Shut up! What do you know?"

"Nothing at all," Cliff said calmly. "I merely—"

"I have not abandoned anyone! I went away when things got intolerable, that's all. My family knew where I was. We simply chose not to communicate! Margaret left a husband and child. All I did was go away to find some room to breathe!"

Cliff's dark eyes were penetrating. "Did you find it?"

"Yes!"

"But the air was a little too intoxicating, wasn't it?"

Liza frowned. "What d'you mean?"

"You couldn't handle it—the freedom you wanted. So now you're back here again."

"That's not it at all!" Liza could hardly catch her breath, she was so angry. "I'm here because of economic reasons—nothing more. Now this lodge idea has grabbed me and...well, I think I can turn it into a job. I'll stay until it's done, but then I'm out of here!"

"If that's the case, I'll do anything I can to speed up the process."

Cliff meant it sarcastically, Liza was sure. But she pounced just the same. "So you'll be my partner, Forrester?"

"I didn't say that," he said, alarmed. "God, being your partner in any venture would be—"

"Wonderful?"

"Hellish," Cliff corrected dourly. "You're a loose cannon, Miss Baron."

"And you're a stick-in-the-mud. You're right, it would be hellish! You'd probably choke my creativity!"

He hooted. "This place needs more than creativity. A lot more!"

"And I haven't got what it takes?"

"Energy doesn't make up for lack of substance."

"Oooh, you make me mad!" Liza stalked to the window and grabbed the latch, determined to get a breath of fresh air. The window stuck, and she smacked it with the flat of her hand. When it finally crashed open, the whole room suddenly filled with a brisk breeze. The flames in the fireplace danced wildly, throwing weird shadows on the walls. Liza leaned on the sill, trying to get a grip on her composure.

"How long are you going to leave that open?" Cliff asked after a time. "It's cold."

"It is not!" Liza snapped, still thoroughly steamed. "It's summer."

"You're so upset you can't feel how cold—"

"I am not upset! I want some fresh air, that's all. Why, I might even sleep with all the windows wide open in my room tonight! What do you think of that?"

Cliff shrugged. "Go ahead, but you'll freeze."

"Oh, don't be such a fusspot!"

"I'm not a fusspot. It gets chilly at night up here, even in the summer. And there's no central heat, you know."

She spun around and sat on the sill defiantly, not sure why she was so infuriated. "Well, I'm not going to invite you into my bed to keep me warm, if that's what you're hoping for."

Cliff's expression hardened. "I was not hoping!"

"No?" Getting to her feet, Liza strolled provocatively toward him. "Come on, Forrester, you think I'm sexy, don't you?"

He folded his arms across his chest. "I think I've made my feelings about you perfectly clear."

Liza laughed at him, one hand cocked on her hip in a deliberately taunting posture. "Your words say no, but your eyes say yes."

"You're impossible!"

"And you're probably dying to be with a real woman after all these years. I'd better lock my door, hadn't I? Just to keep myself safe from you."

"If it will make you happy, I'll move down to the boathouse!"

"Oh, there's no need for that," Liza said breezily, enjoying herself once she had the upper hand again. "I'll lock my door and prop a chair under the knob, just in case you can't control yourself."

He sighed. "Miss Baron..."

"I should warn you, Forrester. I'm not an easy woman. I don't go to bed with anybody on a first date, so don't get your hopes up, all right? I'm very finicky on that point."

"I'm not surprised," he said dryly.

Liza heard his tone and immediately took offense. "What's that supposed to mean?"

"Not a thing."

"Are you insinuating that I'm some kind of tease?"

"No."

"I suppose you think I'm overcompensating for something, is that it?"

"I'm trying not to think about you at all," Cliff returned coolly.

Liza strode to his chair and pointed a long finger at his nose. "You'll think about me a lot tonight, Forrester. I guarantee it!"

Liza stalked toward the door after that, but she couldn't prevent herself from spinning around in the doorway for one last parting shot. "And don't try anything cute, Forrester. I wasn't kidding when I said my door would be locked!"

She marched toward the stairs then, leaving an ominous silence behind in the lounge. Only the gentle crackle of the fire could be heard over her stomping footsteps as she ascended the staircase to the second floor. On the landing, she paused and listened.

From the lounge came the quiet sound of Cliff Forrester clearing his throat. Or suppressing a laugh.

He was laughing at her! Infuriated, Liza slammed into her room and closed her door with a resounding crash. She whirled around, breathing hard, and glared at the door.

"Come on, Forrester!" she said to the door. "I dare you to come up here and make fun of me!"

She paced for several minutes, fuming and rehearsing the kind of remarks that would put Cliff Forrester firmly in his place.

But he didn't come, and eventually Liza let out a huge yawn. She tried to calculate how many hours she'd been awake and realized she couldn't force her brain to concentrate any longer.

Suddenly very tired, she washed up in the small bathroom, then returned to the pink bedroom she'd chosen for herself. She locked the door, as promised, then turned to study the room. It was one of the smaller guest rooms, but had been Liza's favorite when they'd played at the lodge in her childhood. No doubt it had been one of Margaret's pet projects. Unlike the other rustic rooms, which had probably been used by the men in her grandfather's hunting parties, the pink bedroom was cozy and pretty, with a light pink paint, windows festooned with tattered remains of lace curtains, and a set of petite furniture—a small iron bed, a lady's dressing table and a delicate chest of drawers painted white and topped by a porcelain lamp decorated with roses.

The frilly bedclothes had disappeared, of course, and the pastel rug had faded into a pale twin of its former self, but the room still had a certain romantic air that suited Liza's suddenly nostalgic mood.

Though she had never been allowed to spend a night in the lodge, Liza had used the pink room to play pretend games on rainy afternoons. It had also been the hiding place for her collection of paper dolls. Liza hadn't wanted her brother or sister to know she owned such a collection—she had prided herself on her tomboy's reputation—so she'd kept her dolls a secret.

On a whim, she crawled under the bed to look for the familiar shoebox that she'd decorated with pictures clipped from *Life* magazine, but it wasn't there.

"I probably threw it away myself," Liza murmured once she'd extricated herself from under the bed. Still on her knees, she yawned again. "I never did collect anything for very long."

She found a blanket in the chest of drawers and dragged it to the bed, ready to tuck herself in for the night. At the last moment, she remembered her vow to sleep with the window open and hopped out once more, to throw open the casements as wide as they would go. A brisk breeze filled the room, and Liza smiled with satisfaction.

"Good, clean country air! Perfect!"

She climbed into bed then, scrunching her long body under the blanket to keep warm. Smiling, she closed her eyes and let her body relax.

She fell asleep and dozed for a while, but a weird noise suddenly brought her to full consciousness about an hour later. Liza sat up.

"What the hell—"

She heard it again—a soft, mournful sound. Music, maybe? A human cry? *Singing?* Sitting in the dark, Liza listened hard, straining to decipher exactly what she'd heard.

Silence. Then, again, the quiet wail sounded. Liza's heart kicked, and she instinctively hugged the blanket to her chest, shivering with fear as the eerie, musical moan echoed in the empty lodge. The soft, unhappy cry reverberated from a distant room, yet seemed to fill the whole cavernous building with its lonesome lament. Liza couldn't think, couldn't move. Paralyzed, she listened to the echo and felt her skin break out in gooseflesh.

Then her brain snapped back, and she said aloud, "Forrester, you creep!"

He was trying to scare her out of the lodge! That had to be it.

"Oh, grow up!" Liza groaned, flopping back down onto the bed. "If you think you're going to chase me out of Timberlake, Forrester, you'll have to do better than a few stupid ghost sounds!"

She heard the cry again, but this time it made her giggle. Untroubled, she fell asleep in no time.

CHAPTER FIVE

CLIFF WOKE with a jerk and found himself in the pitch-dark lounge, uncomfortably stiff from sleeping in a chair. Instinctively, he didn't move. Holding himself very still, he listened intently, trying to decide what had awakened him.

Sleep was a luxury. He'd discovered that long ago. In Cambodia, he'd been afraid to drift off in the darkness. To fall asleep meant he might die at the hands of an assassin. Back in the States, nightmares kept him awake, sometimes for days at a time. If he dozed off, terrible images filled his head, boiling out of his imagination, his memory, his fears. He'd forced himself to stay awake to avoid the horror of his subconscious mind.

But at the lodge, the nightmares were different.

He listened intensely, half-afraid he had imagined a noise, and finally the sound drifted down to him again. It was a plaintive, almost singsong voice. When he'd first heard it not long after moving into the lodge, he'd been afraid of the ghostly sound. He'd figured it was a new kind of torment generated by the events in Cambodia. But gradually, Cliff had become accustomed to the nightly serenade. It didn't feel threatening. It was . . . well, too feminine to be threatening.

What bothered Cliff most was his inability to explain the sound. He'd searched the lodge thoroughly and found nothing that could rouse him from his uneasy sleep every night. No open windows, no stray animals taking up residence in a nook or cranny. No logical explanation at all.

"Except one," he said aloud. "I've gone crazy."

He stood up quickly and snapped on a light, not surprised to see his hands shaking.

Was he going crazy?

"I can't tell," he muttered wearily, raking his hand through his long hair.

Cliff stumbled to the kitchen and poured himself a glass of milk, spilling a puddle on the counter before succeeding in filling the glass. He tried to drink, but the liquid seemed to congeal in his mouth, so he set the glass down again unsteadily and closed his eyes.

Don't let it happen tonight. Don't go berserk with Liza in the lodge.

He willed himself to breathe evenly, to quiet his pounding heart and empty his mind of the nightmarish images that bombarded him. It took a long time to calm down. When he felt steady enough to move, he went out onto the porch and sat on the steps with his back braced against the railing. There, he heard no more sounds from the lodge. Nor did the bizarre side of his own imagination intrude again. The cold night air helped keep him awake. If he stayed conscious, he couldn't hurt anyone.

He dozed off once, then woke again around dawn. The forest was alive with the chirping of birds, and Cliff listened to their friendly sound while working the kinks out of his stiff limbs. Then he walked down to the lake and cast his fishing line out over the water a few times. He welcomed the peace of the morning and the warmth of the sun. The dawning light seemed to wash away his bad dreams with a kind of golden serenity.

Luck was with him, as it had been the day before. A fat bass took his hook, despite Cliff's lackadaisical technique. Somewhat cheered and relieved that he'd made it through another night, he carried his fish up to the lodge.

He was cleaning it in the sink when Liza came downstairs. She looked bleary-eyed and grouchy—a sight that gave Cliff a surprising amount of pleasure.

"What are you doing?" she grumbled, rumpling her long hair with one graceful hand and crinkling her nose. "It smells awful in here."

She was wearing a snug pair of jeans and the same sweater he'd lent her yesterday. It was an outfit that seemed to suit her better than the short dress and spike-heeled shoes—unaffected, but still magnificently sexy.

"I'm cleaning your breakfast," Cliff said, rinsing his fish under the faucet and trying not to wonder if she was wearing anything underneath the sweater.

She strolled closer. "Why the change in attitude? I thought you wanted me to starve."

"I'm feeling generous this morning."

"How come?"

He shrugged. "I dunno. What's wrong with you this morning? You look like hell."

Which wasn't exactly the truth. She looked very attractive—pretty despite the obvious circles under her eyes and the lack of makeup that emphasized her pale complexion.

Liza climbed onto a stool and glowered at him. "I didn't sleep well," she said flatly. "No thanks to you."

"What do you mean?"

"I refuse to dignify that question with a response. Let's just say I didn't appreciate how annoying you were last night. That, combined with a lousy bed, translates into a body that hurts all over, and my nose is stuffy, too."

"Maybe you're catching a cold."

"That's ridiculous."

Cliff dropped the fish onto a plate and proceeded to wash the scales from his hands, eyeing Liza as she felt her forehead for signs of fever. "You left your window open all night, didn't you?"

Irritably, she said, "People don't catch colds from open windows! I'm not getting sick."

"You're giving a pretty good imitation of it."

"I am not!"

"Your nose is red. Your eyes are glazed."

"Quit trying to sweet-talk me, Forrester."

"Face it, Miss Baron. You're getting sick."

That enflamed her and she sat up straight. "I am not! I never get sick. Never!"

Liza punctuated that definitive statement by letting out an enormous sneeze.

Cliff burst out laughing. He couldn't help it. After a long, unpleasantly sleepless night, the sight of stubborn Liza Baron declaring her good health while snuffling and sneezing like an advertisement for a drugstore...well, it was too funny to ignore. He chuckled and reached for a towel.

Liza stared at him, pink nosed and blinking her wide blue eyes.

"What's the matter?" he asked, still amused.

"You look..." She shook her head as if to dispel amazement. "It's weird to see you laugh, that's all. I wasn't sure you were capable of it."

"Of course I am."

"When was the last time you really laughed like that?"

Cliff considered her question and realized he couldn't answer. "I don't know," he said, surprising himself by telling the truth.

"Well, it's certainly an improvement," Liza responded, and she meant it.

Feeling a lot better, she got down off the stool. Despite a headache and sore joints, her spirits had begun to rise at the sound of his laughter. Cliff Forrester had looked like death warmed over when she staggered into the kitchen, but his laugh sounded very good indeed. His mouth had a distinctly sexy curve to it when he smiled.

She tossed her hair and said, "You look like a normal human being when you smile like that, Forrester."

And just to annoy him, she grasped the front of Cliff's shirt and pulled him down for a kiss. It was an impulsive, thoughtless kiss—the kind that wasn't meant to be sexual, just teasing. It worked, too. The contact was fast and hard and very hot. It gave Liza tingles.

It must have done the same for him. When she released him and stood back, Liza could see that Cliff's gaze had filled with light and his breath had caught in his throat.

"What was that for?" he asked, voice low.

Liza shrugged carelessly. "I felt like it. Besides, it was a way of getting back at you."

"What for?"

"The I-told-you-so about leaving my window open."

"How do you figure?"

"It's simple. If I *am* catching a cold, you'll get it, too. Right?"

She laughed at his appalled expression and skipped out of the kitchen, calling over her shoulder, "I'm not eating breakfast this morning, Forrester. I'm headed into town."

"You're leaving, you mean?"

"No such luck!" Liza started up the stairs and shouted down to him, "I'm going to check on my car and talk to Granddad and run a few errands. I'll be back here by lunchtime. Want to drive me?"

He came out of the kitchen and stood at the bottom of the stairs, looking up at her in his old solemn way again. "No."

"Suit yourself. Trust me with the truck?"

"Of course not."

Laughing, Liza leaned her elbows on the railing. Her hair tumbled around her face. "Would you trust me with anything, Forrester?"

"Not a thing," he said, and smiled again.

LIZA TOOK the rattletrap pickup truck into town in hopes of catching her grandfather at Marge's Diner again. She wanted to extract a promise from him—a promise and a few thousand dollars to fix up the lodge the way she thought it could be fixed.

She wished she could have convinced Cliff to come along. It was obvious that he needed more human contact. The guy really was a certifiable hermit! But she wasn't ready for another marathon argument. Unwillingly, she left him behind and drove into Tyler.

She stopped at the drugstore first and picked up some cold remedies and aspirin. The walk from the drugstore to the diner took her past the old Worthington House, a huge Victorian mansion that had been converted into a retirement home with nursing care for the more frail residents. As she walked along the sidewalk, she gave a tremendous sneeze.

"Bless you!" cried a voice from the screened porch.

"Thanks," Liza called back, not breaking stride as she rounded the corner.

But she could not ignore the quick whispering voices that rose from the porch of Worthington House. They sounded as if they were arguing. At last, an elderly female voice cried, "Is that you, Mary Elizabeth?"

Liza stopped on the sidewalk and peered through the screens just a few yards away. She blew her nose loudly on a tissue and bellowed, "Who wants to know?"

Giggles erupted, and a more authoritative voice declared, "That's Liza Baron, all right. Come up here at once, young lady."

Liza suppressed a smile and did as she was commanded. She recognized the voice as that of Miss Inger Hansen, a formidable woman who had taught a deportment class in Tyler for many years. Half the town lived in terror of Miss Hansen—all the girls who had been forced to attend her deportment class.

"Hello, Miss Hansen," Liza said as she mounted the wide steps of Worthington House, unconsciously straightening her spine into the approved posture. "It's nice to see you."

"Well, I can't see a thing," snapped Miss Hansen. "Come closer!"

Liza obediently opened the screened door and let herself into the porch, where she found herself surrounded by a group of elderly ladies. She was surprised that they were already up and hard at work, all sitting in straight-backed rocking chairs and sewing at the small squares of a quilt. In a flash, Liza remembered the Tyler Quilting Circle, a group of women who had met on a weekly basis for decades to share gossip and create beautiful quilts—quilts that would be worth a fortune in any interior decorator's shop in the world now, but that were usually donated for church auctions or other worthy causes.

At Liza's arrival, all the ladies put down their sewing and examined her eagerly, some taking off their glasses and exclaiming over her appearance.

"Why, haven't you grown up tall and pretty!"

"Liza, I remember when you used to climb my apple trees and steal pumpkins out of my garden. Do you remember doing that?"

"Hello, Mrs. Bauer. Yes, I remember very clearly. Hello, Mrs. Phelps."

"Hello, dear. Aren't you the image of your grandmother! What a beauty!"

Miss Hansen brought the cheery greetings to a halt by rapping her cane on the floorboards. She was an imperious woman of eighty-odd years with a commanding nose and a voice that overrode all the others—not surprising in a woman who had been hard of hearing for most of her life but refused any kind of hearing aid, claiming she didn't need such a thing. Other people should talk louder, was her argument.

"See here, young lady," Miss Hansen demanded. "What's this we hear about you living up at Timberlake lodge with that horrible man?"

"What horrible man?"

The other ladies fell silent, but had the grace to turn pink at Miss Hansen's blunt attack. Miss Hansen did not notice their embarrassment. "That Vietnam person, of course."

"Vietnam person?" Liza laughed. "His name is Cliff."

Miss Hansen's thin brows lowered ominously over her small, dangerous eyes. "I don't care what his name is, miss. You shouldn't be visiting him."

"I'm not visiting," Liza said firmly. "I'm living at the lodge with him, as a matter of fact."

The ladies gasped. Miss Hansen looked thunderous. "Living in sin, is that it?"

"Not at all. We happen to be living under the same roof at the moment, that's all. Why, I barely know the man."

"Well, we know all about him, don't we, ladies? Rose, tell Liza what you saw last spring."

Rose Atkins looked stricken at having been put on the spot. She cleared her throat awkwardly. "It wasn't last spring, Inger. It must have been four years ago, at least."

Miss Hansen pounded her cane in frustration. "I don't care when it was! Tell her what you saw!"

"Oh, I'm sure it was nothing, Inger. I happened to be taking a breath of fresh air, Liza, and I must have surprised Mr. Forrester. It was very late at night, you see. He was...well, he was very upset—"

"Weeping," Miss Hansen snapped. "That's what you said, Rose. He was sobbing like a baby."

"Well, not that hard," Rose said quickly. "He was walking around the park by himself and very upset, so I spoke to him, but he didn't seem interested in—"

"He ran away," said Miss Hansen triumphantly. "That's what he did. Is that strange or not! I ask you! A grown man! Why, he's—"

"He's had a bad experience," Rose said defensively. "I think he's just trying to get over that as best he can. I wondered if someone couldn't suggest a good therapist, but—"

"Therapist!" Miss Hansen snorted. "That nonsense is for weak sisters!"

"I haven't known Cliff very long," Liza said sharply, "but I'm sure he's not a weak sister. He seems like a very nice person, as a matter of fact. I like him."

"He could be very dangerous. Why, I wouldn't be surprised if he was the one who poisoned my cat last year!"

"Inger," said a very patient Rose Atkins, "that cat was nineteen years old. Nobody poisoned him."

"Well, some evil person went around breaking windows once, remember that? I can guess who that culprit was!"

"Three teenage boys from Bonneville," murmured Mrs. Bauer as she picked up her stitching again.

"Honestly, Inger, I don't know why you're having such a hissyfit."

"Hissyfit! Well, don't come crying to me when that man goes on a rampage and murders everyone in town—starting with this young lady right here!" Miss Hansen pointed one bony finger at Liza.

"I can take care of myself," Liza snapped, patience lost. "But if he feels like murdering somebody, I can show him a place to start!"

The quilting ladies burst into giggles at that—all but Miss Hansen, who didn't realize whom the crack was aimed at. She glared at Liza, who marched off the porch with her head held high.

"Come back and visit us again, Liza!" called Rose Atkins.

"Bring us some chocolate next time!" cried another voice.

"Yes, and maybe a pizza pie!"

"Pizza?" Liza heard Miss Hansen demand. "Why in the world would you want to eat a pizza pie, Tillie?"

"Because they're spicy, Inger, and I like spicy things."

"Well, don't come crying to me if it gives you gas," said Miss Hansen.

Laughing, Liza strode down the sidewalk, heading for the diner. She made a mental note to return to Worthington House soon. With chocolates and pizza for everyone.

She hoped she hadn't missed her grandfather, who undoubtedly left Marge's Diner at the same time every day to go to his office at the Ingalls plant just outside town. There Judson, a perpetual tinkerer, worked on new devices and formulas he hoped would help revolutionize the farming industry. Liza quickened her pace and arrived at the diner within a few minutes of nine o'clock.

She found Judson finishing his second cup of coffee and chatting with Marge.

"Back again, are you?" Marge asked, beaming. "More pancakes this morning, Liza?"

"How about a double orange juice and a muffin instead?" Liza asked as she slid into the chair opposite her grandfather.

"Coming right up," said Marge, whisking away to fill Liza's order.

Judson took one impassive look at Liza and said, "What the hell happened to you?"

"I'm catching something," she said, digging another tissue out of her jeans pocket. "A cold, maybe. Do I look that bad?"

"You look like you didn't get a wink of sleep." Judson's face turned dark, and his pulse began to show in one of the veins in his forehead. "Did that Forrester fellow bother you, Mary Elizabeth? By God, I'll wring his neck with my own two hands if he—"

"Take it easy," Liza said, reaching out to cover one of Judson's hands with her own. "Cliff left me completely alone." Remembering her sudden itch to touch Cliff as he'd built the fire in the hearth, she made a face and added wryly, "Unfortunately for me."

Judson looked alarmed at that. "What do you mean? Never mind, I don't want to know!"

Indulgently, Liza propped her elbows on the table and asked, "What's the matter, Granddad? Don't you think your grandchildren have sexual urges now and then?''

Judson's stern countenance began to turn purple with rage. ''I won't listen to that kind of talk from anyone—not even you! Why, I'll wash your mouth out with soap if—''

''Okay, okay, I'm sorry. Cliff didn't bother me a bit, all right? I'm perfectly safe up at the lodge. I'm sure of that.''

''For the moment, anyway.''

Liza decided to ignore that dark remark. ''I didn't come here to talk about Cliff, Granddad.''

''That's a relief. You're going to pay a visit to your mother, is that it?''

Liza sighed. ''No, I'm not.''

''I mentioned to her that you were back in town, Mary Elizabeth.''

She froze and finally managed to say, ''I wish you hadn't done that, Granddad.''

''You can't avoid her forever, you know.''

''I'm not avoiding her,'' she said quickly. ''I—I'm just waiting, that's all.''

''Waiting for what? The moon to turn blue? Listen to me, girl, you get your pretty backside down to the house this morning or you'll have to answer to me!''

''I'll go see her,'' Liza promised sulkily. ''But not this morning. I have too much to do.''

''Too much to do?'' Judson repeated, on his guard at once. ''Do I like the sound of that?''

''I think you will once I've told you everything.''

Marge arrived with Liza's orange juice at that moment, so Liza opened the paper bag of remedies she had picked up at the drugstore and began to outline her plans while she gulped pills. Judson listened to her without interrupting.

"I think it could be a wonderful resort, Grand-dad," she said at last. "It'll be a real showplace once I've finished making it beautiful again. And if we decide not to run it ourselves, the refurbishing will make it much more attractive to a buyer who *could* run it. What do you say?"

Judson was silent. His gaze had wandered away from Liza, and he appeared to be lost in thought.

At last Liza urged, "Say something, Granddad. Is it a horrible idea?"

"It's not horrible," he said slowly.

"Well? Can you give me the money to get started?"

"It's just..."

Liza waited for him to collect his thoughts. It took a while, and she wondered what he was thinking. By the pained expression that flitted across his eyes, he obviously had mixed feelings.

Finally Judson shook his head wearily. "I have too many bad memories of Timberlake. It's hard for me to make a decision suddenly like this."

"It's not sudden. You haven't used the lodge in ages. Why not let someone else enjoy it before it crumbles into dust?"

He considered that, then sighed and murmured, "Things don't always turn out the way you hope, do they?"

"What do you mean, Granddad?"

"Nothing." He appeared to shake himself out of his reverie. "Go ahead and do what you like, Mary Elizabeth. I'll give you money as soon as you draw up a budget."

"A budget?"

He grinned at her. "You don't expect me to hand over a blank check, do you? If you want this to be a job, you had better treat it like a job, my dear. I want numbers—cold hard figures—before you start spending a single penny of my money. And once we've agreed on a budget, there will be no overruns, you understand?"

"But—"

"No buts," Judson announced. "If there's one thing I can teach you before I die, it's how to run a business without going broke. And from the sound of things, it's a lesson you need to learn."

"All right. Anything else?"

"Yes, I have one more demand."

Liza steeled herself to argue with him. "Granddad, I am perfectly safe at the lodge with Cliff. I refuse to move out just because you're afraid he might—"

"I'm not going to tell you where to live," Judson interrupted. "You say you can take care of yourself, and I assume Cliff Forrester can handle *you* if you get too aggressive, so—"

"Granddad!"

"So I'm going to give you a different order. I want you to go visit your mother. At once. Got that?"

CHAPTER SIX

LIZA DISOBEYED.

She checked on her car at Carl's garage, then drove the pickup back to the lodge without going to see her mother. She stopped at the grocery store instead, spent more of Judson's money and headed back to Timberlake with enough food to last several days.

Liza pushed all thought of her mother out of her head. She had more important things on her mind. Fixing up Timberlake was a designer's dream, after all! Her brain seethed with ideas to make the place spectacular. It would be the envy of every designer in the world when she was finished.

"Hey, Forrester!" she bellowed once she returned to the lodge. "Come out, come out, wherever you are!"

She shouted for several minutes and looked for him all over the lodge, but Cliff was nowhere to be found. Chances were he was off somewhere on the lake, admiring his fish. Disappointed that she had nobody to share her excitement with, Liza had to settle for racing around the rooms with her sketchbook, making notes and rapidly drawing when words failed her. Her imagination fairly burned with more and more possibilities as she worked. She grabbed an apple and another cold tablet for lunch and worked all afternoon at getting her ideas on paper.

"A budget can wait," she said to herself decisively. "At this point, it's more important to let my creativity flow!"

The best idea hit Liza when she was studying the entrance to the lodge, blowing her nose. It needed to be grander—large and airy instead of the cramped space that currently served as a foyer.

"It needs a huge chandelier," Liza said aloud. "Nothing ordinary either—something made out of deer antlers, maybe, or—or... Hey! Maybe I ought to tear out this wall! I wonder if it's possible."

There was only one way to find out. In the pickup truck, Liza found a tire iron. With the tool in hand, she began to pry off the molding around one doorway, sneezing and coughing as she worked. The molding came off with a huge crash and sent a cloud of powdery plaster through the air. But underneath, Liza found some loose boards. She was busily hacking at them when Cliff walked in.

He halted in the doorway, his face a picture of astonishment. "Good Lord," he said. "Are you *crazy?*"

Liza sat back on her heels, brushed a dusting of plaster from her face and grinned broadly as Cliff stared at the mess she'd created. He looked very attractive in a short-sleeved T-shirt and jeans that clung to his hips and tapered to some grungy sneakers. He still had the exhausted demeanor of a man who hadn't slept well in months, but he looked pretty good otherwise. From the glow of sunshine on his face and the flecks of paint that covered his chest and arms, Liza

guessed he'd been scraping old paint somewhere outside—the boathouse, perhaps. She was delighted to see
him and sneezed just to prove it.

"What do you think?" she demanded, blowing her
nose lustily. "Isn't it going to be great?"

"You *are* crazy," Cliff pronounced, full of awe as
he stepped over the fallen molding to survey the de-
struction more closely. "Did you set off a bomb in
here?"

"I'm expanding the space," Liza explained, waving the tire iron to show him the lines of the room she
envisioned. "We'll knock down this wall and the one
over there, and throw up another one back here to
keep the lounge intact, and then—"

"Who's going to do all this?"

"You and me, of course. Haven't we been through
this before?"

Cliff stood over her like a disapproving high school
principal. "Miss Baron," he said, speaking carefully
to avoid any confusion, "this job is beyond my ability and yours. You need a real carpenter. An archi-
tect. An engineer . . ."

"What kind of skill does it take to knock down a
wall?"

"It's not the knocking down that's difficult! It's
the . . . Oh, hell, why am I bothering to explain? To you
of all people! It's useless!"

He turned to leave, shaking his head, and Liza
boiled to her feet. "What was that crack supposed to
mean?"

He turned back, his face lined with fatigue. In his
voice, Liza heard the edge of anger along with ex-
haustion. "It wasn't a crack, it was the truth. You've

never listened to anyone in your life, so why do I think I could be the first one to penetrate that thick head of yours?''

"My head is not thick!" Liza tried to jump over the heap of debris she had created, missed a step and lost her balance. When Cliff caught her hand in time to save her from a fall, she threw up her head and snapped, "I'm perfectly capable of doing the job I was trained for! My ideas are exciting and dramatic, so don't go—''

"I have no doubts about your ideas," said Cliff. He helped her over the pile of rubble and added, "It's your common sense that's nonexistent."

"Nonexistent!" Liza yanked her hand from his grasp. "Well, you're alone in that opinion, Forrester. My grandfather has faith in me. He's given me carte blanche—absolute authority to make any changes I see fit—''

"He said that? Those actual words?"

"Well, not those words exactly, but—''

"What words exactly *did* he say?"

"That I have permission to fix up the lodge however I like!"

"And he's paying?"

"Yes, of course. As soon as I prepare a budget, he—''

"Oho," said Cliff, rocking back on his heels. "Maybe Granddad's not a fool after all. He's going to give you just enough money to keep you busy."

Liza felt her blood pressure start to build, and she cocked her fists on her hips. She'd been happy with her day's accomplishments, and Cliff was heartlessly tearing down all her dreams. "What are you suggesting?"

Cliff took an old handkerchief from his pocket and wiped the perspiration and paint chips from his face. "Oh, come on, Liza," he said, sounding tired of arguing. "You know what he's doing. Judson's giving his excitable granddaughter a project to keep her occupied until she settles down—"

"You bastard! Where do you get off saying things like that? This is an honest job—a project I can sink my teeth into! If you think Granddad is...is giving me some kind of charity, you should think again!"

"It'll take millions to fix up this old heap."

"Don't be ridiculous," Liza retorted. "I can decorate this place for—for...well, for lots less than a million dollars!"

"What about the structural problems? The pipes? The roof? The electrical system is something out of the Dark Ages."

"You're exaggerating," Liza said, but her confidence faltered at the suggestion of structural problems. She hadn't planned on those.

Cliff laughed shortly. "Am I exaggerating? Have you tried running the toaster and a radio at the same time yet? And the whole second floor is jury-rigged so badly..."

"It won't take much to fix it," Liza insisted weakly.

"You feel qualified to make that judgment? Face it, you're an amateur. A few curtains and a change of wallpaper isn't going to turn Timberlake into the next Club Med."

A realization struck Liza, and she folded her arms over her chest. "Oh, I get it."

"Get what?"

"You're just trying to make me quit."

"What?"

"You hated the whole idea from the start," Liza accused, jabbing her forefinger into his chest and knocking him back a pace with the force of her poke. "*You* don't want the lodge to become a resort at all. *You* want to have the place to yourself! Of course you'd try to talk me out of my ideas."

"Listen—"

"No, *you* listen," Liza cried. "I'm not some kind of spoiled brat who needs a keeper. I'm going to make something wonderful out of this lodge, and *you're* not going to stop me just because you want to play Rip Van Winkle all alone up here for the rest of your life!"

"That has nothing to do with—"

"Of course it does! If you don't like what I'm doing, Forrester, you can get the hell out! Go on! Go!"

Cliff stared at Liza for several heartbeats, hardly able to believe what she was saying. Her taut face was more angry than ever before.

"No," he began unsteadily, determined to stay calm. Losing his cool around Liza was undoubtedly as dangerous as opening a vein in a shark tank. "Wait a minute."

"You heard me," Liza swept on, unaware of how profoundly her furious words were affecting him. "I'm going ahead with my ideas, and you can pack your bags if you plan to stand in my way!"

"I'm not leaving," he said. "I—"

"And *don't* think you can start any more shenanigans designed to chase me away, because I'm not leaving, either!"

She threw down her tire iron, which bounced with lethal speed and nearly took off Cliff's kneecap. He dodged out of the way just in time to avoid being crippled. Liza spun around, her long hair throwing bits of broken plaster as she whirled and marched for the stairs.

"Liza—"

"And you can forget about that spaghetti dinner!"

"What spaghetti dinner?"

"The one I was going to cook for you!" she shouted. "And believe me, I don't cook for anyone else in the world, buster!"

That declaration rang hollowly in the entrance hall. Watching Liza make her dramatic exit up the stairs, Cliff suddenly felt very unhappy. He hadn't meant to hurt her. Not really. She was so damned explosive!

"Liza," he called tentatively. Then, *"Liza!"*

She turned on the top landing and glared down at him. "You want the last word?"

"I'm sorry," he said.

"What?"

Cliff hadn't noticed how the words stuck in his throat. He coughed and said louder, "I'm sorry for what I said. About Judson giving you a project to keep you busy."

Was he imagining the sudden sheen in Liza's eyes, or had she gone teary as she swept up the stairs? She sneezed abruptly and fished in her pocket for a tissue. She looked about sixteen years old as she wiped her nose. "It's not true, you know."

"I know. I just . . . I shouldn't have said that." He gave a sigh and muttered, "Oh, hell, I'm not very good at this."

"At what?"

"Talking. Explaining. I shouldn't have said what I did."

"Maybe I didn't think about structural problems," she said after a moment. "But you had no right to—"

"I hurt your feelings. I'm sorry. Really."

"Well," she said unwillingly. "That's a start, I guess."

"A start?"

"You're very difficult to get along with, Forrester."

"*Me?*" Cliff waded through the debris she'd created on the floor and stood at the bottom of the staircase looking up at her. "You think *I'm* difficult?"

"Yes." She lifted her pink nose arrogantly. "But I'll admit I can be...well, not easy all the time. I didn't want to hear anything negative, that's all. I'm excited about this project."

"I can see that."

She began to chew her thumbnail—an endearing weakness, Cliff noted—and nodded, surveying the mess she'd made with the tire iron. "Maybe it's going to be a little harder than I first thought. In fact, this may be the toughest job of my life."

"Hmm," Cliff said, trying not to agree too heartily in case she exploded again. He wasn't sure which side of Liza he liked most—her damn-the-torpedoes side or the chagrined little innocent side. Both were appealing.

Before he could think, Cliff heard himself saying, "How about if I cook the spaghetti?"

Liza's face brightened. "You mean it?"

"Well, I can try."

"It's just bottled sauce," she said. "Nothing fancy."

"I can probably handle it, then. How about it? Since you're sick, I'll cook."

Liza smiled tentatively. "I'll go wash my face first."

When she smiled, Cliff's heart turned over. It was a queer feeling—a quick pang in his chest that left him breathless. As she scampered down the hallway and out of sight, he stood at the newel post like a dope and wondered about himself. Things seemed so normal one minute, then frighteningly unreal the next.

The sound of Liza happily splashing water in the bathroom made him feel absurdly happy. After years of cherishing the silence, Cliff surprised himself by feeling glad she had come.

He shook himself and went into the kitchen. He found bags of groceries on the counter—bags Liza had obviously not bothered to unpack. She had been too charged up about the lodge to be bothered with food, he noted. In the bottom of one bag was a quart of melted tin roof ice cream, but other than that, the damage was minimal.

Cliff cleaned up the mess, put the food away and set about making dinner. Liza shyly joined him within a few minutes, and with very little prodding, began to describe her plans for the lodge.

Cliff didn't listen to the details, to tell the truth. Mostly, he watched Liza's face as she talked. The light in her eyes, her quicksilver smile and the animation in her expression were charming. She reminded him of a big, eager puppy, all long legs and enthusiasm. He found himself feeling invigorated around her. Energy radiated from Liza like heat from a stove. It warmed him. Cheered him.

She chattered and got in his way without being much help, so eventually Cliff steered her gently to the stool and plunked a bowl of lettuce in front of her. While she talked, she shredded lettuce for a salad, and didn't seem to notice that the pieces were tiny enough and plentiful enough to feed the Seven Dwarfs.

"Oh," she said, blinking with surprise when she realized what she'd done. "This is an awful lot of salad."

"That's okay," said Cliff, slipping the bowl out of her range. "I'm pretty hungry. Want to butter the bread next?"

She completed whatever task Cliff put in front of her, but he was careful not to ask too much of her while she was so pumped up about the lodge.

At last the food was ready, and they ate without ceremony at the kitchen counter. It felt right that way. To eat together in the cavernous dining room under the chandelier would have been too awkward. Cliff was content to listen and watch, hardly tasting the food in front of him. Liza's energy seemed boundless, her smile infectious, her spirit untamable.

When it was time for dessert, Cliff began to fantasize about what it would be like to make love to her.

She said, "I wish I'd remembered to put the ice cream away when I came home from the store. I was so eager to get started with my sketchbook that I completely forgot to put it in the fridge."

"No harm done."

She propped her chin in her hands and devoted her attention to him fully. Her eyes found his, and she seemed to drink him in the way she'd consumed her dinner—with great pleasure. She asked, "Don't you eat dessert?"

"What? No. Not at all."

"Really?" Her brows puckered with curiosity. "Don't you ever want to break out of this place and go have a piece of pie at Marge's?"

"No," said Cliff. "I don't. But if you'd like to go, don't let me stop you."

"Boy, you're a puzzle. I can never guess what you'll say next. I want to ask you a million questions."

He held his breath. If she prodded him to talk about himself, he might do it. He didn't feel that she'd reject him if he told her about some of the things he'd seen or the way he'd chosen to live his life now. She wouldn't laugh or look at him as if he'd just turned into Frankenstein's monster. Cliff felt that Liza Baron might actually listen and absorb. If she asked a question at that moment, he thought, he would answer.

Liza gave a huge yawn instead. "No trip for pie tonight, I'm afraid. I think I'll take some medicine and go to bed. With the window closed."

Cliff allowed a small smile and let the moment slip by. "Maybe the window had nothing to do with catching a cold."

"Maybe," said Liza, getting to her feet and stretching every muscle in her tall, lean frame. It was a very attractive frame, Cliff decided. Feminine, but not breakable. Sinuous, he thought. And she seemed comfortable in her own skin. She moved with pride, the way a big cat might.

Unaware of his attention, she said, "I'll do the dishes before I go upstairs."

"No," said Cliff, catching himself before he put out a hand to touch her thigh as she stood next to the counter. "Go to bed. I'll clean up."

She smiled at him, a smile at once teasing and grateful. "Okay," she said. "I'll let you."

Liza bent down and kissed him lightly on the temple. It wasn't a gentle kiss, but a quick, teasing one. She caught his earlobe between her thumb and forefinger and gave him a tug there, too.

"Good night, Forrester."

"Good night, Liza," he said. He sat for a long time in the kitchen after she'd left, contemplating women in general.

He hadn't thought about women in a long time. Not the way he thought about them that night. Sex had been a part of his other life. Since he'd come back, there hadn't been anyone. He hadn't let anyone get close enough.

Oh, he'd looked at women once in a while, of course. There was a pretty woman who lived in Tyler. Nora Gates, he thought her name was. Cliff had seen her in the hardware store once and had watched her buy a hammer. She'd made a light remark to him, but he'd been in a bad period at the time and hadn't responded. One thought had occurred to him, however—that Nora Gates had the look of a woman who'd had her heart broken once already. She looked vulnerable and sweet, a combination Cliff certainly couldn't have handled.

But Nora Gates hadn't gotten him thinking about sex. Not the way Liza did.

Sitting there, listening to Liza bathe in the tub overhead, hearing her footsteps pad down the hall and the soft click of the bedroom door, Cliff mused for a while. Had he forgotten how? Had there been new developments in women's underclothes that he might not understand? What did it feel like to hold a woman close and listen to her breathe? To excite her and give her the ultimate of pleasures?

It was all academic, of course. Cliff had no intention of making love to anyone. It was impossible. He might have some kind of breakdown. Or get violent. Heaven only knew what might happen if he quit maintaining his self-control. No, it was best that he keep himself on track.

But Liza Baron was the one woman on the face of the Earth who was probably capable of forcing her way into a man's bed whether she was wanted or not. What if she pushed too hard?

Cliff got up hastily and began to wash the dishes. Here it was again. The same old fear. What if he lost control and hurt someone? He hated the idea of hurting anyone. But hurting Liza? The idea made him shiver.

LIZA SWALLOWED a swig of sickly-sweet medicine and climbed into the pink bed. With a full stomach, her head still pleasantly buzzing with ideas for the lodge and the surprisingly comfortable evening she'd spent with Cliff, she settled down and felt herself begin to doze off immediately. It was the medicine, she decided. She'd sleep like a log.

Sometime during the night, however, she heard a sound. A distant, ghostly voice, singing a song, perhaps. Or maybe she was dreaming.

"Forrester," she mumbled. "Surely you don't think I'm falling for that...."

The sound faded and she went back to sleep. Untroubled thereafter, Liza slept soundly until late the next morning.

When she went downstairs to find Cliff, there was a note on the kitchen counter.

Working on hatching trays in the boathouse. Hope you feel better.

Liza tossed the note down and sighed. "Not exactly a love poem, is it? Well, what did I expect?"

And what in the world were hatching trays? Probably some fish experiment.

She found the keys to the pickup and drove into Tyler once again. Instead of looking for her grandfather, she did some research that led her to the doorstep of Joe Santori.

Joe Santori, Liza learned after asking the opinions of Marge, at the diner, and Rose Atkins, who was pedaling her tricycle around town, was Tyler's best building contractor.

"He's still a small operation," Marge told her. "But he does quality work, and he's honest."

"Besides," Rose Atkins added, "he's just darling."

"Okay," said Joe, when she proposed her idea. He was an attractive man—a big grin seemed to be his best asset—but Liza would hardly have classified him as darling. He was a big, goofy lug who wore his carpenter's apron like a gunslinger, and she caught him singing a noisy, melodramatic song in Italian when she arrived at his office. Every small town has its share of peculiar characters, and Joe Santori was certainly one of Tyler's most colorful.

In a wonderfully mellow baritone voice, he said, "I'll follow you out to the lodge and we'll take a look during my lunch hour."

Pleased that Joe had agreed to examine the project she proposed right away, she led the way back to Timberlake. They parked their trucks side by side and met on the gravel drive to look at the porch.

"Holy Mary," said Joe, taking off his cap and scratching his curly black hair as he stared up at the lodge. He kept a short, unlighted cigar between his teeth and spoke around it. "This is quite a place, isn't it?"

"Isn't it great?"

"Well, it's spectacular, I'll give you that," said Joe. "I heard it was in pretty bad shape. I can see my source wasn't too far wrong. Does that nut still live here?"

Liza ground her teeth. "There's no nut here. Cliff Forrester is the caretaker."

"Yeah, that's him. The crazy vet."

"He's not crazy," Liza snapped. "He's perfectly nice! If you'd just…oh, here he is. You can judge for yourself."

Cliff came out onto the porch with a half-eaten sandwich in one hand. He stopped dead and looked stricken when he realized that Liza had brought an invader.

"Hi," Liza said, bounding up the steps to Cliff before he could duck back into the lodge. "This is Joe Santori. He's a contractor who's going to give me some estimates for fixing up the lodge."

Cliff didn't speak. His expression was stunned and a little frightened.

"Hello," Joe drawled, mounting the steps warily and putting out his hand. "Anyone who's brave enough to live in this old wreck must be pretty tough, I guess."

Silently, Cliff shook Joe's proffered hand, and Liza wanted to scream at them both. Cliff was acting weirder than ever, eyes cast down and his body stiff as a toy soldier's, which was only going to cement Joe's opinion that he was loony. Joe, for his part, seemed to think Cliff ought to be shipped off to a padded cell.

She made an effort to cover for Cliff, saying rapidly, "The lodge isn't really a wreck. It looks bad, but I think you're going to find that the structure's okay."

"Let's get started, then." Joe pulled a battered notebook from his hip pocket and shifted his cigar to the other side of his mouth. "Let's see. How about the roof? Does it leak?"

"I'm not sure. I..." Liza noticed that Cliff had started to slip away, so she grabbed one of his belt loops. "Cliff could tell you that kind of stuff. Right, Cliff?"

He didn't respond until Liza goosed him, then he said, "The roof might leak. But I don't know how to get into the attic."

"Uh-huh," said Joe, glancing doubtfully at Cliff over the rim of his notebook. "Maybe I'd better take a look."

Cliff shot Liza a deadly look, then led the way into the lodge without a word. Joe and Liza trooped after him. Liza finished the sandwich and prayed that Cliff would loosen up.

It took about an hour, but he did, thanks to Joe. Liza thanked her lucky stars that she'd chosen Joe Santori to come to the lodge, because he was a kind-hearted fellow with a breezy sense of humor. In fact, Liza doubted he had a malicious bone in his body. Joe stopped acting nervously and made a few light remarks that gave Cliff a chance to relax, too, so that in time, the two men were talking as if they'd been working together for a long while.

"The porch is sound," Cliff said in response to one of Joe's questions when they came downstairs again. "It's the water pipes that concern me most."

"There's a well?"

"Only for drinking water. The rest of the water comes from the lake."

"When were those pipes laid?"

Cliff shrugged. "Fifty years ago, at least. Maybe Liza knows."

Liza hadn't been listening. Instead, she'd been watching covertly as Cliff became more natural talking business with Joe. He didn't seem crazy at all, just uncomfortable. And who wouldn't be after spending so many years all alone looking after fish?

Both men turned to her expectantly, and she said, "I'm sorry. I didn't catch that."

Cliff grinned. "I forgot. You can't bother Liza with boring details. She's in charge of creative thinking around here."

Joe chuckled. "Well, somebody's got to be the man in charge—or woman in charge, I guess. I'll take a look at the pipes myself before I give you a final opinion."

"Thanks," said Liza gratefully.

"It may take some digging. Should I bring my backhoe and look around a little?"

"You'd better do whatever you have to do." Then Liza sneezed.

"Wow, that's some cold you've got."

"I'll get over it. In the meantime, Cliff and I will keep trying to find a way into the attic. I'm sure I remember going up there when I was a kid. I can't believe I don't remember where the staircase is."

"It'll come back to you."

"Assuming the roof will need to be replaced, can you give us a rough idea of how much the repairs will cost?"

Joe took off his hat and slid his stubby pencil behind his ear. Frowning professionally at the lodge and chewing on his cigar, he said, "It's a big job, no doubt about it. There's lots of stuff we should do to modernize the place. The good news is that we won't have to tear off half the structure before we start, since the foundation and basic framework are sound."

Liza blew her nose and wished she'd remembered to take her cold tablet. "That's a relief. How about putting some numbers on paper for me?"

"Sure thing. It'll take a few days, since I'll have to come back with the backhoe. Is tomorrow a problem?"

Liza held her breath and looked at Cliff.

"No problem," said Cliff. "Come anytime."

Liza let out her pent-up air while the two men made further plans. They strolled over to Joe's truck as they talked, and Liza followed in their wake, blowing her nose.

At last, Joe climbed into his truck. "You know," he said, casting a final look up at the lodge. "This could be a great place once you're finished."

"I hope so."

"Yep, I'm sure the two of you will be happy living here together."

Liza blushed and said quickly, "We're not living here together."

Joe looked puzzled. "No?"

"Not like you think. We're friends. Not even friends, really—we're acquaintances, that's all." Liza sneezed again and fumbled for a tissue. "There's nothing at all going on between Cliff and me."

"Nothing at all," Cliff agreed.

"We barely tolerate each other, in fact."

"That's right."

Then Cliff sneezed. A tremendous, explosive, sinus-rattling sneeze that echoed in the trees overhead.

Joe laughed. "Nothing going on, huh?" He started the truck, continuing to chuckle at the picture they made standing together on the drive, both sniffling. He said, "There's nothing more romantic than sharing a head cold, is there?"

"We aren't sharing anything!"

"That's the trouble with kissing, you know. It spreads germs."

"This is not what you think!" Liza bellowed over the roar of the truck's engine.

Cliff sneezed again.

"Stop that," she commanded. "You're embarrassing me!"

"I can't help it," Cliff said as Joe's truck started down the drive. "Hell, *you* gave me these germs!"

"I did not!" She grabbed a fresh tissue and pushed it into his hand.

He sneezed three more times and looked dazed when he'd finished. "I can't believe it! You gave me a cold. You really gave me a cold."

"It was an accident! Oh, heavens, now we don't dare go into town together. The gossips will have us married by the end of the week."

"I can't hear you. That last sneeze plugged up my ears completely."

Liza bellowed, "I said we don't dare be *seen* together! Everybody will think we...that we've been..."

"What?" Cliff sneezed into his tissue and came up with watery eyes. "I can't hear a thing!"

"Oh, never mind," Liza snapped, grabbing his arm and dragging him toward the lodge. "Come inside for a cold tablet. Luckily, I bought a whole bottle."

Cliff's health went downhill very quickly after that. As Liza predicted, his first illness in several years laid him flat out. He drank two glasses of orange juice and swallowed a tablet and some aspirin, but those medicines had little effect. Liza sent him to bed for the rest of the afternoon, and without arguing he staggered up the steps like a drunken man.

While he rested, Liza spent a couple of hours trying to find her way into the attic. The longer she looked for the narrow staircase she remembered from her youth, the more disgusted she became with herself. How could she have forgotten something as big as a staircase?

"I *know* it's here someplace," she grumbled to herself. "We used to play dress-up in the attic all the time."

Amanda would remember, Liza decided. Her older sister had a steel-trap mind—perfectly suited for her chosen profession in law—and could recall nearly any fact she ever heard in school. Where Liza had been a less than sparkling academic student, but a hit on the social scene, Amanda had lived a quieter adolescence and become a successful lawyer.

But paying a call on Amanda to find out the location of the attic staircase meant coming face-to-face with the conflict that had driven Liza from Tyler in the first place. She had no intention of setting foot in her mother's house until she was ready for the confrontation that was sure to take place.

Liza didn't want to talk to Amanda or Alyssa about anything. Especially after being bombarded by the memories of her childhood at Timberlake! Everywhere Liza looked were things that reminded her of the carefree days of her youth—the days when she couldn't even imagine something as terrible as her father's death. That wound still felt fresh to Liza, even though the rest of the family had obviously put the event behind them. Perhaps she'd been closer to her father than anyone else in the family.

"I won't ask any of them for favors, that's all. I'll just keep looking for the staircase on my own," Liza said to herself.

By nightfall, she hadn't found anything but a lot of dust. She gave up and went to the kitchen to heat some soup. When Cliff awoke, surely he'd be hungry, she thought. He didn't come downstairs, however, and Liza eventually assumed he was still sleeping off his head cold.

Wisely deciding to pamper herself with a good night's sleep that might knock the cold out of her for good, Liza went to bed early.

But at midnight, the strange singsong voice woke her.

CHAPTER SEVEN

"THAT DOES IT!"

Liza flung herself out of bed and snapped on the bedroom light. "That idiot is sick as a dog, but he's got enough energy to try chasing me out of this lodge? Ooh, I'll show him a thing or two!"

She stomped across the floor and threw open her bedroom door. The eerie noise Cliff was making was louder in the hall, but Liza marched undaunted toward his room, snapping on the hall light as she passed the switch.

"There's no polite way to do this," Liza muttered, lifting her fist to pound on the door. "Get out of there, you coward!" she bellowed.

Beating her hand faster and faster on the door, she shouted, "If you're going to play stupid games, Forrester, you had better have the guts to face me! Come on, open up!"

He shouted something, but Liza didn't understand. She grabbed the doorknob and shoved her way inside. Instantly sensing something was wrong, she stopped dead in the doorway. The room was completely dark, but a jagged triangle of light from the hallway zigzagged across his bed.

Cliff came out of the darkness like a springing tiger. He wore a pair of jeans and nothing else. His chest was bare. His long hair was rumpled, and his eyes were wild—with anger and something more.

"Go away," he ordered thickly, breathing in ragged gasps.

Too furious to see straight, Liza exploded, "You're damn right I'll go away, but not until I'm good and ready! You can stop this ghost nonsense right now, Forrester, because I—"

"Get the hell out of here!"

"You can't order me—"

Cliff grabbed her arm, his grip so tight Liza cried out. It wasn't until that moment that she saw the sweat glistening on his face, felt his muscles bunched so tightly they could have snapped any moment. His dark eyes were wide and swimming with unfocused anger.

"Go away," he rasped. "I don't want to hurt you!"

"Forrester—"

"Don't argue, dammit!"

"Let me go!"

But he didn't hear. Her words didn't penetrate the demons that had taken over his brain. Liza struggled against his grip. "That's my arm you're breaking, Forrester!"

He was dreaming—that had to be it. Or having some kind of breakdown. *Flashback,* Liza thought suddenly. Didn't some Vietnam vets suffer from flashbacks? This one was driving him over the brink of sanity.

Liza tried to stay calm and forced her voice to sound reasonable. "Let me go, Cliff."

But he shoved her against the open door and pinned her there, his face only inches from her own. "Damn you, don't you see how dangerous it is for you? You could be killed, for God's sake!"

Liza wriggled to be free. "Stop it! First that stupid ghost routine and now—"

"Ghost?" he repeated.

"It was a stupid and immature trick, you know."

He blinked, fighting to regain his composure, his grip slackening. "What are you talking about?"

From the attic above, a weird cry suddenly silenced both of them.

Liza's heart stopped beating and seemed to expand in her chest. All of a sudden she was glad Cliff had grabbed her, and she hugged him hard, listening to the crying song from above. The sound faded almost as quickly as it started, but it left Liza shaken to the bottom of her soul. For a long moment, she strained to listen, and she could feel Cliff listening, too—his every nerve stretched.

At last Liza found her voice and croaked, "What was that?"

Cliff's chest felt warm and solid, but she could feel a shudder go through him before he broke the silence with a ghastly whisper. "You heard it?"

"Of course I heard it! I'm not deaf!"

"It's not . . . you didn't imagine it or—"

"Imagine it! What kind of idiot do you take me for? Ouch! That hurts, dammit!"

Cliff sucked in a hissing breath. Liza winced as he tightened his grip on her shoulders and twisted her until their faces were only inches apart. His expression scared the daylights out of her.

On a rasp, he said, "Tell me what you heard."

"For Pete's sake, it was plain as day! Somebody singing or playing music..."

Cliff's eyes narrowed in a way that made Liza wonder if she had spoken in a foreign language. His grip contracted.

"*Ow!* That *hurts!*"

All of Judson's warnings came back to Liza in a rush. At that moment, Cliff *did* look dangerous. With his tangled hair and blazing black eyes, he looked wild—and on the verge of losing his sanity. His whole body had turned to stone, and his face was drawn in a feral tautness. Violence burned in his gaze.

Fighting her instinct to hit him and run, Liza forced herself to say calmly, "It's okay, Cliff."

"No," he growled, then began shaking his head as if to rid himself of the devil. "Damn, damn, damn—"

"Cliff, please."

Suddenly he shouted, "Don't do this to me!"

She flattened her hands on his chest. "I'm not doing anything, Cliff. It's me."

"I can't—I can't—"

"Cliff, it's only me—Liza!"

Her voice must have penetrated at last, because he focused, and his gaze cleared, searching every inch of her face, seeking answers, looking for the truth.

Gently Liza said, "Let me go. I'll get you a drink of water."

Cliff didn't move, and Liza put her free hand on his shoulder to give him a little shake. "It's okay," she said. "I'm Liza, remember?"

"Liza..." he whispered.

"Right. You're scaring me, Cliff."

He released her so fast Liza fell back against the open door. Sounding almost dazed, he said, "I thought it was a dream."

"What was a dream? The noise?"

"I heard it, but I never... I couldn't..."

Abruptly he began to shake, as if seized by a feverish chill. Liza had never seen anything so frightening—not in a full-grown man who a minute earlier had looked capable of tearing a whole house apart.

She pulled herself together and rushed across the hall to the small bathroom there. Quickly she filled a drinking glass with water from the tap, grabbed a towel and returned to Cliff's room. He had staggered to the rumpled bed and was sitting on the edge of the mattress, holding his head in his hands.

Liza snapped on the bedside lamp. Taking one of his hands, she pressed the glass into it. "Take a sip," she commanded.

She had to assist him, holding the glass against his mouth as he drank. He sipped the water, then choked.

"It's okay," Liza soothed, smoothing his hair back from his temple as if he were a sick child.

Cliff shook his head and gave an odd laugh. "Sorry," he said, sounding strangled. "Give me a minute."

"Take all the time you need."

While he worked at composing himself, Liza said, "I guess I woke you too fast. I shouldn't have pounded on the door. It shook you up, huh? You must be a sound sleeper."

He shook his head. "I hardly ever sleep."

"What?"

"I can't sleep. That voice. It talks to me every night."

Liza blinked and tried to understand. "It talks to you?"

He nodded, rubbing one hand across his eyes.

Liza wondered if she had miscalculated where Cliff was concerned. Maybe everybody in Tyler *was* right. Maybe Cliff was off his rocker.

"Uh," she said tentatively, "what does the voice say when it talks to you?"

"It doesn't *say* anything," he replied, an edge finally creeping back into his voice. "It just makes me..."

"Crazy," Liza supplied.

The distant, musical noise suddenly began again, breaking off any sensible thought and sending Liza's heart into a painfully frightened rhythm.

"Oh, God," she said, leaning close and gripping Cliff's hand for courage.

Cliff raised his head and listened tensely as the sound died away. "If you hear it, too, maybe I'm not...maybe I'm—"

"You're not nuts," Liza breathed. "Unless I am, too."

Her knees gave out at that moment, and she sat down on the bed beside him, shivering. Awkwardly, Cliff put his arm around her shoulders and they sat together as the creepy sound diminished into a faraway, mournful note that wavered and finally died. Silence reigned once more. Then, somewhere else on the big house, a loose shutter slapped the cedar siding.

"Sweet *heaven*," said Liza, trembling with the urge to run screaming from the lodge and never come back. "People used to say this place was haunted, but I never believed it. How can you stand this every night? My God, Cliff, it's a wonder you're not a raving lunatic!"

Sometimes Cliff *felt* like a raving lunatic. But this time he knew he had weathered the event pretty well. His stomach still fluttered, but he hadn't lost control. He hadn't gone crazy and hurt Liza in a fit of anxiety. The relief that washed over him felt like a rush of soothing water.

Thank heaven he hadn't snapped. Liza was safe.

She stayed snug in the curve of his arm, but half turned toward him. "Cliff." Her voice was gentle but firm. "Talk to me."

"I can't explain."

"Try. Tell me what you're feeling."

Without thinking, he said, "Scared most of the time."

Liza had a small towel in her hands, and she used it to sponge some of the sweat that had sprung out on his face. "That sound—what is it?"

Cliff couldn't swallow, couldn't find his voice for a moment. "Until tonight, I—I wasn't sure it was real."

"Are you serious?"

"Nothing's been right," Cliff said lamely.

She stroked his neck and chest gently with the towel. "What hasn't been right?"

"Everything. Since I got back from Cambodia, everything has been . . . different."

"Different?"

"Unreal," he corrected.

Liza digested that for a moment, then asked softly, "Have you seen a doctor?"

Cliff shook his head, lulled by her ministrations as she dried his shoulders with the towel. "I used to, but I—I never felt any better. Then I came here, and I was able to handle most of it."

"Except you don't sleep."

"It's the dreams," he said, and suddenly shuddered uncontrollably.

"That was no dream!" Liza cried, holding his shoulder. "It was real—I heard it! Cliff, what *was* that sound?"

"I don't know." He laughed shortly, marveling at his helplessness. "A ghost, I guess."

"Don't be silly!"

"I'm not."

Liza used her fingers, firm and reassuring, to turn his face toward hers. Her quirky brows were gathered tightly over curious blue eyes. "You really think there's a ghost in the lodge?"

"No," he said at once, but she must have read his expression and known he was lying. He relented and added, "Maybe. It's nonsense, but sometimes I can't help feeling . . ."

His voice trailed away, and Liza urged, "What do you feel?"

"Like there's someone else here sometimes."

"Besides you and me?" Liza prodded, starting to look doubtful. The towel lay forgotten in her lap.

"I've felt it from the start. Sometimes I think it's why I liked the lodge in the first place. She was welcoming me, you see, and—"

"She?"

Liza obviously didn't understand. Cliff wasn't sure he did, either. He tried to put his impressions into better terms. "I always thought there was a woman here. A female presence to help me with the dreams."

"Cliff, ghosts don't exist, female or otherwise."

"I know that, but I—I was never sure. About myself, I mean."

Liza considered his words solemnly. But she didn't run laughing from the room, and for that, Cliff felt infinitely grateful. She believed him—or at least parts of his story. She chewed on her thumbnail, frowning at him, and in that moment Cliff saw the qualities that made Liza Baron the most unique woman he'd ever met. She wasn't as tough as she pretended. She wore that rough-talking, streetwise disguise like her own skin, but it wasn't the real Liza.

The real Liza was the sensitive young woman who sat close beside another human being when she was needed. Her slender hand curled inside his, comforting and firm. She devoted her incredible energy to him, and Cliff felt warmed by the burning embers of her concern.

At last, she said, "I think you need to see a doctor."

"No."

"Cliff, it's obvious you need some help! If you've been living here for years believing that sound is your own imagination—well, it's a wonder you haven't gone completely around the bend. You just *think* you've gone around the bend."

"I don't need a doctor. I've heard everything I need to hear from doctors. I can't afford one, anyway."

"Oh, every veteran's hospital in the country would provide the kind of help you—"

"I'm not a veteran."

Liza's lovely mouth stayed open several seconds. Then she said, "But I thought you were in the war."

Cliff shook his head. "Nope. My father was."

"Your father?"

"He was a career man and served in Vietnam. That's why I went."

Liza frowned deeply. "I don't understand."

"Look," he said, drawing a long breath. "I don't want to talk about this."

"You think you can scare the hell out of me tonight and not explain?"

"It's none of your business—"

"So sue me!"

"I don't owe you any explanations!"

"The hell you don't! You've been acting like a monster ready to break his chain any minute, and it's high time you spilled your guts, Forrester. I want some answers, and I want them now!"

For good measure, she punched him on the shoulder. Hard.

Instinctively, Cliff seized her hand. "Stop it!"

"No, *you* stop it!" She threw up her head and said, "You can't say anything that's going to shock me. I know you've been through something terrible. That's obvious. Tell me, for crying out loud. Maybe we *both* need to hear it."

Cliff fought the urge to push her away. It had been years since he'd told his life story, but even when he had, he'd never felt as if his audience truly cared what had happened over there. Liza's intent face bespoke more than a clinical interest, however. Her beauty had never seemed more radiant than in that moment. Beneath her show of anger lay a concern that felt genuine.

Slowly Cliff released her. He pulled the towel from her hand and finished wiping some of the drying perspiration from his forehead. "My father disappeared in Nam," he said.

"Disappeared?"

"We were told he'd been taken prisoner."

"Who's we?"

"My family. My brother and my mother and I."

Liza nodded. "Go on."

Cliff cleared his throat, uncomfortable telling the story, but compelled to do so by Liza's palpable interest. The trust that showed in her gaze gave him the courage to speak.

"My father disappeared just as the American forces were pulling out completely. We weren't told what had happened to him. The government declared him missing and presumed dead. But I couldn't let that stand. Losing my father that way—not knowing what became of him…it almost killed my mother. I had to know what happened."

"So you went to Vietnam to look for him."

"Yes. He—he disappeared over Cambodia," Cliff said haltingly. "So that's where I went."

"And?" Liza cocked her head. "Did you find him?"

"I found the people who had helped him after he crashed—the people who were with him when he died."

"Oh, Cliff."

She was quick to empathize. Liza wore her emotions very close to the surface. She wasn't afraid to let the turmoil of her feelings show.

He shook his head, unable to react in kind for fear of letting down a floodgate that held back emotions he'd been trying to control for years. He was able to say calmly, "By the time I learned what really happened, I was ready to hear the truth. I grieved for him, but I—I needed to stay. To help his friends."

"What do you mean?"

Cliff found himself explaining, "Cambodia was in trouble then. The people were being overrun by the Khmer Rouge. Women and children were being slaughtered by the tens of thousands, so I stayed to help."

"What kind of help?"

"Guiding families over the mountains, mostly. Protecting them as they traveled. We smuggled whole villages to boats that could take them out of the country."

"How long did you do that?"

"Two years. Then I was wounded and—"

"Wounded?" Liza looked shocked.

"It was a war, Liza."

"But not your war," she murmured, watching his face. "How badly were you hurt?"

"Not too badly." His hand crept unbidden to the back of his head, where he'd been hit by a piece of shrapnel. Hardly a scar remained—just a jagged ridge of tissue on his scalp. The memory of the pain was still very real, however, and the anguish of leaving his friends before the work had been finished was a wound that had never healed.

Without an invitation, Liza covered his fingers with her own and found the evidence beneath his hair. Her touch was very gentle, but not tentative. It felt like a caress.

Softly, she murmured, "You stayed to fight someone else's war to help people you didn't know."

"I did know them. They were my father's friends. Besides, if you'd been there, seen those children..."

His voice shook, and Liza sat very still, listening.

When he could speak without trembling, Cliff said, "I spent a couple of months in a hospital in the Philippines. After that, I couldn't get back into Cambodia, so I came home. Not home to Rhode Island, exactly, but back to the States."

"Why not home?" Liza asked, quick to catch his slip.

"I couldn't," Cliff said simply. "I wasn't the same person who'd left."

"But your family? You told them about your father?"

"Oh, yes. I went to see them, but I...well, I couldn't stay. I needed to be alone. I still do."

"Why?"

"Because I can't be around people!"

"But why? Are you embarrassed by the flashbacks?"

"My dreams are my own problem. It's ... I don't want to hurt anybody, that's all."

"Why would you hurt people?"

"I can't control it. It's...I'm—"

"You're not exactly a murderer, for Pete's sake!"

"I have been," Cliff said quietly.

Liza watched him for a long time.

"No," she said, shaking her head at last. "I don't think so."

"You know nothing about me!"

"I know enough," she replied, her expression turning furious again. "You're a good man, Cliff Forrester. Any fool can see that. If you used a gun, it was for a good reason—the only good reason! To help innocent people."

"Is that an excuse for killing?"

Liza broke out of his grasp and stood up, agitated. "Now I understand what's going on here."

"What?"

"You're punishing yourself, aren't you?"

"I'm staying away, that's all. I know what I'm capable of doing. And I can't always control myself."

It was too hard to explain. Control was what mattered most. Out in the world, there were too many unknowns. Something simple might set him off, make him crazy. But trying to explain that to Liza—Liza, who was stronger than anyone else on the face of the earth—felt like an impossible task.

She said, "You're not one of those guys who climbs a tower with a high-powered rifle and starts shooting."

"I *could* be. I know what those men are going through. I dream their dreams, I've seen the same darkness—"

"You haven't hurt me."

"Not yet," Cliff said.

Liza laughed harshly. "You're not *that* crazy. Anybody who'd try to hurt me is going to end up with his butt in a sling. I doubt there's anything wrong with you at all. You've had a little too much solitude, that's all.''

"Liza . . ."

"Get dressed," she commanded.

"What?"

"Put on a shirt and some shoes. You're coming with me.''

"What the hell are you talking about?"

"We're going to prove you're not crazy. We're going up to the attic to find out what's been haunting you.''

"I've already searched the lodge—every corner!"

"Not with me, you haven't."

She hauled Cliff to his feet and slid her arms around him as naturally as if they'd been lovers. It felt strange to be held by a woman. The sensations her embrace evoked felt stranger still. Bewildered by the barrage of conflicting emotions that swept over him, Cliff automatically let his arms enfold Liza's slim body. Her curves stirred him and befuddled him at the same time.

She was speaking, and it took Cliff several seconds to catch up with her conversation.

"We'll have to get into the attic," she said, her words tumbling over themselves. "Ever since Joe was here today, I've been trying to remember how we used to get up there to play. As I was drifting off to sleep tonight, I started remembering. . . ."

Dazedly, Cliff wondered what Liza looked like as she drifted off to sleep. The thought struck him like an arrow between his shoulder blades.

She chattered on, breathlessly unaware of the nosedive his thoughts had taken, saying, "My grandmother used to sleep downstairs in her own bedroom.

You know that little room off the veranda? It was her boudoir—near the French windows so she could run out to meet her lover, I suppose...."

While she talked, Cliff wondered if Liza had lovers. Real lovers, or just boys.

"And there was a staircase from her room," Liza continued. "A narrow set of stairs that ran up to the attic. It's behind a panel, and I'm sure I can find it. Shall we try? Cliff? Are you okay? Cliff?"

He'd become aware that Liza was wearing nothing but the sweater he'd lent her the moment she'd arrived at the lodge. Did she wear that old rag all the time? he wondered. The lines of her body—so lean and taut in appearance—felt soft and feminine against his harder frame. Would her skin feel soft beneath the sweater?

Without thinking, he filled his hands with the knitted fabric and crushed it in his grip.

Maybe he wasn't crazy. Maybe there was a chance to be normal. To be a whole man again.

Liza tilted her head up to his and watched his face as he did it. There was no fear in her expression, however. Questioningly, she said, "Cliff?"

"Liza," he said. "Liza, you should go."

"Let's not start that again."

"There's no need for you to stay. Go home to your grandfather."

"I don't want to leave." She touched his face with her fingertips.

Cliff shuddered under her touch. It was a tender gesture. One that battered at the wall of his self-control.

Softly she said, "I want to stay."

"Why?"

She answered his question with a rhetorical one of her own. "Why did you take care of those children in Cambodia?"

"But I'm not a child."

"No, but you need me just the same."

Cliff said, "Maybe I need you in ways that are far from childlike."

Her blue eyes began to flicker, and her saucy mouth curled up at the edges. "What are you saying, Forrester? Do you think I'm sexy after all?"

He let out his pent-up breath. "God, you're trouble!"

"Don't change the subject. Do I turn you on or not? Yes or no?"

"Yes," he said.

"Good," said Liza, firmly pushing herself out of his embrace while smiling provocatively at him. "That's the best sign I've seen so far."

She found a shirt for him and shoved it into his hands. "Get dressed," she commanded. "Then we'll play ghostbusters."

To punctuate her command, she kissed him on the mouth, wrapping one hand neatly around the back of his neck and letting her long fingers play into the strands of his hair. Her lips tasted warm and delicious, and her tongue swiped across Cliff's mouth languorously before she broke contact completely. She looked deeply into his eyes and smiled.

Gazing into her face, Cliff felt the stirrings of desire. Maybe he *could* be a man again.

CHAPTER EIGHT

LIZA KNEW she was being rash. Plunging into a ghost hunt at midnight wasn't exactly the most sensible act she'd ever proposed. But she had to do it. Seeing the pain that dilated Cliff's black eyes when he talked about his sanity was motivation enough. He wasn't crazy. And she intended to prove it to him.

"Let me get dressed," she said, and slipped into her room to pull on jeans. Then, barefoot, she scampered back into the hall, only to discover that Cliff had gone downstairs alone.

"Wait!" she called. "Forrester!"

He was bending over the pile of rubble she'd left after ripping down the wall in the entry hall. From the debris he pulled the tire iron.

"What are you doing?"

"I'm going to get some answers of my own," Cliff said, an undercurrent of determination flickering through his voice as he led the way down the passage to the abandoned bedroom.

"Have it your way," Liza said, nervously following.

Margaret Ingalls had chosen the first-floor location of her bedroom herself, so the family legends said, because she liked the noonday sunlight to awaken her. Margaret slept late, bossed her family unmercifully and enjoyed a good party more than anything.

But, Liza had suspected since first hearing about her headstrong grandmother, there was more to Margaret Ingalls than good times. She played too hard, it seemed. She had been hiding something, Liza believed. She enjoyed hiding things.

Which was one of the reasons she'd concealed the staircase to the attic.

"This room used to be kept locked," Liza said, peering around Cliff's body at the darkened bedroom. "My grandfather ordered it shut up forever, but I picked the lock one summer and my sister and I sneaked in here to play. He never knew what we were doing."

"Why did he order it locked?"

"I suppose because he was furious with Margaret for running off. He probably locked it so he could forget her. It's easier to forget something you don't look at every day."

Under his breath, Cliff murmured, "That's not been my experience."

"The attic door opened by a hidden mechanism," Liza went on as she eased into the bedroom behind Cliff. "I hope I can remember how it worked."

"If you don't," he said, fingering the heavy tire iron, "I'll take care of it."

Liza swallowed hard and followed cautiously in his footsteps. "God, it's dark in here. I don't suppose the old light bulbs work. We'll need a flashlight."

"In the kitchen drawer."

Though hesitant to leave him, Liza hurried to find the flashlight, and when she returned, Cliff was standing in the middle of Margaret's bedroom with the moonlight slanting through the French windows. He stood very still, and the milky light that poured over his body turned him into a rugged marble statue, the tire iron held loosely at his side like a ready weapon.

"Cliff?"

Shivering from the chill in the room, Liza flicked on the flashlight. Immediately, the dancing beam caught the painting that hung over the fireplace.

Cliff had been staring at the painting in the darkness. As the light struck it, he let out his breath in a slow hiss.

Liza padded to his side, keeping the flashlight trained on the portrait. By instinct, she lowered her voice to a whisper. "Haven't you been in here before?"

"Yes," Cliff responded slowly, distractedly. "I used to come in and look at that painting. I'm not sure why, but now... God, she looks like you."

The young woman depicted in the painting smiled at them from the mantel. It was an odd smile, Liza thought as she allowed the flashlight beam to trail the contours of the pale face and offcenter mouth. A secretive smile.

"That's Margaret, all right," she said uneasily. "My grandmother."

"She was beautiful."

Liza tipped a glance up at Cliff and was surprised to find that he was mesmerized by the face in the picture. What did he see? A pretty face, a lace dress, graceful hands adorned by rings, slender wrists weighted down with gold and silver? Or did he read something in Margaret's expression? Did he like the subtle sensuality in her posture? The suggestion of Margaret's gaze? Or did he see the cold determination that gleamed behind those tantalizing blue eyes?

"Cliff?"

Still staring at the portrait, he asked, "She wasn't a nice woman, was she?"

"I don't know. I never knew her. But Granddad loved her, and I trust his opinion. She must have had some good qualities."

"But she left him."

"Yes," Liza said, knowing he'd hit upon the one act for which Margaret would never be forgiven.

Cliff must have heard something change in Liza's voice—a change she couldn't control. He put his hand on the back of her neck and squeezed gently. "I can see why you don't like to be compared to her," he said softly. "She didn't have your heart."

The remark buoyed Liza. She felt like an autumn leaf suddenly launched from a tree branch. At last someone understood.

"Margaret was a shallow person."

Cliff nodded. "I can see that in her face. It's the difference between the two of you."

Liza's eyes stung, and her throat was suddenly very tight. "Thank you."

Cliff didn't hear her words, though. Shaken by his perception as she was, Liza hadn't made them audible.

As if waking from a dream, Cliff released her and abruptly asked, "Where's the door?"

Liza pulled herself together, too. "This way."

She led him to the north wall and fingered the panels of wood, knocking occasionally as she sought the hollow area she remembered from her childhood. At last she found the spot and pressed the panel. It popped smoothly, but opened no more than a few inches.

"Let me," Cliff said, shouldering Liza aside and wedging his hand into the opening to force the door wide.

"Wait," Liza urged, suddenly seized by anxiety.

As her hand touched his back, Cliff swung on Liza in the half-light. His face was tight, his gaze sharp. "What's wrong?"

"Nothing exactly. I—I just wonder if we shouldn't wait until morning."

"What for?"

"Because it might be dangerous up there. The floor might be rotten, or—"

"Will you be able to sleep in this house until you know what causes the sound we heard?"

"No, I guess not."

"Then what do you propose?"

"I don't know. I—I guess I'm scared."

Cliff smiled thinly. "You? Scared? I didn't think it was possible."

"Forrester..."

He caught Liza's chin in his hand and tilted her face to the light. "You're not as tough as you pretend, are you?"

"I'm tough enough," she retorted, the moment of ambivalence passing as quickly as it had come. "Let's go."

Cliff held her hand as they ascended the narrow staircase. Under most circumstances, Liza would have walked alone. But tonight she appreciated the snug pressure of another hand around hers. She clung to Cliff's shadow as they crept up Margaret's stairs to the attic.

"Give me the light," Cliff said. "Your hand's shaking too much."

"It is not!" Liza argued hotly. But she passed the flashlight to him anyway when they reached the landing and stopped.

Cliff cast the light around the attic—the eaves first, to check for bats, perhaps. Then, slowly, he allowed the beam to play over the shapes of junk piled high in the long, narrow space. Old furniture, several trunks, a rolled-up carpet, bales of yellowed newspaper, a broken bird cage. It could have been a dusty antique shop or a haven for children playing dress-up.

In one corner lay a heap of tattered dresses left in exactly the same place where Liza and her sister had dropped them nearly twenty years earlier.

"Oh," breathed Liza, remembering the hours she'd spent trying on one lovely silk dress after another. "We never put anything away. What a shame! All these dresses have been ruined. They were so beautiful."

Perhaps her perception was clouded by the memory of the happy days she had played in the attic, but Liza felt transported in time as she stood at the top of the staircase with Cliff, gazing at the jumble of forgotten possessions. The place seemed very romantic suddenly—not frightening at all. A lace shawl had been tossed over a crooked lampshade, abandoned by Liza's sister, Amanda, always the romantic at heart. A cracked mirror with a gilded frame—no doubt one of Margaret's extravagant purchases, hung from a stubby nail that had been haphazardly hammered into the wall. How many times had Liza gazed at her own reflection in that glass? A second mirror, eerily clouded with age, stood propped against a rocking chair with a broken arm. Another shard of reflective glass lay in a distant corner. If a ghost resided in the attic, it was a very vain ghost indeed. The idea amused Liza.

"Whew," she said at last. "No evil spirits up here, I guess."

"Not evil," Cliff said under his breath.

"What?"

She realized Cliff was seeing the place for the first time, and he seemed dazed by the riot of Margaret's things. Quickly, Liza said, "This stuff was my grandmother's. Granddad had it all carried up here, and we played with it years later without his knowing. I'm sure he'd have killed us if he ever knew...." Her voice trailed off. "Cliff, what's wrong?"

"I don't know," he said carefully. "It's queer, though, isn't it?"

"Oh, God, you're not feeling that presence again, are you?"

He put out his fingers and caressed the forgotten shawl. "I'm not sure anymore."

"What's that supposed to mean?"

Cliff shook his head. "I feel...oh, hell, I can't tell. Did you and your sister play here for very long?"

"One summer, I think. Then we forgot about it, I guess. Or found other things to do. It was a long bike ride out here to the lodge. I'm sure Amanda found more interesting ways to pass her time besides baby-sitting me out here. You know, at the time, it never occurred to me that we were disturbing my grandmother's things. Now it feels a little like grave robbing, doesn't it?''

"It feels okay," he said quietly. "I think she would have wanted us to be here."

Liza watched him move tentatively into the attic, shining the flashlight here and there. "You're giving me the creeps, Forrester. You're not communicating with 'the other side,' are you?"

"It's not that," he said seriously, not responding to her taunt. "But I can't help feeling she might have been calling me here."

Perhaps Cliff had a side Liza hadn't expected—a spiritual part of his personality.

"Margaret was calling you?"

He shrugged. "I know it sounds strange. In Cambodia, people believe that spirits exist in our world, especially spirits of people who have left unresolved problems behind."

"Do you believe that?"

With a short laugh, he said, "I don't know what to believe. I just . . . If I'd known how to get into this attic, I'd have done it long ago, that's all."

"To be with Margaret?" Liza asked, studying him.

Cliff didn't answer. He looked like a man in a dream—moving with care, his expression puzzled.

"You know," she said finally, "I have a feeling you've been a little in love with her."

Cliff bent and plucked a pale green dress from where it had been carelessly discarded years ago. His hands toyed with the delicate fabric.

She added, "You're showing all the classic signs, you know. Maybe you've been obsessed by a dead woman."

"Is she dead?" he asked quickly.

The question caught Liza off guard. "We always assumed so. After she ran off, no one in the family ever heard from her again."

"I wonder..."

"What do you wonder?"

"What became of her. Where did she go? What happened?"

"It's obvious, isn't it?" Liza asked lightly and laughed. "Margaret died and came back here to haunt Timberlake for eternity. She's probably been up in this attic for years, singing her sad songs just to get you to come up and play. Why, she's probably been infatuated with you from the start! You're just her type, Forrester. She had lovers—"

"Stop," said Cliff, sounding unamused.

"Sorry." When he turned and she saw his expression again, Liza immediately regretted baiting him. Cliff wasn't strong enough yet. He was still confused about his own life and didn't need to hear theories about Margaret's.

Trying a new tack, Liza said, "We ought to be looking for something that could have caused that weird sound. A loose windowpane, maybe, or—"

"Here." Cliff was already rummaging in a pile of broken furniture. "Look at this."

"Be careful! That squeak in the floor doesn't sound safe."

"The roof's been leaking. See?"

With care, he stepped over the weak spot toward an old phonograph player, the kind with a huge horn attached almost directly to the needle. A long-playing record still lay on the turntable, and sure enough, the needle was resting on the record.

"There's no dust," Cliff said, hushed. "See that?"

His hand moved to crank the machine, and Liza said quickly, "Cliff, don't."

He glanced up at her. "Why not?"

"I—I'm not sure I want to hear the music." Liza began to shiver. Suddenly she didn't feel as confident as she usually did. The talk of ghosts with unresolved troubles made her nervous.

"We came for answers," he said darkly. "Go downstairs, if you like."

"But—"

"I've been haunted, as you said, for years by this. Now's my chance to find out what's going on."

"Okay," Liza replied, chastised. "If you can take it, so can I."

He proceeded then, giving the crank a slow turn and setting the turntable in motion. The music blared out at once, so loud that Liza jumped and cried out. Cliff stood up quickly and took her into his arms as the attic filled with the strains of a blues tune straight out of the past.

"Please don't leave me," sang the throaty female voice, while a wailing saxophone echoed her tune. "Please come—"

Then the record caught and skipped back, so that the singer began again. "Please don't leave me. Please come—Please don't leave me. Please come—"

"Shut it off!" Liza urged as the voice repeated the same phrases over and over. "My God, Cliff. Make it stop."

He was trembling almost as much as she was, but he stooped over the phonograph and lifted the needle clear. Welcome silence filled the attic once more, and Liza released a shaken sigh.

"That's it," she said, her voice quivering. "That's the sound we heard!"

"But how does the phonograph work without anybody cranking it?"

"Who knows? Probably the wind. This place is as drafty as a barn. Look, you can see those scarves moving even now." Liza let out a nervous laugh. "You've been haunted by the wind, Forrester."

Cliff couldn't think straight. Maybe Liza was right. But for years he'd been sure the soft sounds that emanated from the attic hadn't been totally outside his own mind. Something *had* been haunting him—not a ghost exactly, but some kind of spirit.

For so long, he had thought it was the lost part of his own soul.

Maybe, he mused now, it had been some queer, unexplainable connection to Margaret Ingalls.

Cliff didn't believe in ghosts or reincarnation, but in Cambodia he'd seen events that couldn't be explained in terms he understood. In the mountains of that faraway land he had learned that the spiritual side of life couldn't be ignored. Maybe a part of Margaret, Liza's grandmother, *had* wanted him to come to the attic.

He couldn't help sensing that there was something in the long, dark room that could tell him what he needed to know. Cliff pushed into the jumble of furniture, brushing the cobwebs aside. What had happened to Margaret Ingalls? he wondered.

"What are you doing?" Liza asked, sounding far from her usual cocky self as she edged after him.

"Looking around."

"Be careful!"

"I'm okay. The water damage is minimal. Joe will be glad to hear that."

"Cliff, can't we go downstairs now?"

"Just give me a minute."

"Aren't you convinced that the phonograph has been causing all the noise?"

"I want to see what else is here."

She sighed as Cliff began to explore the rest of the attic. He shone the flashlight over the objects stacked around them—a lady's writing desk, a chest of drawers, some chairs with curving legs, a jewelry box with a tarnished silver clasp. Liza glanced at everything in a desultory way, no doubt because she had seen all these things before. As a child, she hadn't recognized Margaret's belongings for what they were—a chance to get to know a woman who had disappeared long ago.

Liza asked, "Exactly what are you looking for?"

"I'll know when I find it," Cliff said, flashing the light around. "Hey, there's a nice old rug. See it?"

Liza knelt down and uncurled the end of a rolled-up Oriental carpet. Its deep colors shone like jewels in the flashlight's beam. "Oh, it's beautiful! Maybe I should have it cleaned up, find a place for it once we finish with the lodge."

"Good idea."

"I'll take it downstairs tomorrow. What else can we find?"

Cliff had opened one of the drawers in Margaret's tall chest and was running his hands through the lacy garments that lay in the drawers to find what might have been hidden underneath. "Aha."

"What is it?"

"A book, for one thing, and—"

"That's a diary!"

Cliff turned the small, leather-bound volume over in his hand, revealing the tarnished clasp. "So it is. And some other papers, too. Here's an envelope and..."

Liza reached past him and drew one of the garments from the drawer. It was mauve silk embroidered with a fine, feminine design and snippets of delicate lace. She hummed lightly and held the slip of silk against her body, turning toward the mirror to study her reflection.

"Now this is more like it! What do you think?" she asked. "Is it me?"

"It's pretty," Cliff agreed.

"Look at the workmanship." She held the silk out to him to display the embroidery. "Isn't it amazing?"

Cliff's voice seemed to thicken as he said, "Very nice."

"My sister and I used to try on all kinds of things like this and play tea party."

"That doesn't look like a tea party outfit to me."

Liza laughed and draped the slip against her long body again, turning this way and that as she looked in the mirror. Suddenly, she was the picture of a Victorian lady with her hair tumbled around her shoulders like a golden cloud. Cliff watched her for a long while, his dark eyes flickering.

Suddenly feeling shy under his gaze, Liza let the slip slide down.

"I like it," she said, mustering some normalcy in her voice. "What else is in that drawer? Oh, hand me that white thing!"

Mechanically Cliff did as he was commanded, taking a long satin gown out of the drawer. It was as light as a scarf and felt odd in his hands.

"Oh," she cried, taking the negligee from him and spinning toward the mirror. "I have to try this on! Turn around for a minute, will you?"

He seemed to pull himself out of a daze. "I'm not going to stand here while you play dress-up."

Liza looked in the mirror and laughed at his reflection. "What's the matter, Forrester?"

Frowning, he snapped, "I just don't want to watch you take off your clothes, that's all."

"Then turn around!"

"I'm not doing that, either," he said stubbornly. "I'll go downstairs if—"

"You wouldn't leave me up here alone, would you?"

No way. Leaving her was the last thing Cliff wanted to do. She looked so innocent and so damn sexy at the same time, standing there clasping her grandmother's negligee to herself and smiling at him in a way that caused an uproar inside him. He almost didn't recognize the feeling at first, it had been so long since he'd felt genuine sexual attraction—the kind that was so powerful it made a man's throat catch.

Liza's smile was genuine—teasing and trusting. Cliff's voice didn't work for a moment. Then quietly he said, "Thank you."

"What for?"

"A lot of things."

She turned around slowly, smiling. "For barging into your hideaway? For giving you a cold?"

"For other things?"

"Like what?"

"I—I—"

"Oh, never mind," she said, letting the negligee slip from her hands and stepping toward him. Getting a grip on the front of his shirt again, she turned up her face to his and said, "Why don't you just shut up and kiss me?"

There was no stopping her, so Cliff let Liza fit herself against his frame. Automatically, he slid his hands up to grasp her shoulders. Holding her was so easy, so tantalizing. It made him want more. And she was ready to give it.

"Why now?" he asked, his voice hoarse.

Her smile flashed. "Because you look like a man who needs kissing."

He let his fingers explore the soft flesh of her arms. "Any other reason?"

Responding to his caress, she let out a slow, unsteady sigh. "Because," she said, her smile fading, "I think we're starting to understand each other a little."

"Liza..."

"Just kiss me. We don't have to talk anymore."

Cliff closed his eyes, and his brows came together painfully. "Liza, it's been a long time for me."

"A long time since you kissed anybody?"

"A long time since I did anything."

"Shall we find out what you've forgotten?"

There was so much to tell her. So much to warn her about. Inadequately, Cliff said, "I just don't want to hurt you."

"I know," she murmured soothingly, lifting her mouth to meet his. "I know."

Liza felt Cliff's hands bite into her arms, and she braced herself for a hard, powerful, passionate kiss. She could feel his heart beating in painful throbs beneath her hand and knew he was barely holding on to the threads of composure. He was very strong, and the war of his emotions played across his rugged face. She watched as his self-control began to crumble.

But Cliff didn't snatch her into a kiss that packed a wallop of sexual messages.

Instead, he hovered over her mouth for a heart-stopping moment, his dark eyes seeking hers as he gathered Liza into a firm embrace. Awkwardly at first, his hands smoothed down her body, but finally reached the most sensual curves and clung there. Almost tentatively, he drew Liza closer until the heat of his frame melded with her own. Then he lowered his head and brushed her lips as lightly as butterfly wings.

Liza clung to him, suddenly weak in the knees with the force of her own shattered emotions. She could feel Cliff check the forces inside himself, holding back, trying hard to be gentle. His kiss was sweet. It was slow. Gentle. Thorough. The care with which he held her, kissed her, caressed her, made Liza's heart turn over.

She might have whispered his name. Either that, or the word became imprinted in her mind at the exact moment his mouth caught hers, as if giving a name to the myriad sensations that washed up from inside her soul as Cliff kissed her there in the attic.

She felt a ripple of tension pass through him, too. As her senses awoke, Liza felt Cliff come alive as well—years of loneliness falling away as soundlessly as a dark shadow. The pressure of his hands, his lips, his body, grew more sure with every passing heartbeat. But Liza relaxed and gave herself to him completely, knowing she was safe, sure she didn't want to stop what was happening.

Cliff took his time, the kiss turning more passionate until Liza's mouth slowly parted and allowed him entry. Rhythmically, he savored the contour of her lips, the warmth of her breath as it mingled raggedly with his own. His tongue swirled gently across her lower lip—seeking, exploring, enjoying.

Stretching on tiptoe, Liza aligned their bodies, delighting in the perfect symmetry. Her breasts swelled deliciously against his chest, and her belly fit into the curve of his as perfectly as if they'd been created for each other. She loved the excitement created by his hard thighs as they rubbed her softer ones. She slid her fingers into his hair and prolonged the kiss until she was drowning in erotic sensations.

She blew a soft sigh when he drew back.

"Again," she whispered, gazing into his desire-darkened eyes.

"You're so soft," he murmured, delving into her lips for another kiss. "Soft and beautiful."

She strained against him then, urging his tongue deeper into her mouth and swirling her own with playful abandon—teasing, coaxing, encouraging. He turned hot and possessive, and Liza's blood was soon thundering in her veins. If the kiss had started out in her control, he soon made it clear that they would share the dominant role.

Their play might have gone on for hours or mere minutes, but at last Cliff broke the kiss. The contact of their mouths diminished until finally the wonderful sensation was no more than an imperceptible touch.

He bumped his forehead against hers and seemed unable to catch his breath. Raggedly, he said, "I can't believe what you're doing to me."

"I love your body, too, Forrester. It's making me wild. Can you feel my heart beating?"

She lifted his hand and placed his palm against her breast, causing Cliff to groan.

"Liza," he said, his voice catching. "Liza, I can't do this."

"Then you're doing a damn good imitation of it." She arched as his fingertips caressed the curve of her breast, the touch more erotic than any she had ever known. The gentle contact had her seething inside so that she closed her eyes to enjoy it completely and sighed, "A damn good imitation."

He stopped caressing her and traced a line up Liza's chest to her cheek before lacing his fingers in her hair. For an instant, Liza thought he meant to kiss her again.

But he said softly, "Liza, I want to make love to you."

She opened her eyes. "Yes. I can feel how much you want me."

She could, too. The powerful way his body rode against hers allowed no secrets. Liza felt scorched by the heat of him. He was no awkward boy anxious for quick release. Although Cliff hesitated, she could sense he was no amateur in the art of love. Lovemaking had come easily to Cliff at one time in his life, she knew. He was a powerful man—full of all the basic desires, despite his wish to keep those desires in check. His other hand moved hungrily down her back, effectively pinning Liza's body to his own.

Huskily, he said, "I do want you. So badly. But we can't do this."

"Why not?"

"I can't explain. Not exactly."

"Cliff, I'm practically melting!"

"I don't want to hurt you, Liza."

She bit her lips to keep from crying out her frustration. Then she managed to say, "But I trust you. I trust you completely."

The turbulence in Cliff's gaze pierced Liza as sharply as any knife, and the rigid control that quivered in his body bespoke a conflict that still raged inside him. His face looked so ravaged that Liza suddenly wanted to cry.

He traced the line of her cheek gently and then released her. Standing back, Cliff said quietly, "But I don't trust myself."

CHAPTER NINE

ALTHOUGH SHE HATED to admit it, Liza was afraid to go back to her bed for what was left of the night. She was too churned up—sexually as well as psychologically. The idea of a ghost rattling around in Margaret's attic made sleeping alone impossible. But the chances of sleeping with Cliff were even more remote. She didn't dare press him on that.

Exhausted and still drugged with cold medicine, Liza couldn't keep her eyes open, however. She crawled onto the sofa in the lounge and tried to stay awake while theorizing with Cliff about her grandmother, but it was a losing battle. At last she crept into Cliff's arms, put her head on his chest despite the immediate tension she felt in him and fell soundly asleep.

Sometime during the night she was aware of Cliff pulling something warm over both of them.

"Don't go," she murmured. "I don't want to be alone."

"I'm not leaving," he whispered back, taking her languid body into his arms again and settling into the cushions once more. His long legs tangled with hers, and Liza's hand lay over his heart. "Go back to sleep."

Before she lost consciousness, Liza wondered if Cliff had slept at all. Perhaps he'd sat up all night, holding her, watching her sleep, still afraid to let his guard down.

In the morning, she woke and found herself alone. She pushed the mop of her hair back from her face and checked the time. Nearly ten.

"Cliff?"

No answer.

Liza pushed out from under the tattered blanket he'd carefully used to cover her, and called his name again. Hearing no response, she padded to the kitchen for a large glass of orange juice.

"At least I'm starting to feel better," she noted, sipping the juice.

On the kitchen counter sat a bottle of cold tablets, and Liza picked them up. "I guess Cliff isn't so lucky."

Cliff. She shook her head, remembering the events of last night. She had learned so much about him. Yet there was more to learn. Much more.

Had he meant what he said when he'd told her he didn't trust himself? She wondered if he feared suffering a flashback at the wrong moment. Had he abstained from love—from life itself—because he was afraid he'd go crazy and hurt someone?

The need to find out everything there was to know about the man burned inside Liza like a candle flame.

"He's going to be okay," she murmured to herself. "I'm going to make sure of it."

She poured another glass of juice and went looking for him. The sound of a tractor engine drew her outside, and she stepped through the front door.

Liza hoped to find Cliff on the veranda.

She didn't expect to find her mother there.

"Mom!"

Liza almost panicked. She wasn't ready yet. Too many years of turmoil between herself and her mother couldn't be resolved easily. She needed more time to prepare!

"Mom—"

Alyssa Ingalls Baron had turned hastily. She looked lovely, of course. She always did, Liza thought. She was wearing immaculate white trousers with a starched white shirt, a simple belt and large gold earrings. Elegant, but casual. Perfectly combed and lightly made up, Alyssa didn't need to rely on elaborate hairstyles and expensive cosmetics to look wonderful. But she did look pale and unnaturally agitated. Under most circumstances, Alyssa Baron looked cool and composed. This morning, however, she could not conceal the anxiety that lurked behind her wide blue eyes.

"Liza," she breathed, frozen to her spot on the porch.

Stupidly, Liza blurted out, "What are you doing here?"

"I came to see you." Alyssa ventured a smile, but it quivered at the corners of her mouth. "Your grandfather told me you were here at the lodge."

"Just for a little while," Liza said hastily. "I—I should have come to see you, I guess. I'm sorry. Really. I've been busy."

Her words sounded lame, and Liza felt a pang of guilt for even trying to lie. She could see her mother knew exactly why she hadn't made any effort to stage a reunion. There was still too much tension, too much that hadn't been spoken between them. Liza flushed.

Quickly, Alyssa took a step forward and grasped
Liza's free hand. Her own was trembling. "You look
lovely, darling. Your hair is so much longer than the
last time—why, I can't believe how much you look like
your grandmother!"

It was exactly the wrong thing to say. Without
thinking, Liza snapped, "Don't start that already,
please?"

"I'm sorry," Alyssa said, contrite at once. She
turned pale and released Liza's hand. "I forgot. You
like to think of yourself as your own person."

"I *am* my own person!"

"Of course, of course." For once, Alyssa looked
flustered and she backed up a pace. "It's... well, it's
wonderful to see you again."

"It's nice to see you, too," Liza murmured,
ashamed that she'd lost her temper already. It had always been that way. Alyssa was so damned gentle and
controlled all the time. Trying to communicate with
her was like trying to knock over a brick wall. Even as
a little girl, Liza had been determined to batter down
her mother's cool facade. But she'd never managed,
never been strong enough to penetrate her mother's icy
shell. Now she felt foolish for trying.

Alyssa pasted another quivering smile on her face
and forced her voice to sound bright. "I thought I
might coax you into having lunch with me in town today. What do you say? We could have a salad and
talk—"

"Actually, I've got things to do."

"Oh."

"There are some workmen coming, you see. Joe
Santori's doing some preliminary work so he can give

me an estimate on the cost of fixing up the whole place."

Alyssa controlled her expression to avoid showing disappointment. She looked across the lodge yard and nodded. "I noticed Joe's truck. He's got a good reputation around town. And your grandfather told me about the ideas you've had for refurbishing the lodge. It all sounds very nice. Very nice indeed."

"Do you mean that?"

Alyssa's light blue eyes touched Liza's. "Of course."

Liza couldn't think of a thing to say. If only she'd had a chance to prepare! She stood on the veranda in her bare feet, holding the glass of juice and feeling foolish.

Alyssa managed to fill the awkward gap by waving a hand at the lodge and saying cheerily, "The old place looks pretty good, doesn't it? It's been a long time since I've been here, but it hasn't changed much."

Liza decided to try making conversation and said, "I can't remember ever seeing you at the lodge when I was a kid."

"No, I never came up here." Alyssa might have blushed, but she hid that reaction by trying to laugh. "I like to stay close to home, I guess."

"You spent hours in the garden, and you love walking outdoors," Liza argued automatically. "I'd have thought the lodge would be the perfect place for you. How come you stayed away?"

Alyssa avoided Liza's gaze by looking out at the lake. "Oh, bad memories, I guess. My mother used to live here. Coming to the lodge just reminded me of her, so I—I stayed away."

Funny, Liza thought, how she'd never really noticed how much the whole family seemed to suffer from mother-daughter conflicts. She had forgotten that Alyssa's relationship with Margaret had been practically nonexistent.

"How old were you when Margaret disappeared?"

"Seven," Alyssa said, smiling weakly. "A very impressionable age, you see. I suppose I've stayed away all these years because of some silly, emotional childhood vow I made to myself."

"Hmm," said Liza, thinking about Cliff's questions last night. Here was a chance to learn more about Margaret's disappearance. Feeling her way cautiously, she observed, "You and Granddad have both avoided the lodge."

"Until today," Alyssa said, changing the subject adroitly. "Today I woke up thinking I just might burst if I couldn't see my dear Liza, so...here I am!"

Liza contemplated her mother, who showed every evidence of trying hard to be cheerful. But the signs of tension were unmistakable. For once, Alyssa looked surprisingly uneasy. Was it the lodge? Or did stouthearted Alyssa Baron feel nervous about seeing her rebellious daughter after their long estrangement?

The sight of her mother's anxiety caused another twinge of guilt in Liza. Abruptly, she said, "Why don't you come inside, Mom? I'll make a pot of tea."

"Oh, no. I couldn't—"

"Sure you can. I've been fighting a cold, and some tea would do me some good."

"You've been sick?"

"A little cold, that's all. Come on."

For an instant, Alyssa looked as if she might refuse, but her motherly concern took over.

She followed Liza to the screen door. There, she balked on the threshold and said quietly, "I haven't set foot in the lodge in more than forty years."

Liza laughed and pushed the door wide. "Well, don't be shocked. Yesterday I got a little carried away. Take a look at the results."

"Goodness!"

Alyssa stepped over the threshold and gaped at the mess Liza had created the day before. "What happened here?"

"I had an idea for opening up the entrance. What do you think?"

For an instant, Alyssa seemed at a loss for a suitable compliment. Then she said, "Uh, very...interesting."

"I think it's going to be a national showplace. C'mon into the kitchen."

Liza led the way to the kitchen, not noticing at first how Alyssa lagged behind and glanced curiously into the lounge. She peeked briefly into the dining room, too. Her footsteps were hesitant, her posture almost cringing as she walked through the lodge, which struck Liza as odd. She was startled to see her mother gripping the trim around the kitchen doorway to keep herself upright.

"Mom! What's wrong?"

"I'm fine," Alyssa said hastily. "Just a little dizzy, for some reason. Goodness, I didn't expect to react to these rooms this way."

"What way?"

Alyssa smiled ruefully and entered the kitchen. "I don't know. It's just odd. I would like that cup of tea you mentioned."

"Okay. This way."

Moving efficiently, Liza put the kettle on the stove and rummaged through the meager supplies in the refrigerator, looking for something she could offer her mother. "How about some toast? We've got whole wheat bread and some jam, I see. Or maybe a piece of fruit—"

"Just the tea, I think."

With a kick, Liza closed the fridge. "Tea it is. Maybe I'll gulp a cold tablet while I'm at it."

"I hope you're taking care of yourself."

"I'm doing the best I can."

Alyssa put her handbag on the counter. "I guess you've made friends with Cliff."

Proud of herself for remaining calm, Liza said, "I'd hardly call us friends. He tolerates me, that's about it."

"He's a very nice young man, you know. Just misunderstood."

Liza eyed her mother curiously. "Do you understand him?"

"Not entirely. He's...complicated."

Very complicated, Liza wanted to say. She found the tea bags in a cupboard.

Alyssa said, "I hope you're being kind to him."

"Not especially kind, no."

"Liza, Cliff has been through some terrible experiences. We owe him some peace, I think."

"Maybe he's had too much peace."

"What do you mean?"

"I'm no expert, but it doesn't take a psychiatrist to figure out that several years of solitude haven't done him a hell of a lot of good. I think it's time somebody tried shaking him up a little."

"Liza—"

"Maybe he needs to confront some of his problems to get rid of them. And you know me. I'm great at stirring up problems."

Alarmed, Alyssa said, "Liza! Surely you're not—"

"You don't need to give me any advice about Cliff, Mother. You always had your say about the boys I dated in high school, but this—"

"Because you always managed to pick the most inappropriate young men to date."

"What's appropriate for a high school girl?" Liza demanded.

"A young man who doesn't have a jail record," Alyssa said promptly. "Remember that boy who stole motorcycles? Oh, what a character! Why you brought him home, I can't figure out even now."

"Because he was fun," Liza said sharply.

Alyssa gave her a cool look. "I assumed it was because he made your father angry."

"Dad didn't mind him. It was you who hit the ceiling."

"I never..." Alyssa caught herself and sighed. "Why are we arguing about a relationship that's been over for ten years at least?"

"You brought it up," Liza said sulkily.

"Yes, I did, and I'm sorry."

Several moments passed, then Alyssa squared her shoulders. "I didn't come to upset you, Liza," she began. "I came for a very different reason. I thought we could patch things up."

At once Liza tensed for another fight. "Mother—"

But Alyssa overrode her protest. "Just let me say a few things, all right? I hate confrontations, as you know, so I'd like to speak my piece first and you can explode afterward. I'm glad you've come home, darling. In fact, I hope you'll decide to stay."

"Mom—"

"I know, I know. I shouldn't apply any pressure. If I do, you're sure to do exactly the opposite—"

"I'm not as ornery as you think. I just—"

"We've got different styles," Alyssa cut in gently. "We're different people. I know you hate hearing it, but you're a lot like my mother that way. Margaret was always a firecracker. Everything had to be a turmoil for her. Well, I can't stand it, Liza. I couldn't stand it then, and I can't take it now, either. I'm just not the kind of person who can shout and—"

"I don't shout."

"No, but you make your opinions known. I can't do that."

"So what's the point? I'm not going to change, Mother."

"I'm not asking you to," Alyssa said. "Just be a little more understanding, can you?"

"I understand plenty."

"Do you?"

The teakettle began to whistle at that moment, and Liza snatched it off the burner. She grabbed the box of tea bags, trying to decide how to play the scene. Concentrating on the act of dropping the tea bags into cups, she gritted her teeth and said, "I understand my own feelings, if that's what you mean. But I haven't any idea where you're coming from. You don't say what's on your mind, so I have to guess. It's always been that way."

Tightly Alyssa said, "I know we've always had our differences. Maybe because we have different ways of handling our emotions. But I think it all boiled down to your father, didn't it?"

"We don't have to talk about him. That's not where our problems began."

"Maybe not. But that's what drove you away in the end, wasn't it? Your father's death."

In the act of pouring boiling water over the tea, Liza splashed the counter and cursed softly under her breath. Sometimes her father seemed like a distant memory, almost as if he had never existed. His face, his voice, the way he walked or read his newspaper on the porch swing on summer evenings—those things Liza could hardly envision anymore. But the pain that squeezed up from inside her was real indeed.

She set the kettle down with a crack and faced her mother, suddenly ready to speak the truth. "Daddy's death didn't drive me away, Mother," she said. "Your attitude did."

Alyssa didn't speak. Her large eyes grew glassy with tears, though.

Liza planted her palms on the kitchen counter. "All right, I was upset when Daddy died. We all were! But *you*—you hardly shed a tear, did you? Sometimes I wondered if you ever really cared for him at all."

"How can you say such a thing?"

"Because it's true!"

"Liza—"

"No, it's my turn to talk now! I've always wanted to say these things to you, but you never let me have a chance. Yes, I was angry with you, Mom! I couldn't believe the way you behaved when he died."

"Was I supposed to throw myself on the pyre?"

"Of course not! But I expected some pretense of grief! A little compassion for—"

Still damnably cool-voiced, Alyssa said, "I don't expect you to understand how I felt, Liza. My relationship with Ronald was my business, not yours. How I grieved for my husband was—"

"Did you grieve at all?"

"Of course I did!"

"You never showed it."

"Then you weren't very observant."

"I was plenty observant! You played the charming hostess at the funeral. You even attended a charity dance the same week!"

"I could hardly avoid going. They gave your father an award for community service. It was painful, but—"

"You could have sent somebody in your place! It was a selfish, rotten thing to do to the rest of us. I hated you that night, Mother. You left us alone with our grief and you got all dressed up and went to a dance! And Daddy hadn't been dead for a week! I hated you for that!"

A soft scrape sounded in the doorway, and Liza found herself whirling with her mother to see who had arrived in the kitchen. It was Cliff, standing stock-still ten feet away and looking comically guilty for materializing at such a melodramatic moment.

He cleared his throat and said, "Uh, hello."

Alyssa backed up until she collided with the kitchen counter, then looked as if she wished she could melt through the floor.

Cliff said, "I'm sorry. I'll come back later."

"No, no," said Alyssa, collecting herself and going to his side. She drew Cliff into the room by slipping her hand around his arm. "Please, come in before one of us says something we'll regret."

"At least it will be said," Liza muttered. "I hate keeping things bottled up."

Alyssa smiled at Cliff, which infuriated Liza even more. How could she pretend everything was all right? Cliff looked extremely uncomfortable and—as usual—as if he hadn't slept in months. His dark eyes were heavily ringed, and his illness had given him a slightly reddened nose.

Other than those details, however, he looked magnificent to Liza. His jeans hugged his narrow hips, and his plain, time-softened T-shirt gave her a chance to admire the ropy length of muscle in his arms and shoulders. He hadn't shaved yet, and the bristle on his face combined with his too-long hair gave Cliff a decidedly sexy, to-hell-with-it appearance on a summer's morning. Judging by the hammer that swung from his belt, he'd gotten in a few hours' work.

But just a few hours earlier, he'd cuddled Liza in his arms, kept her warm and safe through the night. Lying snug against his long body had felt better than she'd imagined. And staring at him as he sauntered into the kitchen, Liza wanted nothing more than to throw her arms around his neck and kiss the stuffing out of him.

Not with her prim and proper mother standing there, however.

To Cliff, Alyssa said, "We're not an average family, are we, Cliff? Are you sorry you've gotten mixed up with us?"

"He's only sorry about getting mixed up with me," Liza retorted, turning away before her mother saw how Cliff's arrival affected her. "Right, Forrester?"

Cliff heard the edge in Liza's voice and wasn't sure whom she was most angry with—Alyssa or himself. He'd walked in at exactly the wrong moment, of course, but he had a feeling she wasn't just furious with her mother. She refused to meet his eye.

With some surprise, Alyssa said, "*Are* you two mixed up with each other?"

Still sounding angry, Liza snapped, "That's my mother's polite way of asking if we've hit the sheets yet. No, we haven't, Mother."

Last night shouldn't have happened, Cliff told himself. *We went too far, and now everything's ruined before it even got started.*

Liza turned her back on him, and the stiff set of her slender back sent Cliff all the message he needed. She wanted no part of him this morning. Why should she? She probably had men swarming all over her in Chicago. What would she want with a sleepwalking emotional cripple?

She thought he was a charity case, he supposed. She figured she could use her sex to ease his pain. Or maybe she really got her kicks from dangerous men. Clearly, Liza liked walking on the wild side. Which was it for her?

Part of him wanted to snatch Liza by her shoulders, whirl her around and make her understand how he felt. He *wanted* her, for God's sake! She was the first woman to affect him that way in a decade! Lord, how many hours had he held her last night, listening to her breathe, aching to touch her body all over, wondering what her breasts felt like, fantasizing about the texture of her skin? But he'd settled for burying his face in her long hair and holding her tight.

And for the first night in hundreds, Cliff hadn't experienced a nightmare. It was magical. He'd actually slept for a while, then awakened early and decided he'd better get up before his desire for Liza overwhelmed both of them. She'd been so beautiful curled against his chest. So pliant. How easy it would have been to slip her clothes off, kiss her awake and slide himself into the sweet core of her soul.

But he'd played it safe, thank heaven, and crept out before she woke up. Good thing, too. Obviously, Liza didn't want any part of him this morning.

Alyssa flushed. "That's not what I meant at all! I only—"

"We're not mixed up with each other," Cliff said gently. "We're just living under the same roof temporarily."

Liza slammed a teacup down on the counter. "That's right. There's nothing going on between us."

"Not a thing," Cliff agreed.

Then he sneezed.

"Oh, Lord!" Liza groaned, spinning on him. "Don't do this again! Joe Santori already thinks we're passing germs back and forth—"

"It's your fault for bringing the germs in the first place!"

Cliff sneezed again and reached into his hip pocket for a handkerchief.

Liza said, "For heaven's sake, didn't you take a cold tablet this morning?"

"I forgot."

She grabbed the bottle of tablets from the counter and pushed it at him. "What do I have to do? Shove the pills down your throat?"

"I can take care of myself!"

Their hands collided, fumbling for possession of the medicine bottle. Liza looked up, and at the moment their gazes clashed, Cliff realized he'd been wrong. She didn't despise him. Far from it. Liza was blushing like a teenager—a becoming pink that heightened the brilliance of her eyes—and her fingers began to tremble in his hands. Her mouth opened—that lovely, lush, delicious mouth of hers—but no sound came out.

Well, well, Cliff thought, dazed by the desire he saw clearly in her eyes. *I've miscalculated again.*

Liza drew back quickly, as if a spark had ignited when they touched.

Feigning a brusque temper she obviously wasn't feeling, she said, "Well, you're doing a lousy job of taking care of yourself. Did you have any breakfast?"

"Well . . ."

"You ought to be loading up on vitamin C, you know. I'll pour you some juice. Lots of liquids, that's important. I'll have to get some herbal tea, too, I suppose."

"Don't do me any favors," Cliff replied mildly.

"Favors! Who will suffer if you're sick for days?"

"I'm not going to be sick for days. I'm getting over it already. Stop fussing!"

"I'm not fussing!"

Smiling, Alyssa said, "You two sound like an old married couple."

"We are not a couple!" Liza shouted.

Cliff couldn't help himself. He laughed at her.

Astonished, Alyssa looked at him and said, "Why, Cliff! I don't think I've ever heard this much conversation out of you at one time, and now you're actually—actually..."

"He laughs at me all the time," Liza said in a grouchy voice. "Apparently I'm very comical."

"You're not comical," Cliff said. "Not all the time."

She couldn't prevent a grudging smile. "I hoped to be taken seriously around here."

"Believe me," he replied, "I take you very seriously. And so does Joe Santori, by the way. He's been here for a couple of hours."

"A couple of—! Why didn't you call me?"

"Because you needed some sleep. Joe started digging down by the lake to find out about the water pipes."

"What did he find?"

"All kinds of stuff. He wants you to have a look. Maybe you ought to come, too, Alyssa. You probably know more about how things are laid out for the lodge."

Alyssa's smiled faded. "Oh, no," she said. "I don't know anything."

"But the water pipes from the lake—"

"Really," she insisted faintly. "I don't remember anything about Timberlake. I was a child. I just came to see Liza. I can't stay."

"Well, how about the electricity?" Cliff asked, trying again. "Do you remember when the lines were installed—"

For once Alyssa's voice rose and cracked with emotion. She cried, "I don't remember anything!"

Liza looked surprised by her mother's outburst, and Cliff found himself wondering, too.

"It's okay," he said, surprised to find himself soothing her for once. "We'll figure it out, I'm sure."

Alyssa reached a shaky hand for her purse. "I'd better be going. You obviously have work to do, Liza."

"Mom—"

"I'm sorry I can't stay for that cup of tea, but I have things to do, as well."

She turned to leave, almost rushing to get away, and Cliff did something he had never done before. He put out his hand and stopped Alyssa by touching her arm. In all the years he'd known her, he'd never initiated any physical contact, but this morning he found himself moved to comfort her.

She hesitated and turned her face up to his, as surprised as he was.

Cliff said, "Come back some day soon, Alyssa. It's good to see you here."

She smiled fleetingly and broke the contact. Without a word, she led the way through the lodge to the veranda. Liza followed her mother, and Cliff brought up the rear, puzzling about many things.

When they arrived on the porch, a shout sounded from the yard.

"Forrester! Miss Baron!"

Joe Santori rushed up to the steps, out of breath and windblown. He grabbed the porch railing, panting almost too hard to speak. Obviously, he had run up from the lake.

Liza found her voice first. "What's wrong, Joe?"

The building contractor looked past Liza and straight at Cliff. He said, "You'd better come down. We've hit something."

"Hit what?" Liza demanded. "Have you broken a pipe?"

Cliff read the expression on Joe's face and started down the steps at once. Something was very wrong, and Joe didn't want to say it in front of Liza and Alyssa. Cliff had seen the same expression before—on the faces of men trying to spare their women from terrible things. In Cambodia, that expression had been the forerunner to many atrocities. He steeled himself to cope with what lay ahead.

Liza caught his shoulder. "Cliff—"

He turned and held her arms tightly. "Stay here," he ordered. "Don't move, understand?"

Liza hated being told what to do. For half a minute, she stayed on the porch and watched the two men hustle down the lawn. Cliff's easy stride matched Joe's as they ran down to the lake.

The suspense was too much. "I'm going down there," she said.

"Liza, wait," Alyssa begged, gripping the porch railing with both hands. "If there's something really wrong..."

"What could be wrong? Why are they acting so weird? I'm going."

"Liza!"

She didn't wait around to argue. Leaving Alyssa on the veranda, Liza clattered down the steps and set off toward the lake, where Joe and his men had been working with the backhoe.

Four of them were hunkered down around the hole that had been dug. A pile of fresh earth lay where the equipment dumped it. Liza made a beeline for the spot.

Cliff looked up, hearing Liza's approach. He got up and moved fast, intercepting her on the lawn.

"Don't," he said, blocking her path. His face was set.

"Don't what? Dammit, what's going on, Forrester?"

"Liza, don't look."

She tried to brush past him, but Cliff caught her in his arms, stolidly preventing Liza from taking another step. "Stop," he said. "You don't want to see it."

"See *what?* Damn you—"

"It's a body." Cliff's grip changed, turning gentle as Liza stopped struggling against him.

"A—a body? A dead—?"

"A person," Cliff agreed. "I can't tell how long it's been here, but for a lot of years. You don't want to see it. Go back to the house. Get the truck and drive to the nearest telephone. Then call the police."

"The police?" Horror and revulsion filled Liza with the speed of rushing floodwater. "What do we need the police for?"

"Liza," he said severely, "just *do* it!"

The shock of hearing Cliff take command was enough to send Liza scampering back to the lodge. She fought down her fear as best she could. When she reached the veranda, her mother cried, "What is it?"

"A body," Liza said unsteadily, trying to compose herself. "It's been down there a long time, Cliff says."

"A body," Alyssa repeated.

Liza heard her mother's tone, and it stopped her cold. Alyssa Baron wasn't surprised to learn a body had been dug up on the family property. She didn't sound shocked.

She sounded scared.

CHAPTER TEN

LIZA FOLLOWED Cliff's orders to the letter and drove to the nearest house in Tyler, then pounded on the door and asked to use the telephone. She phoned the police, then rushed back to Timberlake so she could guide the officers to the lakefront where Joe had been digging.

Alyssa must have left the lodge during the initial excitement, but Liza didn't notice her mother had slipped away until nearly an hour later, when she saw her grandfather arrive behind the police car.

Judson climbed out of his pickup, but didn't follow the police—Liza recognized Chief Schmidt and Brick Bauer—down the lawn. Judson stayed by the truck, gripping the open door. Suddenly he looked frail and shaken, like an old man.

"Granddad!" Liza hurried to his side. "What are you doing here?"

"Chief Schmidt called me," he said gruffly, pulling himself together for Liza's benefit. "He said there was an emergency out here. It's my property, so I came."

"There's no emergency. Maybe twenty years ago it was, but not anymore. Joe Santori was digging and—"

"I never gave you permission to dig up the grounds!"

"It's no big deal," Liza snapped. "We're checking the water pipes, that's all. Except Joe found a body."

Judson's sharp gaze traveled past Liza to the knot of men standing around the hole by the lake. His already pale face turned gray, and he asked hoarsely, "Whose body?"

"I don't know. Cliff won't let me down there."

Judson cleared his throat. "Good man," he said.

Warily, he turned to look at the lodge then. His eyes scanned the empty windows, the weathered roof and sagging porch with an expression that Liza read as ambivalence. He hadn't visited the lodge in forty years, Liza remembered. What kind of memories did he have of the place? she wondered.

Watching her grandfather's face harden, Liza guessed the memories weren't happy ones.

She stepped toward him and took his arm. "This is a historic day, I guess. Both you and Mother have come to the lodge for the first time since...when, I wonder? When were you last here, Granddad?"

"I don't remember," Judson rasped, though it was clear to Liza that he remembered very well indeed.

"What's wrong, Granddad?"

"Nothing. It's—it's just a shock to see the place again, I guess."

"Do you want to talk to the police?"

Judson glanced across the lawn again, his brow furrowing with pain as he watched the two police officers crouch down. "No," he said more softly. "I don't need to go down there."

Liza started to ask more questions, but Judson broke from her clasping hand and strode into the middle of the driveway. He seemed shaken, she decided. Or angry.

"Dear heaven," he said, as if Liza wasn't there. "I never expected to feel this way."

"What way, Granddad?"

He ignored her and walked to the veranda, his steps surprisingly uncertain for a man as vital as Judson Ingalls. Liza followed, suddenly afraid he might fall on the stairs. But he climbed them quickly, then stood on the old porch for a long moment, breathing the forest air in gulps and fighting down the emotion that obviously threatened to overwhelm him. He seemed unaware that Liza had followed.

He stared at the glistening lake and sighed. "Margaret," he said softly, "you shouldn't have gone."

Then Judson turned on his heel and went into the lodge. Liza knew she should let him have his first look at the place in peace. But her curiosity was too aroused, so after a few moments, she followed her grandfather inside.

She found him standing in the middle of the hallway, looking at the debris.

"What's the problem here?" he demanded.

"No problem. I was trying to see if the room could be expanded. I guess it looks like a wrecking ball came through the window, but—"

Judson grunted. "A wrecking ball is what this place needs, all right."

"Granddad, it's a beautiful building!"

He shook his head, growling deep in his throat.

Liza stepped closer so that she could see his face. "Are you having second thoughts about refurbishing Timberlake?"

"Maybe," he said shortly. "If you ask me, some things in this world are better left buried!"

Judson didn't give Liza a chance to respond to that. Instead, he turned and made a quick tour of the downstairs rooms, glancing into the dining room and running his fingers clumsily over the keys of the piano in the lounge. Liza followed at a respectful distance, giving her grandfather a chance to wrestle with his memories. He seemed very emotional, despite his obvious effort to hold his feelings in check.

After stumbling across Margaret's things in the attic the night before, Liza found her own thoughts drawn to her grandmother. She had never really known what kind of relationship her grandfather and Margaret had had. Her family never spoke about it. They must have been in love once, she thought, but how had Judson felt when his wife ran away? Had they quarreled? Had Margaret really run off to meet a lover? Or had Judson driven her away?

Why has Granddad never talked about her? Why the big secret?

Judson hesitated in the hallway, staring at the door to Margaret's bedroom, which had been left open the night before.

"Who's been in there?" he demanded.

"Cliff and I," Liza answered at once. "We heard noises, so we had to look around."

"What kind of noises?"

Liza shrugged. "Some junk in the attic was settling, I guess. I hope you don't mind, Granddad. I know you didn't want this room disturbed."

"I suppose it doesn't matter now." He pushed open the door and stood on the threshold of his wife's boudoir. On a quiet note, he said, "I never thought I'd see this room again."

The portrait over the mantel caught his eye, and for the first time in forty years, Judson looked at the face of his wife. Margaret's picture smiled wickedly back at him, her long, fair hair curling innocently around her less-than-innocent face.

"She was a vain woman," Judson said abruptly. "Who hangs a picture of herself in her own room except a woman like Margaret?"

Liza followed Judson into the room, but stayed near the doorway. "She must have had some good qualities, Granddad."

Judson laughed sourly. "Oh, yes. Lots of good qualities. She was a beauty, of course. And a woman with spirit. She was a lot like you in many ways, Mary Elizabeth."

"I'm not vain!"

"No, but you're impetuous. You like to take risks. She was like life itself—full of exuberance and fire. "God," he said, his voice rasping suddenly. "I miss her sometimes!"

"Granddad..."

Liza caught herself, unable to find words that could comfort Judson Ingalls. He gripped the bedpost and his shoulders slumped, as if weighed down by the memory of the woman he had once loved.

"Margaret," he said. "I did love you. I know you thought otherwise, and God knows we had some terrible fights..." He laughed shortly. "The night you threw me out into the snow—remember that? I tried to walk to town across the lake and fell through the ice. I'd have died, but you followed me and...well, we ended up on a blanket in front of the fire for the rest of the night, remember?"

Liza froze. She felt more than ever like an intruder. And she felt another emotion she wasn't used to— guilt. Perhaps she'd been neglecting her family for too long.

Judson continued to speak, as if unaware that Liza wasn't the woman he'd married so long ago. He bowed his head and said, "I can't remember how our marriage started to fall apart. I thought we were wildly in love. Then... Well, maybe bringing you to Timberlake was a mistake. It was too isolated for a woman like you. You didn't have any friends here. And I...maybe I wasn't enough of a husband to make up the difference."

Liza wished she could stop him. She had never seen her grandfather so upset. Judson was the strong one— the patriarch who ruled his family with an iron fist. His word had been gospel when she was growing up. But today he seemed broken. Were those tears shining on his rugged face?

Judson whispered, "Margaret, I'm sorry. For what I did to you, I'm sorry."

Liza strode forward and seized her grandfather's hands. "Granddad, stop this!"

He looked into her eyes, and cried, "I hope you forgive me, my love. I've forgiven you long ago. I don't care anymore about what you did. I wish it was over."

"It's over, Granddad."

Judson shook his head and turned away. "Sometimes I'm afraid it's only beginning."

He blundered out of the bedroom, shoving blindly past Cliff, who had soundlessly come to the doorway.

Cliff said, "What's going on?"

"I'm not sure. Granddad, wait!"

Cliff caught her wrist, looking after Judson's departing figure with understanding in his gaze. "Let him go, Liza."

"He's upset. Something's very wrong, Cliff. I don't understand."

"Give him a break. He doesn't want to talk right now."

"He thought I was Margaret!"

"No, he didn't," Cliff said firmly. "Believe me, I know what I'm talking about. He was just rambling—letting off steam. He's an old man, Liza."

Furiously, she cried. "No, he's not! He's as strong as he ever was!"

Cliff sighed. "Well, something's got him churned up, and I'm betting it's the lady of the lake."

"The what?"

"The body Joe dug up."

The wind knocked out of her, Liza sagged against the doorjamb. "What makes you think it was a lady?"

"I don't know," Cliff said at once. "Just an instinct, I guess. Maybe I'm wrong." He watched her, then used his fingertips to gently brush some wisps of hair away from her eyes. It was a tender gesture that spoke volumes. "You okay?"

Liza nodded and tried to relax. "I'll be fine. I'm just worried about Granddad. Something's wrong, Cliff. I can't figure out what got him so upset."

"He hasn't been to Timberlake in a long time. Maybe seeing the place again caused him to snap."

"There's a connection to Margaret," Liza said, frowning hard. "I'm sure of it."

Cliff met her gaze, and they stared at each other for a long frozen moment. Something clicked in Liza's brain, but she couldn't accept it.

"No," she said to Cliff. "I know what you're thinking."

"I'm not thinking it," he said. "You are."

"You don't suppose—"

"The lady of the lake is—"

"Margaret?" Liza breathed.

It seemed impossible. For years, she'd been led to believe that her grandmother had run away with one of her lovers, leaving her husband and young daughter, Alyssa, behind.

"What does it mean?" she asked Cliff.

"It doesn't mean anything," Cliff said quickly. "It's your wild imagination at work again, that's all. The woman can't be Margaret. There's another explanation, I'm sure."

"How will we find out?"

"The police have taken the body away. They'll see that some kind of autopsy is performed. We'll have some answers soon."

"Cliff, I..."

His hands smoothed gently up her arms to quell her agitation. "It's okay," he said.

"No, it's not! Oh, my whole family is so screwed up sometimes! I want Granddad to be himself again. My God, he's the only sane person in the bunch!"

Cliff smiled slightly. "Present company included?"

"Are you calling me crazy?"

"No," he said at once, turning solemn. "You're a lot of things, but not crazy."

Liza peeped up at him shyly. "You think that after you heard my argument with Mom this morning?"

"I wasn't eavesdropping, you know," he said. "But you were bellowing loud enough to—"

"Don't tease me," she said, slipping out of his grasp and turning restlessly into the bedroom. "I don't have a sense of humor where my mother is concerned. Damn, I wish she hadn't surprised me!"

Cliff folded his arms over his chest and leaned against the open door. "She didn't surprise you, Liza. You came back to town on your own, so you must have assumed you'd bump into her eventually. You just weren't ready to face the conflict."

"You're right," Liza said slowly. "I wasn't. I'm not sure I'll ever be."

The trouble with Alyssa went back farther than Liza could remember. She had sensed tension from the beginning, it seemed, from the time she was a toddler. How could she have ignored the faraway look in her mother's eyes as she watched Liza play? Or the worry in her face when Liza got dressed up and went out on dates? Love. Pride. Anxiety. And fear, too. Liza felt all those emotions from her mother.

But the real problems surfaced during Liza's teenage years. Their relationship had turned volatile then.

Cliff said, "Your mother isn't an ogre."

"I know that."

"So what's the big deal between you two?"

"I don't want to talk about it."

"Why not?"

"Look," Liza snapped, releasing her anger. "I don't push you for details of your most painful memories, do I? Just leave it alone, okay?"

Cliff wasn't ruffled by her rising temper. "What did you tell me last night? That maybe I needed to hear myself say what was bothering me?"

Lisa sighed. Summarizing the history of her family would be a tough job, especially since no member of the family ever did anything the easy way. Nor did the family communicate. Maybe they were all repressed, or maybe just unfailingly polite, but Liza couldn't remember any of her relatives actually fighting. Except when she was around. Liza prided herself on her ability to start open warfare within ten minutes of encountering any of them.

But her conflict with Alyssa was the most complicated of all.

Liza sighed. "It's my father, I guess."

"Your father? I thought he was dead."

"He is. It's the way he died that—that . . ." She let out a faint laugh when she realized she couldn't say it. Perhaps she had some of Alyssa's genes after all!

"Liza," said Cliff, patiently waiting by the door. "How did your father die? What's gotten you and Alyssa so furious with each other?"

"My father killed himself," Liza said. "Simple as that. And it was my mother's fault."

She didn't want to say more. There was no use, really. And oddly enough, she found she wasn't capable of speaking after that, either—her throat closed up completely. Liza brushed past Cliff, hurrying to put some distance between herself and her grandmother's bedroom. Suddenly it seemed too full of ghosts.

CLIFF FELT THE STORM coming long before he heard the first rumble of thunder. The warm summer air was heavy with moisture, yet charged with the kind of electricity that sent birds chattering to their nests. Though he wanted to seek out Liza and press her for the truth, he waited, hoping she'd return of her own free will. She didn't come, however.

At seven o'clock that evening, Cliff began to wonder if she had decided to go back to Chicago. He couldn't find her anywhere. Not in the lodge, not sitting on the veranda, or knocking down walls in the hallway.

He began to worry, and then he found himself beyond worrying. Where could she have gone?

Finally, he laughed at himself. "What is this? A week ago you'd have been scared to death of having somebody around the lodge. Now you go *looking* for her?"

At last, he found her, skipping stones on the lake from the boathouse dock. With her back to the lodge, Liza seemed oblivious to everything but her own thoughts. Cliff's relief at seeing her slender frame silhouetted against the low-hanging sun that shone through the bank of oncoming storm clouds was like a huge rock being lifted from his shoulders. And dropped on his chest.

God, she's beautiful.

Her stone-skipping technique was good—lots of body English and a quick flick of the wrist. Her hair cascaded around her shoulders with each throw.

Cliff stopped at the edge of the lake and put his hands into the front pockets of his jeans, watching. Not only was she beautiful, but a kind of energy surrounded her like an aura. She was full of fire inside. A formidable woman. An irresistible force.

She must have felt his gaze, because she turned a minute later and examined him from the end of the dock.

"I'm sorry," she called. "I'm a jerk."

"You're not a jerk."

"I feel like my whole life's blowing up. I thought I came back to Tyler by mistake, but so much is happening. I feel—I feel like I'm coming apart."

"It's okay."

Cliff waited while she sauntered the length of the dock toward him. She was barefooted like a woodland sprite, and the slanting evening light illuminated her pale complexion in an oddly incandescent way. It took Cliff's breath away. She was winsome, yet womanly.

She stopped a yard away, frowning. "No, it's not. My family's a mess. And now this body's been found."

"Maybe that has nothing to do with your family."

"But maybe it does. Oh, Cliff, maybe I'm all messed up. Finding that body has upset me. But tonight, I've been thinking about you."

"Me?"

"Well, you in the context of me. It's true, I think, that a person needs to get all the ugly stuff out. Say what's bothering you. Speak your mind. Let it all hang out. If you don't, things just fester."

"Okay," Cliff said warily. "So?"

Liza took a deep breath and said slowly, "I don't hate my mother, you know. Not really. But I'm mad at her for the way she handled things before my father died."

"You said this afternoon that he took his own life."

Liza nodded. "He did. And when he did, my mother . . . well, she didn't seem to grieve for him."

"Some people grieve differently."

"But she didn't even cry, Cliff. And she could have stopped him from doing it."

"Is that what you meant when you said she killed him?"

Liza nodded. "My father needed help. Financial help, mostly. And she could have fixed everything for him with her money."

"Alyssa had money?"

"Oh, yes. She inherited a lot from an aunt in Margaret's family, and she certainly could have asked Granddad for a loan."

"Maybe your father was too proud to take her money."

"That's stupid! I . . . Oh, hell, I can't explain."

"Yes, you can. Talk to me."

Cliff took Liza's hand. She resisted for a second, but he remained firm. He pulled her to a patch of grass beneath the tallest oak tree, and they sat down together. Liza folded her limbs and sat cross-legged, facing him attentively.

Cliff started slowly, feeling his way carefully through his thoughts. "Maybe you just never saw things objectively. I wasn't here at the time, but I know a lot of men would have a hard time asking their rich wives for financial help."

"I can't accept that. If she'd really loved my father, she would have forced the money down his throat. To save his life, for Pete's sake! Shouldn't she have offered, at least?"

Cliff still held her hand and had linked his fingers through hers. "Liza, it's impossible to guess the circumstances. You were young when all this happened, right? Maybe your perspective wasn't as clear as you think."

She pulled her hand away and muttered, "I should have known you'd take her side."

"I'm not taking anybody's side!"

"Aren't you?" Sparks flew from her eyes. "Exactly what goes on between you and my mother, anyway?"

"We're friends," Cliff said. "Maybe she's my only friend."

Liza looked tart, stretching out her legs and bracing her weight on the outstretched arms. "Thanks a lot. I thought I had made a little headway with you, but I guess—"

"That's not what I'm saying, and you know it. I'm glad you're here."

She laughed. "I never thought I'd hear that!"

Cliff had to agree. Until Liza showed up, he hadn't wanted anyone trespassing on his privacy. Even Alyssa had kept her distance, and he'd been relieved that she stayed away from the lodge. But he said, "Alyssa's been good to me. I think we've come to understand each other a little. And I can't imagine that she'd deliberately ignore your father's troubles to—"

"Maybe she didn't love him."

"Don't talk nonsense."

"I'm serious," Liza insisted, sitting up straight. "I never felt as if they had a grand passion."

"A grand passion?"

"You know. The kind of love that just burns you up! It didn't exist between them."

"How can you be sure?"

"I just am."

Cliff couldn't help smiling a little. "What does a grand passion look like?"

"It's marvelous," Liza said impatiently, clasping her hands to her chest in an unconsciously romantic gesture. "It looks . . . it's like—like . . . Oh, I can't explain it!"

"Try."

"Well, it's . . . To be honest, it's like the way I felt last night."

Cliff fell silent.

"And the way you looked at me this morning," Liza said, her gaze suddenly smoldery in the slant of evening light. "It's sex that comes burning out of a person's soul. I saw it in your face today."

"Liza . . ." Cliff began, then couldn't finish.

She smiled. "Are you embarrassed?"

"No, I just—I don't think we ought to pursue this line of conversation, that's all. We were talking about your mother and father."

She studied him whimsically for a long moment. "I'm tired of talking about all that. It makes me sad. I'd rather talk about us."

"There is no us!"

"Maybe there should be. You're the only thing that kept me from going nuts today."

"Liza, I must be ten years older than you are...."

"So what?" She allowed her long forefinger to draw an imaginary line along his kneecap, and her voice dropped to a soft murmur. "I want us to be together, Cliff."

"I thought I made myself clear on that."

"You said you're afraid you could hurt me." She slanted an inquiring look up at him.

"I'm not the most stable person you've ever met."

"You'd be surprised," she said dryly, snatching up a piece of grass and chewing on it. She sat back and contemplated him with amusement written on her face. "I've been living in the big city, you know. Have you ever spent an evening in a singles' bar?"

"No." Making his voice as neutral as he could manage, Cliff said, "Look, I just don't want to ruin what we've started."

"What have we started?"

"I don't know! But for the first time in a lot of years, there's someone for me to talk to and...well, it's okay."

"Just okay?"

"Frankly, it's been downright terrible from time to time, but—"

"All right," Liza intervened. "But I could be your lover and still talk to you."

Cliff's mouth went dry. Quietly, he asked, "What if things go bad?"

Languidly, Liza climbed to her knees. Bracing her hands against Cliff's shoulders, she toppled him onto his back in the cool grass. She straddled his torso in a trice and stayed there, pinning him to the ground and smiling that odd, exciting smile that was purely her own. The longest tendrils of her hair teased Cliff's face as she leaned close.

"What could go bad?" she whispered, her lips brushing his.

She kissed him on the mouth. Cliff couldn't suppress a groan, and Liza laughed. An instant later, her tongue probed his, swirling erotic messages that arrowed directly into the part of his brain he had been trying to ignore. He felt the softness of her breasts against his chest and the long length of her legs clasping his hips, and he found himself responding. He ran one hand into her hair, holding Liza inescapably to the delicious kiss. With the other, he found the hollow of her back, the smooth curve of her hip, the round shape of her bottom. She smiled against his mouth and breathed some words of encouragement as he explored her body. She arched like a cat against his caressing hand.

In time, Cliff felt her tug his shirt from his jeans, and then Liza's long fingers slid up his belly, tracing a tingling path through the hair on his chest. All the while, her tongue played hide-and-seek with his own, and he could feel the heat of her body beckoning him closer, deeper.

"What could go bad?" she murmured again.

A lot.

Cliff felt his brain shut down—he almost heard the click as a deluge of memories suddenly swam up from his subconscious. He tightened his grip on Liza's head and heard her sharp intake of breath.

Cliff grabbed her and rolled. Liza flailed once, and then he pinned her roughly to the grass. He trapped her legs with the weight of his body, spreading her thighs so that he rode hard against her and making no secret of his superior strength. He didn't kiss her into submission, but trapped her arms over her head.

"You don't understand," he muttered.

Liza blinked once, trying to catch hold of her courage before it fled. "You won't hurt me," she said, but didn't sound convinced.

"I can. It's possible."

"No, it's not. You're no rapist."

"I've hurt people before, Liza."

"Not women."

"No, but—"

"And not for this reason," she said, relaxing in his grip. "You're attracted to me, Cliff. You *want* to make love with me."

"But if we start, if things get out of hand—"

"You're afraid you'll lose control."

"You can't expect any man to keep his head during sex."

"Cliff," she said, slipping one hand free and touching his face, "sex isn't about control and power and who's going to win. It's about pleasure. It's about love." Her voice turned husky. "Let me give you pleasure."

"I can't," he said.

She stroked his face gently. "I can be kinky, if that's what you want."

He closed his eyes and cursed. "That's not what I want at all. I need . . . I just want some peace."

Then, revulsed by his own behavior and the kinds of thoughts that rampaged through his mind, Cliff got up quickly.

Liza sat up and seized his hand before he could leave.

"Don't run away from me," she commanded. "Talk to me. Tell me what was so terrible in Cambodia."

"It will make you sick."

"I'll get over it. And so will you. But not if you let it eat you up, Cliff. Just say it."

CHAPTER ELEVEN

"I NEVER HAD TO KILL a human being until I went there," Cliff said eventually. "It never entered my head."

Liza heard the pain in his voice and she climbed to her feet. She hugged Cliff fiercely, catching him around his waist and holding him tight. He reacted like a robot—with mechanical motions that showed no feeling underneath. Overhead, a wall of gathering clouds began to blot out the brilliant colors of the sunset. The air turned chilly, and Liza pressed close to Cliff to warm him.

"Tell me," she whispered.

He talked then. In halting sentences, and with a volcano of emotions boiling behind the words but never exploding. Looking out over the lake, he told Liza of his friends, Cambodian people who had been simple folk.

"Good people," he said. "Honorable people."

He told her how they had been battered by the Vietnam war and their own government before the Khmer Rouge invasion blasted their lives beyond belief. Families were torn apart as fathers were conscripted into the army, death squads murdered innocents senselessly, and black-market thieves smiled one minute and plunged a bayonet the next. Children had been slaughtered by the thousands.

It had been more than the young, idealistic Cliff Forrester could stand.

"I don't know what happened to me," he said. "I reacted, that's all. I remembered all the skills I'd learned in the woods at home, the silly games I used to play with my brother—and suddenly it was real. I had to use every shred of intelligence I possessed or die. If I made a mistake, I was shot at. Or worse yet, someone I'd come to know, someone I'd shared a meal with or slept beside was blown to bits in front of my eyes."

He passed one hand across his brow and went on. "One day I snapped. I went crazy."

"Did something trigger it?"

It took a long time to pry the story out of him, but at last Cliff said, "There was a girl. She couldn't have been more than fourteen years old, and she'd been nice to me—I guess you could have called it a kid's crush. She followed me around, found me some food. Every morning when I woke up, she'd be sleeping beside me. It was like having a kid sister tagging along all the time."

His eyes seemed to mist over at the memory of his little Cambodian sister.

"What happened, Cliff?"

He sighed. "She was captured. We went after her, but the men who'd taken her kept us pinned down with their automatic weapons. We could hear her screaming, though."

A shudder racked his body as the memory bombarded Cliff. Slowly, he said, "I don't know what they did to her. When we finally got through, she was dead.

And she'd been burned. They must have doused her with gasoline and—and—''

He couldn't go on after that.

But he didn't break down. Cliff didn't cry or shout or burst into a rage. His whole body felt as hard as steel, and his face became a mask of control.

Liza looked away so he wouldn't see how powerfully his tale had affected her. ''Cliff,'' she said when she trusted her voice to sound normal, ''you can't blame yourself.''

''I do!''

''What would you have done differently?''

''I should have taken her away! We could have run ahead of the rest of the villagers or slipped past the enemy. We could have done something!''

''And left the rest to fend for themselves?''

Cliff shook his head. ''We could have done something. I tried avenging her death. We tracked those men for days and picked them off one by one. But there were thousands more to take the place of every man we killed. We couldn't stop a whole army. So we turned south and headed for the sea.''

''And that's when you were wounded?''

''Eventually. Funny, but I didn't mind getting hit. By that time, I was ready for anything. I was surprised to find myself alive. And part of me was sorry I was.''

Liza gulped—only it sounded like a sob and she choked down another at once. ''Don't say things like that, Cliff.''

For a long time, the storm seemed to mesmerize Cliff. A stiff, cool wind rustled the forest around them, then suddenly began to hiss ominously. The lake's gleaming surface turned gunmetal-gray beneath roiling clouds. But Cliff did not see the last dazzle of sunlight fade from the lake, nor did he notice how quickly the storm swooped down upon them. His gaze was turned inward.

Roughly, he said, "I did some terrible things, Liza. I don't want to be that crazy again. I've got to stay in control."

At that moment Liza realized she wasn't capable of helping Cliff overcome his problem. He needed professional help far superior to anything she could offer. She had been foolish to imagine that she had the power to heal his psychological wounds.

Had her blunt and reckless style made things worse for him? She had bullied her way into his life. Was he better off alone?

I don't think so, she thought. *My mother's been kind and gentle to him for years, and look what's happened—he thinks he's barely holding on to his sanity.*

"Cliff, you can't take responsibility for a whole war."

"I must take responsibility for my own actions."

"Sometimes circumstances make us do things we regret. But you have to put it behind you!"

"I can't," he said simply. "I can't forget any of it."

Alyssa had been too kind, Liza decided. She had never pushed him, never demanded that he change. So Cliff had gone deeper into his hiding place. Tenderness and understanding hadn't helped him at all.

"Come on," she said, taking his hand. "Let's go get something to eat."

He resisted her automatically. "I'm not hungry."

"Force yourself," she said, managing to grin. "You'll need your strength if you're going to continue fighting me off."

He disengaged her grasp easily. "I don't want to fight you."

Liza's temper snapped inside, and she let the anger lick through her words like brushfire. "Dammit, Cliff, you've got to fight something!"

"I've done enough fighting for a lifetime."

"So what are you going to do now? Wait here until your bones molder? Forget it! I'm not going to watch you give up your life to bad memories!"

"I'm not asking you to watch. I just want to be left—"

"I don't want to hear it! I don't know why, but suddenly you're important to me." She raised her voice and lectured, "You're not crazy and you're not stupid. It's time to get your act together!"

"I like my act the way it is."

"You're wasting your life! Don't you know how precious it is? Life's a gift! You've got to use it! Abuse it! Love it!"

"That's the Liza Baron philosophy. But me—I've had enough of life."

Conscious of her own cruelty, she said stonily, "You sound like my father."

Cliff eyed her, nonplussed. "I'm not your father."

"You know what I mean. He gave up. Nobody was there to push him when he needed it, so he took his own life. Well, I'm going to give you something to push against."

"I want you to leave me alone."

"Well, I won't," Liza declared. "What are you going to do about it?"

Another heartbeat passed, and then a rumble of thunder echoed down from the forested hillside. The sound was enough to galvanize Cliff. Silently, he turned on his heel and began walking away.

Boiling with fury, Liza followed, shouting, "Don't turn your back on *me*, Forrester! I'm one woman you can't ignore!"

He laughed shortly. "That's certainly true."

Liza ran after him. "I'm going to torment you, y'know."

"Maybe I'll leave Timberlake."

"Good! At least you'll have to function in the real world again!"

"Can't you just leave me alone?"

"No!"

Cliff halted and wheeled on her. "Why not? Why can't you just focus on your own business and leave me out of it?"

There were lots of ways to answer that. Liza wasn't sure of all the reasons she couldn't leave Cliff alone. She didn't want to admit how important he'd become to her in a very short time. So she said simply, "Because I need you."

"Like hell. Maybe you need a trainer with a whip and a chair, but you don't need me."

"Look," Liza said determinedly, "I can't finish the lodge on my own. I know that now. I've bitten off more than I can chew this time and I—I hate to admit it to Granddad. I need help, and I don't have anybody else to turn to."

"My God, woman, you almost knocked the whole place down single-handedly with a tire iron yesterday! What else do you need?"

"I—I—"

"Yes?"

"All right," she ground out, unwilling to admit a weakness but seeing no alternative. "I need your common sense. Maybe you've got problems, but you've also got something I need. Yankee practicality. I have good ideas, but I...well, that damned budget, for one thing. I don't know where to start."

Impatient, he said, "Just get a piece of paper and start writing down what needs to be done."

"See? That's easy for you to say, but it's beyond me! Help me with this one thing, okay? Then maybe I'll leave you alone."

"Maybe?" he repeated dangerously.

"Maybe," Liza reaffirmed, not about to give him an inch. "I never make promises I can't keep."

Cliff looked away and sighed.

"Please?" she asked, stepping closer. "I do need you. Come on, I'm trying to be as polite as possible, aren't I?"

"I suppose I should be thankful for small favors," he said sourly.

She grinned, and another rumble of thunder shook the ground under their feet. Cliff glanced up at the sky, as if seeing the descending storm for the first time. A huge thunderhead had boiled up from the leaden clouds.

"We're going to get wet in a minute," he said.

"I don't care. I want an answer. Will you help me or not?"

The first drops of cold rain splashed down, striking Liza's shirt. She didn't flinch, but waited for his answer. The rain fell sharply around them, turning Cliff's dark hair slick. He didn't seem to notice, but studied Liza's upturned face for a long moment—examining her expression for signs of deception.

He said, "I don't really have a choice, do I?"

Liza grinned. "Not really. I'm going to make your life miserable, one way or another. Come on, let's go inside before we get soaked."

They ran for the lodge, dashing through the raindrops and sliding on the wet grass. Cliff reached the porch first and put out an automatic hand to help Liza up the steps. They staggered inside and headed for the kitchen.

Liza prepared the food while trying to coax Cliff out of his dark mood. Relentlessly, she teased him, forced him to respond, asked questions and waited for answers. *Like pulling teeth,* she thought. Gradually, however, Cliff began to thaw.

Dinner turned out to be a surprisingly delicious omelet with a salad and buttered bread. They ate together companionably in the kitchen. At least, Cliff ate. Liza scribbled notes on a scrap of paper torn from her sketch pad while Cliff outlined a preliminary budget for the refurbishing of the lodge. Mind you, she had more experience with budgets than she'd let Cliff believe. But she'd always had a staff of accountants to supervise before, and she didn't feel capable of organizing figures on a project as big as Timberlake without some help.

"Once Joe figures out how much some of these things will cost," Cliff explained, "you can plug in the numbers. If the cost of repairs is too high, you'll just have to figure out what work can wait."

"But I want to do all of it at once."

Cliff looked amused. "If you're a millionaire, you can do that. If you aren't, you need to learn some patience."

Liza tossed down her pencil. "Not one of my best qualities."

She reached for the bottle of catsup on the counter and poured a liberal dollop onto her omelet. "I hope Joe will hurry up and figure out how much the repairs will cost. I want to get started."

"He seems like a hardworking guy. I'm sure it won't take him long to work up an estimate."

Liza used her fork to smear the catsup evenly over her omelet and said musingly, "I bet poor Joe freaked out when the backhoe hit that body today."

Cliff studied her splash of catsup and said, "He was upset, of course. I gathered it wasn't something that happens to him every day."

Once her omelet was smothered in catsup, Liza reached for the jar of pickle relish. "It sure scared the hell out of me. I never thought of Timberlake as having a dark side, but I guess some terrible things must have happened here once."

"It scares *you?*"

"It makes me think. I hope it won't keep Joe from coming back to work at the lodge."

"He'll be back," Cliff said, drinking the crown of foam off his beer. "He didn't strike me as the kind of man who gets rattled easily."

"Still, I'm glad you were here when it happened," Liza said truthfully, slathering relish on top of the catsup that coated her omelet. "I couldn't have handled it alone."

"You did okay. I noticed Alyssa slipped away pretty quickly. She didn't even stick around for the police to arrive."

"She really hates this place, I think."

"Bad memories for her here?"

"I guess so." Liza sighed. "I wish I knew more. Maybe I'll look through Margaret's diary tomorrow."

"I left it on the table in the lounge."

"Thanks. If I look through it, I might be able to find out a few things about my family."

"Maybe you won't like what you learn."

Liza smiled and forked up some of her omelet. "I think I can handle just about anything. At least I hope so. Mmm. Delicious. But I sure wish I had some onions!"

"Onions?" Cliff asked, eyeing the concoction on Liza's plate. "That looks like an explosive combination already. You're not actually going to eat it, are you?"

Liza paused, her fork halfway to her mouth. "Sure."

"With all that gunk on top?"

"Gunk? It's wonderful!" Liza cleaned off her fork and dug into the omelet for more. "You don't know what's good, Forrester. Here, try some catsup—"

"Whoa!" He caught her wrist before she could up-end the bottle.

His grip was quick and firm, and Liza felt her pulse jump against the pressure of his fingers. Laughing, she lifted her gaze to his dark eyes, but suddenly found herself tongue-tied. Surprise flickered across his face, too, but Cliff was careful to release her hand gently. But the moment had happened—a brief instant when time seemed to stop and a funny electrical current passed between the two of them.

Liza cleared her throat. "How about some ice cream after I finish this?"

"The ice cream melted. Remember? You forgot to put it into the fridge."

"We'll go to town, then. I bet the Dairy King still makes great banana splits. When was the last time you had a banana split?"

"I don't like bananas."

"Really?" Liza laughed. "That's odd. What else don't you like?"

"Beets," Cliff responded, going back to the last few bites of his omelet. "And mincemeat pie."

"What's wrong with mincemeat pie?"

"I don't know. It's probably something from my childhood. My Grandmother Pierce used to make it and force it down my throat on holidays. I was always sick afterward, though probably not from the pie. My brother and I used to steal her shortbread cookies before dinner, you see."

Liza liked the visual image of a young Cliff Forrester stealing cookies from his grandmother's kitchen.

"Were you afraid of your Grandmother Pierce?"

"Terrified. She was a very tall New England lady with a big voice. She was a little deaf, I think, and always shouted."

"She's gone now?"

"Yes. Half the Daughters of the American Revolution mourned her passing, since she'd been the driving force of the organization for many years. She was quite a woman. I was named after her father.''

"He was a Cliff?"

"Clifton. Clifton Rutherford Pierce."

"Clifton," Liza repeated, trying the name on her tongue. "That sounds very blue-blooded. Are you?"

"Blue-blooded? I don't know. What does that mean?"

"Do you come from a very old and venerable Boston family with lots of money and a collection of silver that would sink a yacht?"

"Yes," said Cliff, and they laughed together. Quickly, he added, "My family had money a long time ago. But my father became a career man in the air force, so he wasn't exactly rich. His choice of careers was a disappointment to my mother's family, who wanted him to quit flying airplanes and join the family business.''

"What kind of business?"

"Publishing. You ever heard of Pierce and Roth-childe's?"

"Good grief, you're from *that* Pierce family?" Genuinely startled, Liza exclaimed, "Heavens, Forrester, you could be rubbing elbows with rich and famous authors instead of counting rainbow trout or whatever you do here."

"I like working outdoors," said Cliff shortly. He finished his meal with a couple of quick bites and carried his dishes to the sink.

Liza ate in silence after that, pleased that she'd made a little headway with him despite the abrupt end to their conversation. Talking about his family hadn't made him too uncomfortable, so she decided to try another idea.

She dropped her plate into the sink and dusted off her hands. "Let's go for ice cream."

"You go," said Cliff. "I'll wash up."

She shut off the water faucet and steered Cliff away from the sink, his hands dripping soap bubbles on the floor. "No, I want you to come along. I don't remember the road exactly. I might get lost."

"You won't get lost!"

"I might," she insisted, lying cheerfully. "Come on, I'm dying for something sweet. Don't fight me on this, Forrester. I can be a bear unless I get my chocolate fix."

He gave in reluctantly, and Liza led the way, dashing through the rain to the pickup truck. Cliff drove, and Liza propped her sneakers on the dashboard and turned up the volume on the radio. As they splashed through puddles on the highway, she sang merrily along with the Beach Boys and Tommy James and the Shondells, tapping her toes and drumming her fingers on the seat between them.

Cliff found the Dairy King quite easily and parked under the flickering neon sign with half a dozen other cars.

"I see a little rain can't keep the citizens of Tyler away from their ice cream," Liza noted. "Ready?"

"You get what you like," Cliff said, suddenly tense once he turned off the engine. "I'll wait for you here."

"No way!" she cried, reaching past him and popping open the door on the driver's side. She pushed him out and scrambled after him, saying, "I'm not going to pig out on dessert all by myself. What will you have? A chocolate sundae? A diptop? Maybe a scoop of strawberry with sprinkles and whipped cream?''

"Liza—''

She refused to listen to his protests and propelled the reluctant Cliff through the steamed-up glass doors of the ice cream shop by pushing the backside of his jeans.

The place was nothing fancy—a fake marble counter and a few cheap tables with plastic chairs grouped on a checkered linoleum floor. Behind the counter stood a pair of overworked teenagers who struggled to keep up with the orders fired at them by the phalanx of customers crowded into the Diary King for a rainy night snack. A jukebox played noisy rock and roll in one corner, and the smell of French fries hung in the air. In a booth under a root beer sign, a group of teenagers lounged over greasy paper plates and nearly empty paper cups of soda pop. They shouted laughing insults at one another.

Liza hooked her arm through Cliff's and dragged him to the menu board. "Let's see. I'm definitely in the mood for a banana split. But should I get the regular or the jumbo? Decisions, decisions. A jumbo, I think. What about you?''

"I'm not very hungry.''

Cliff looked pale in the glaring fluorescent light, so Liza shoved one of her hands into the hip pocket of his jeans just to jar him out of the anxiety that looked ready to overwhelm him. "Baloney! You could have eaten a dinner twice the size of the one I made. I saw the way you were looking at my plate until I spread catsup all over everything.''

Her hand in his pants did the trick. It felt good to Liza, and it must have electrified Cliff, too.

"Well..." he said. "I guess I have a little room for something sweet."

"Great!" Liza led him to the counter and prepared to abandon him there. "Order for both of us, will you? I'm going to the ladies' room. Got enough money?"

Cliff wanted to yell at her. But Liza disappeared in a flounce of blond hair that drew the appreciative gazes of every teenage boy in the room. She left him alone.

At once Cliff started to sweat. He didn't venture far from the lodge very often, and he stuck to the same routes every time. It was safer that way. He didn't like new places, new people. They scared him, though until lately he hadn't recognized the feeling that gripped him as fear. He never knew if something ordinary might trigger a memory and send him spinning into the past. He might snap into a flashback, an idea that terrified him now that he'd seen how close he'd come to violence with Liza. What if he lost his marbles in a public place with a lot of innocent people around?

Damn Liza for dragging me here!

The walls of the Dairy King suddenly seemed very close. And the floor wasn't steady under his feet. Cliff crossed his arms and hooked his shaking hands under them, afraid to take a step. He closed his eyes and tried breathing deeply, emptying his mind of all conscious thought. Sometimes that technique worked—it often helped him fall asleep when he thought relaxing wasn't possible.

But a large family burst in through the doors at that moment, and Cliff realized he was blocking the entrance. He pulled his wits together and stepped aside.

"Oh, were you in line?" the harried father asked.

"No, no." Cliff gasped.

"Waiting for someone?"

"Yeah."

The father nodded and herded his brood to the counter. Automatically, Cliff got into line behind the family. There were several wailing children who wanted their ice cream immediately. One of the little boys wrestled out of his mother's grip and threw himself on Cliff's leg, bawling his lungs out.

"I want choclit!" he howled. "Want it now!"

"Sammy, you'd better behave," snapped his exasperated mother. "Before that man gets angry at you."

The boy's sticky-fingered grasp on Cliff's jeans loosened at once, and he cast a scared look upward. His tears evaporated, only to be replaced by fear. But he couldn't drag his hands off Cliff's leg. He was frozen with panic.

Before Cliff could speak, the mother yanked the boy's arm, pulling him against her side. "Don't touch strangers!" she admonished. "What if that bad man decided to steal you?"

Little Sammy started to cry in earnest then. His chest heaved in terrified sobs, and he buried his face against his mother's skirt.

Cliff wanted to say something. To explain that he wasn't bad, at least. But he was afraid his voice would roar out like hideous fire from a dragon's mouth. Cliff couldn't even smile to reassure the little boy. The fear he had seen in that small face paralyzed him.

"Can I help you, sir?"

The girl behind the counter raised her voice and repeated, "Can I help you? Mister?"

Cliff tried to shake himself out of the trancelike state and grabbed the edge of the counter to hold himself upright. Hoarsely, he said, "A banana split."

The girl was chewing gum and cracked it loudly, making Cliff jump. "What size?" she asked.

The question baffled him for a moment before he remembered what Liza wanted. "A—a large one."

The girl's elaborately made-up eyes narrowed on Cliff after his long hesitation. "Okay," she said with exaggerated patience, as if she was speaking to an addled old man. "You want chocolate, vanilla and strawberry ice cream?"

Cliff nodded numbly. His mind was suddenly filled with a harsh buzzing sound.

"Whipped cream?"

Cliff's head swam. He hadn't realized ordering a banana split for Liza was going to be such an ordeal.

"Whipped cream, sir?"

Liza materialized at his side just then, and she leaned over the counter with her earrings dancing in the bright lights. "Extra whipped cream," she said with authority. "And some peanuts, but no cherry, okay? I hate those canned cherries. They hardly qualify as real food."

The counter girl dragged her puzzled gaze from Cliff and shrugged. "Okay. Anything else?"

"What are you going to have, Forrester?"

Cliff couldn't think of anything he wanted except to get out of the Dairy King as quickly as possible. The awful buzzing in his head had started to build to a roar. It was a sound like pulsing thunder.

When he didn't answer, Liza laughed. "I guess he's just going to share mine. Give us two spoons."

"Coming right up."

Liza jiggled his arm. "You okay?"

Cliff almost couldn't hear her. The thunder in his head was so loud he was sure everyone in the building could hear it. He put one hand to his temple, hoping to hold in the turmoil of emotion that threatened to break through at any moment. But it was no use.

He tore out of Liza's hold and gasped, "I'll wait for you in the truck."

He escaped then, blundering out of the ice cream shop and elbowing aside the throng of teenagers in his path. He heard a few outraged cries, but he didn't stop until he was safe behind the wheel of the pickup again. Breathing hard, he gripped the steering wheel as if it were a life preserver. The neon lights of the Dairy King flashed in his eyes, so he put his forehead down on the wheel.

The thunder in his head matched the sound of the rain as it pounded on the roof of the truck. Cliff felt as if the sound might knife through his skull at any moment.

"Move over," said Liza beside him. She had opened the driver's door and was pushing him with one hand, forcing him to slide across the seat. "Take this," she ordered, shoving the plastic dish into his hands.

Cliff took it woodenly and nearly spilled a river of chocolate into his lap.

"I changed my mind," Liza said lightly, "and ordered a hot fudge sundae since you don't like bananas. Start eating it before it melts. Here's a spoon."

"I—I don't want it. Let's just go."

"You're not in any shape to drive," Liza said matter-of-factly. She slammed the door. "So eat. What happened in there, anyway? You looked like you were ready to climb the walls."

He didn't know what had happened. The only thing Cliff was sure of was that if he'd stayed in the Dairy King for another moment, he'd have exploded.

Beside him, Liza said, "You know, it looked like you were having a panic attack."

"A what?"

"It's an anxiety thing. All this tension builds up inside and just about bursts you open. My friend Gracie used to get them all the time. They scared the hell out of her. It got so bad she was afraid to leave her house."

Cliff looked up at Liza and found her studying him intently.

"I wonder..." she murmured, then smiled suddenly. "You better start eating that thing, okay? It's *melting!*"

She started the truck with a roar, then reached across and dug into the ice cream with a little plastic spoon. She scooped up a huge mouthful and ate it with delight, humming happily.

"Now you," she said, feeding him a bite of ice cream. "Taste good?"

Cliff couldn't taste a thing, and the cold lump that oozed down his throat almost came back up again. He choked.

"Okay," Liza ordered, wedging the spoon into his hand, "just nibble around the edges so it doesn't overflow while I drive."

The plastic dish did overflow, however, just a few miles down the road. Liza laughed when she saw the mess, then pulled over under some trees and tried to mop up the worst of the melted chocolate. She used a paper napkin to wipe the mess off the seat and set to work on the leg of his jeans.

"Stop," Cliff said at last, finding enough breath to speak.

"Aha, you aren't giving me the silent treatment after all, huh?"

"Take this thing!"

She accepted the ice cream, then folded up her long legs and sat eating it while Cliff tried to get his brains in order again. The noise in his head had begun to abate. Now only the rain overhead made the drumming sound he heard. But he remained shaken. Never had he come so close to disaster with so many people standing around. Never had he felt so damaged. So abnormal and horrible. He squished himself into the corner of the seat, unconsciously trying to escape the soft glowing light of the dashboard.

While he collected himself, Liza waited patiently and ate her dessert.

In a few minutes, with her mouth full, she asked, "You okay now?"

Cliff nodded in a series of jerks. "I think so."

"Does that happen a lot? When you go into public places?"

"I don't go into public places," he replied, relieved that his voice sounded normal. "I stay at the lodge."

"You leave it occasionally."

"Not often."

Liza frowned. "But you must go to the grocery store, right?"

"Now and then, but it's...I've been there before. It's not so bad."

"It's a safe place for you?"

"Yes."

"And the truck must be safe, too."

He nodded and realized that he had eased into the light once more, to better see her face.

Liza ate more ice cream thoughtfully. "Is it the places you're afraid of? Like Marge's Diner and the garage? Or do the people make you nervous?"

"Not exactly."

She skewered him with a wise look. "Then you must be afraid of what you might do to them?"

"Yes," said Cliff, letting out an unsteady breath.

Liza sat in silence while they both got used to the idea. Then she leaned closer.

Her voice was barely a whisper. "Want a bite?"

She held the spoon out to him, smiling. Her blue eyes shone brilliantly in the light of the dashboard. "You're not going to make me eat this whole thing alone, are you?"

Cliff stared at her, trying to decide if she'd simply decided to ignore what had just happened in the Dairy King. "Aren't you afraid?"

The question surprised her, and her brows rose prettily. "Of what?"

"Of me. Of what I might do."

She shrugged and laughed, devil-may-care as she spooned more chocolate into her mouth. "What's the worst that could happen? If you have a fit in the Dairy King, we'll just pretend you're an actor practising an important movie role. I hear Robert De Niro does it all the time."

She dug into her ice cream again and ate ravenously, apparently unconcerned. "Look," she said, "it's no big deal. I can accept you the way you are. If the rest of the world can't, who cares? We've got each other, right?"

"Liza," Cliff said, struggling to communicate. "Don't you wonder if I—if I might truly hurt you? Does it never enter your head?"

"You can't hurt me," she said, turning to look at him with all traces of her casual attitude suddenly gone. Solemnly she said, "You can't hurt me, Cliff, unless you throw me out of your life."

She wasn't afraid at all. Liza was strong and willing and determined, and nothing could prevent her from getting what she wanted, once she set her sights on it.

Cliff couldn't stop himself then. The feelings inside him overflowed completely, and he saw himself reaching for Liza across the seat. Unsteadily, she set the sundae dish on the dashboard, then slid into his arms, warm and slightly flushed with emotion. Her smiling mouth joined his, tasting cool and sweet.

"Ah, that's better," she whispered against his lips, "but let's do it just once more. And this time, really put your heart into it, all right?"

Cliff began to laugh helplessly, drunkenly, and Liza responded with a husky laugh of her own, sliding deeper into his embrace and lifting her mouth to be kissed properly.

In two seconds, they were necking like teenagers.

CHAPTER TWELVE

LIZA LET HERSELF be carried on the wave of Cliff's raw release. He needed her—and nothing had ever given her such pleasure before. She could feel his heart hammering and heard his breath rasping in his throat. His hands bit into her flesh, and he groaned aloud as they kissed. Liza felt cherished, adored, impassioned.

She felt her own tension peak and burst, too, then spread like seafoam through her veins. Suddenly Liza couldn't hold back anymore, and she wound her arms around Cliff's strong neck and pressed her body into his. Their kiss turned wild and exciting. Cliff drove his fingers into her hair and tilted her head, making the coupling more firm, more sensual. She arched against his chest, smoothing her hands all over his shoulders, his back, memorizing the contour of muscle and bone, soaking up the vitality that glowed from inside him. All the while, she kept hearing the same message. *He needs me. He needs me.*

The windows of the truck began to fog up, and the thrumming of the rain on the roof seemed to echo the thunder of Liza's pulse.

Cliff pulled her across the seat, and in a moment Liza was straddling him, her knees jammed into the seat cushion, her long legs capturing his thighs.

"Yes," she whispered, throwing her head back so that he could nuzzle the length of her trembling throat. "The answer is yes."

"I haven't asked the question," he breathed.

"You don't need to. I want to make love with you, Cliff."

"Liza—"

"Stop worrying. Stop analyzing. Stop *thinking!* Just do what you feel like doing."

"I feel like—like—"

"So shut up and *do* it!"

He did, pushing her shirt up and sliding his hand under it to caress Liza's bare back. It wasn't enough. Frustrated, she sat up straight and took his hand in her own, guiding him until he cupped her breast and found the nipple with his fingertips. Shivering with pleasure at his touch, Liza forced him to rub her breast in slow circles. Her nipple grew hard beneath his warm palm, and Cliff gave a soft exclamation. When she released his hand, he went on caressing her.

Liza sighed and opened her eyes. "That's what you want, right?"

His dark gaze burned into hers. "That and more."

Leaning forward, Liza bumped her forehead against his. Her long hair made a curtain around them. "Much more," she whispered. "We could be good together, Forrester. I've been thinking about it since we met. I knew this had to happen between us."

"So did I."

"But you're fighting it."

"As hard as I can."

She laughed unsteadily as he pushed her shirt higher still and found her breast with his lips. It was going to happen, all right. He began to kiss her rhythmically. "I'm a very demanding woman, you know."

"I can be a demanding man," he said, his voice fading to a murmur, just before closing his teeth with excruciating gentleness on her engorged nipple.

Liza melted into a boneless collection of female hormones as Cliff nibbled his way from one breast to the other. Then he eased her down onto the seat and began to work magic with her nerve endings. His weight felt good, his body fitting perfectly into the shape of her own. She felt his fingers, his mouth, his tongue, his teeth, start to unfasten all her clothes and warm every inch of her skin. He pressed kiss after molten kiss into the places where her pulse beat fast. She found herself writhing like a cat beneath his caresses, and the last of her doubts seemed to drain away.

Her own hands cruised unbidden to unbutton Cliff's shirt and find the springy hair of his chest. His back was a strong curve of muscle that tempted her touch, too. His skin was warm beneath her palms, and she felt his breath catch as she drew lazy, exploring circles around the small of his back. She slid one hand lower, hesitating at his belt.

Cliff shuddered with anticipation, but Liza did not venture farther. Not yet.

"Wait," she whispered, wriggling uncomfortably. "We're both too tall to wrestle in a truck."

"I can't stop now," he said, feverishly kissing her neck and earlobes.

Liza laughed breathlessly. "We can't manage this, Cliff, not here. I want to see you when we make love, to watch everything you do, everything you feel."

When he lifted his head, she traced the hard line of his cheek with one finger and smiled into his eyes. "Let's go home and make love properly."

The idea began to appeal to him. "I could make a fire."

"You already have!"

He laughed unsteadily and relented. Liza clambered up, tugging her shirt back into place. Cliff slid behind the wheel of the truck. But Liza had left the headlights on, and the stupid battery was dead. Cliff couldn't get the engine started.

"Damn!" she cried, laughing helplessly when he gave up trying. "Finally, I get you in the mood, and we find ourselves stuck in a contortionist's pickup truck!"

"We'll manage," Cliff growled, reaching for her again.

Liza evaded his grip. "I know a shortcut through the woods," she suggested. "We could run for the lodge. Maybe we won't get too wet. It'll only take five minutes, and then we'll be alone together."

Cliff sent her a smoldering look that scorched Liza to the marrow of her bones. He said, "I don't want to wait five minutes."

She smiled and popped open the passenger door. "I'm afraid you don't have a choice. I'm making a break for the lodge."

"Liza, come back here!"

But she slid out of the truck and into the driving rain. She was soaked immediately, and when Cliff climbed out of the other door, she could see his shirt was soon plastered to his skin, too. It was an appealing sight—all that perfectly honed muscle displayed for her pleasure.

She grinned and shouted, "Catch me if you can!"

She raced up the hillside and plunged into the trees, laughing and dodging raindrops in the darkness. Branches snatched at her clothing, and the storm filled the night with the steady thunder of falling rain. The earth was slippery beneath Liza's sneakers, but she hurried onward, conscious of nothing but the powerful man who ran half a step behind her—the man who wanted her badly enough to chase her through the dark forest on a stormy night.

It felt like a game, and God knew Cliff needed something as foolish as a game. She could feel him watching her hips, wanting to seize her from behind, debating about throwing her to the ground and making love in the rain. What would it be like? Naked bodies washed by a warm summer rain, their cries of passion muffled by the drumming of thunder. Cliff needed to let go, to have fun, to take his pleasure in the heat of the moment.

Liza nearly fell coming out onto the gravel driveway. She snagged her soaked shoe on a root—or maybe the pursued woman simply wanted to be caught at last. Cliff swooped Liza into his arms, breathless from exertion. She felt his heart pounding against her own through the drenched fabric of their clothing, and the tension in his body was unmistakable. She could feel how aroused Cliff was and laughed with delight.

But when she looked up and their gazes met, her laughter died in her throat. Desire was carved plainly on Cliff's face, and fire burned in his gaze. Suddenly he seemed capable of taking what he wanted. He was tall and strong, every inch a man. A life force she could not resist.

A tingle of excitement shot up from inside her body, and Liza heard herself whisper his name.

Without a word, without tearing his hungry gaze from hers, Cliff slid his callused hands around her face and tipped her mouth to his. Their lips met ravenously, fused by the rain that suddenly rushed down from the heavens. The sky opened and poured upon them, melting body to body, mouth to mouth. Liza felt as if she'd been swept into a vortex, and she was powerless to stop it. She had aroused something primitive and unstoppable, and the consequences made her tremble.

Cliff tore free from the kiss and pierced her gaze with his, asking a last question. *Now?* But Liza couldn't find her voice. She nodded her answer, and Cliff seized her hand, turning for the lodge. They ran lightly over the drive and hustled up the steps of the veranda. Liza's usually steady hand fumbled with the catch on the door, and Cliff ground out a harsh word of impatience. In the next instant, he bent and snatched her off her feet. With a cry, she wrapped her arms around his neck. Then Cliff gave the door a resounding kick and sent it slamming back on its hinges. A moment later, he strode into the lodge with Liza trembling in his arms.

He headed for the old lounge—the small room with the stone fireplace and comfortable furniture. But he didn't bother with the furniture or with building a fire. Liza felt she might have screamed if he'd stopped to do anything but make love to her.

He halted and set Liza on her feet once more. She clung to him, wet and shivering with anticipation. His hair was sleek against his head, and the rainwater on his body made him slick and hot to her touch. Unsteadily, Liza began to unfasten the rest of the buttons on his wet shirt.

"You're so beautiful," he murmured, passing his hands over her wet T-shirt.

"Undress me, Cliff," Liza begged, unable to wait any longer. She wanted to feel his skin against hers.

In one smooth motion, he pulled the shirt over her head, and Liza stood very still as he dropped the garment and absorbed the sight of her bare breasts. She had never felt so much like a woman as at that moment. Riveted by the male hunger she read clearly in his gaze, she allowed him to unhook her jeans and plunge his hands into her panties, filling his palms with the curve of her buttocks.

"It's been so long," he murmured, barely audible.

Liza worked his shirt off and unsnapped his jeans. Though his flesh felt hot, he shivered as she undressed him, kicking his wet shoes aside and running her hands down the powerful muscles of his legs before smoothing her caress upward once again. She found him hard and pulsing.

Stretching on tiptoe, Liza aligned herself with him, and felt Cliff shudder as their rain-slick bodies connected. For a moment Liza feared he couldn't control himself, that he was overcome by desires too long suppressed. He ran his hands down her hips and kissed her hard and hungrily. Growling words she couldn't understand, he pressed against her soft body, holding her inescapably against the proof of his own excitement. Wet skin against wet skin, he hugged her hard and poured a liquid kiss into Liza's mouth.

Too fast, too fast, Liza wanted to cry. *Make it last all night.*

Perhaps he heard her plea or his own instincts took over at that moment, because Cliff suddenly slowed and a long, tormenting pleasure began. He stroked her, explored her secret places, admired her body with his hands, whispering words that soothed and aroused at the same time. Liza found herself shaking weakly as she responded in kind, caressing Cliff's lean frame and learning every detail of his still-moist skin. Her feathery touch led him to the brink of desire time and time again.

At last, Liza pulled away and reclined on the rug, inviting Cliff with outstretched arms. His gaze was dark with tumultuous desire as he knelt above and stared at her languorous, naked body.

"I want to make you mine," he said on a rasp, parting her knees and caressing the inner flesh of her thighs.

"I'll always be myself," she whispered.

"God, Liza, you must stop me if I—"

"You can't hurt me, Cliff."

With a groan of surrender, he came down to her then, gripping Liza's shoulders with hands that bit hard. Liza reached for him, welcoming him with a soft murmur. He lost control and thrust inside her at once, driving deeply until he reached the place that made Liza cry out.

He tensed at once, frozen above her like a beautiful, erotic statue.

"No!" she choked, already floating on the brink of something wonderful. "Don't stop."

"But I—"

"You're a man making me feel like a woman. Please don't stop."

He buried his face against her breast. "I couldn't stop now. You feel too warm, too good."

Liza held his tousled head and wondered if she'd ever felt so deeply moved. How profoundly this man needed her. And he needed her in every way.

There seemed no way to express how much she needed him, too, except by physical communication. Liza held him and rocked her hips—slowly at first, then building to a delicious dance that dragged a groan of pleasure from Cliff's throat.

The sound of his voice gave her a thrill of feminine triumph. For him, she was the only woman in the world. When he raised himself and began to thrust powerfully into her, a delightful tremor grew inside Liza. Mindlessly, she arched to meet his next plunge, wrapping her slim legs around his hips to make each surging connection more perfect than the last. She wanted to give him everything, to ease his pain and make him whole again. His intense gaze burned with conflicting emotion, emotion she longed to assuage.

But silhouetted against the rain-streaked window, Cliff's face soon began to swim in a haze of sensual pleasure, and she could not find her voice to ease his troubled soul. Liza lifted her fingertips to his cheek, then had to close her eyes as waves of delight racked her body. Tears of joy and release burned behind her lids. Over and over, she felt Cliff find the sweetest spot inside her—sometimes tenderly, sometimes sharply—

and her throat contracted with emotion. How could a man so full of pain give so much pleasure? How had he learned so quickly the things that she loved most? Yet she felt attuned to him, too, and knew exactly how to make him respond. They moved with eerie syncopation, rushing higher and higher, hotter and hotter, as they soared toward satisfaction.

At last, the world contracted and seemed to explode around them, shimmering in tiny fragments of light and darkness. Liza clutched Cliff tightly, and they plunged off the edge of the earth into darkest space. Perhaps she called his name, for Cliff answered with a deep, hoarse cry of his own.

A long time later, Liza became conscious of floating back to reality. Cliff remained deep inside her for a long while, then reluctantly shifted, tucking her body against his own lean frame. Exhausted, yet revitalized, Liza lay snugly with him, listening to Cliff's breathing steady and wondering if he'd been as racked by emotion as she had been. Her whole body still throbbed with pleasure, and unshed tears filled her eyes. Puzzled, she tried to remember if she'd ever felt such deep emotion before.

She shivered, and Cliff mistook that reaction. He left her for a few minutes to light a fire, then returned with the worn afghan from the sofa. He wrapped her in the warm folds and held her as the flames sprang up. Liza hugged him fiercely. She didn't dare look at his face for fear he'd see how profoundly she'd been affected by their lovemaking, but she relaxed into his arms again and marveled at how natural it felt to be so intimate with Cliff. He toyed with the long strands of her hair, content to bathe in the glow of the fire.

What had happened? Liza wondered. How had something usually as uncomplicated as sex turned into something so amazing? Inside, she felt churned up. Her heart was still beating erratically.

Maybe it was foolish. Stupid, even. But Liza felt the urge to say the words.

"Listen, Forrester," she whispered, fighting to keep her voice steady. "I—I think I must be falling for you."

She felt his arm go tense beneath her head.

"Liza—" he began, voice rough.

She covered his mouth with her fingertips and avoided making eye contact. "Just listen a minute. I'm not asking for your eternal love or anything. I just . . . it's funny, that's all. Don't you think so?"

"Hilarious," Cliff said, sounding anything but amused.

"Don't get bent out of shape." She sat up quickly, wishing she hadn't tried to explain her feelings. She kept her face turned away.

Cliff pushed up on one elbow and touched her bare back hesitantly. "Liza . . ."

"I'm not trying to get you to say something you don't mean. I just wanted you to know, that's all. I really care about you."

Cliff's touch was gentle but firm as he turned Liza around to face him. He brushed her hair from her temples, and his dark gaze was solemn on hers. "You know I'm not ready for any of this—not even for what's already happened."

The truth hurt, even though she already knew Cliff wasn't capable of declaring any deep feelings. He had too many problems to overcome before he could recognize love when it stared him in the face.

"Sometimes," he said, "I've hated you. You make demands and push your way into things that—"

"I'm a pushy broad."

"Yes, but you're other things, too. Whether you admit it or not, you're sensitive and caring. I know that, Liza. I just...I can't give you the things you need. Not now, anyway. I'm not ready."

The mood had changed too quickly for Liza to stand. She swallowed hard, attempted to grin saucily and slid her hand down his body. "Oh, yeah? A few years of celibacy seems to have made you ready for just about anything."

"That's not what I mean," he said, catching her hand before she could tease him erect again. "I can't make you any promises, Liza."

"I'm not asking for anything. Relax," she said, playfully extricating her hand from his grip and brushing her nose against his to coax a grin. Her own mouth trembled with the effort of keeping a smile pasted in place. "Let's just see what happens, okay?"

"But—"

"I just want to have a good time," she lied. "Let's just fool around a little and see what develops. When was the last time you enjoyed yourself? Or played a game?"

"A game?" he repeated blankly.

She laughed and caressed him boldly, anxious to restore the mood she'd broken by making premature declarations. Her fingers toyed with the hair on his chest. "Yeah, a game. A sexy game."

Cliff was at a loss. "You mean like spin the bottle?"

"No, you dope! I'm talking about grown-up games. Like you pretend you're a gunslinger, and I'll be the saloon girl who ropes you—"

He began to laugh helplessly. "Liza, I don't even know who I am under normal circumstances!"

"I know who you are," she said softly, nibbling his jaw and planting tiny kisses on the curve of his mouth. "You're a sexy, wonderful man, and you turn me on, Cliff Forrester."

"You can't be as turned on as I am."

"You make me ache inside and tingle when you touch me—"

"Like this?"

Liza shivered as he feathered a caress down her belly. "Yes, like that."

"We don't need games," Cliff murmured, his mouth centimeters from capturing hers.

"Maybe not," Liza agreed, opening her mouth as he crushed her lips with his. She pulled Cliff over, and they tumbled onto the soft afghan once again.

IN THE MORNING, Cliff awoke to the sound of a car crunching on the gravel of the driveway. He sat up groggily, and found himself alone.

"Liza?"

She called from the kitchen. "I'm going outside! Carl's here with my car!"

She slammed out through the door, and he could hear her bare feet thudding quickly on the porch.

Knowing she was outside, Cliff leaned back on his elbow on the floor. After making love a second time, they'd spread their damp clothes in front of the fire and made a kind of nest on the floor, complete with pillows and cushions from the sofa and extra blankets to snuggle under. In fact, the blanket was still warm where Liza had slept. Cliff ran his hand over the place where her body heat remained and closed his eyes, remembering how good it had felt when she stirred against him in the night.

God, she'd been sweet. And spicy, too. The many flavors of Liza—delicious as honey one minute and piquant with sensual curiosity the next.

Her sexuality burned like a flame inside her. Shedding her clothing had been natural for her. Cliff remembered the openly lusty look in her eyes when she lay back on the rug and beckoned him down. Just thinking about the expression on her face made him hard again. She was beautiful and she enjoyed it. Some women liked sex, Cliff thought, the way they enjoyed chocolate. It was quick and refreshing.

But not terribly lasting.

That was probably the way Liza looked at it. Good, quick, fun sex and no regrets.

That business about falling for him—that had been an afterthought. Maybe she'd figured he needed to hear that after their first wild coupling.

"She can't mean it," Cliff murmured. "Love doesn't happen that fast. Besides, she seemed very willing to change the subject when I called her bluff."

That was what it had been, no doubt. A bluff. Liza's sexual appetite was probably like her appetite for everything else she enjoyed in life. Large and insatiable. And saying she cared for him afterward—that was probably part of modern bedroom etiquette. Saying the right words at the end was surely as obligatory as a postcoital cigarette, and Liza had obliged. But it didn't mean anything to her.

Cliff felt changed, however.

Liza romped into the room, her hair full of sunshine and her blue eyes throwing sparks. She had pulled on her T-shirt and jeans again, and looked unbearably sexy.

"Hi," she said, falling to her knees and giving Cliff a sizzling good-morning kiss. Her voice was husky, and she looked deeply into his eyes. "Sleep well?"

"Yes," Cliff answered, surprising himself with the truth. "I haven't slept like that in years."

Her brows waggled suggestively. "A little exercise is good for you, I guess. Carl brought my car. He's gone back to town with his assistant. It's all fixed. Want to go for a spin?"

"I'd rather stay here with you." He filled his hands with her hair and tugged her close, wanting nothing more than to spend the rest of his life making love to this wonderfully uninhibited young woman.

She laughed, looking beautiful as she curled into his arms. "That's a switch! You don't want to get rid of me anymore?"

"Don't tease a naked man, my girl."

"Why not?"

"Because you'll find yourself in a compromising position."

He pinned her unresisting body to the cushions and rode into the valley of her thighs. Liza sighed and settled provocatively beneath him, slipping her arms around his neck.

"Listen," she said, fondling his hair and smiling. "Before we start making a regular thing of this—"

"Yes?" he asked, already easing her shirt off to explore her body again.

"I think we ought to talk about a few issues."

Cliff stopped trying to strip her naked and eyed Liza warily. "What issues?"

"Birth control, for one thing. It slipped my mind last night, what with all the excitement, you understand. And believe me, I've done a lot of calculating this morning before coming to the conclusion that this is probably a safe time for me, but..."

Cliff stopped listening for a second, his own thoughts superseding Liza's chatter. Birth control! He hadn't even thought about it last night. And the idea of fathering a child at this stage in his life was more frightening than facing a platoon of soldiers with automatic weapons.

What kind of father would he make? He could hardly look after himself, let alone a child!

Liza prattled on obliviously, saying, "I think condoms would be best for the moment, since it'll take a few days to get a doctor to prescribe the pill for me again—"

"You were taking birth control pills?"

"For a while," Liza replied, meeting his gaze without a blink. "When I had a steady boyfriend a couple of years ago. Want to hear about him?"

"No," Cliff said hastily.

"It's considered common sense to ask your lover about former affairs, you know. Just to be safe—"

"I don't want to hear anything!"

"What's the matter?"

Cliff sat up, feeling shaken. "Nothing."

How complicated life was! He'd almost forgotten. In the real world, every action resulted in a reaction. Consequences. He should have remembered that.

"Don't forget who you're talking to," Liza said, watching him try to collect himself as she lay quietly on the cushions. Softly she said, "I can see you're upset."

"I'm not. I just— This is more complicated than I thought." Cliff passed his hand through his hair. "I wasn't thinking at all last night, I guess."

"I'm glad," Liza murmured warmly.

"No, I mean, I— Lord, birth control!"

"That's the easy part," Liza replied. "It's the sexually transmitted diseases that scare the heck out of me. I figure you're as safe as they come since you've been such a monk lately, so I didn't grill you like I usually—"

"I don't want to hear about what you usually do."

Liza fell silent for a moment, then she said, "Cliff, I wasn't a virgin last night. I'm a grown woman, and I've had some affairs before that didn't work out. You're not the first for me."

"I know that."

"And I wasn't the first for you. That was obvious. What's nice is that we've been bumped around a little, and we've found something nice together that—"

"I don't think we've found anything, Liza."

"What do you mean?"

Cliff reached for his jeans and found them dry. "I mean I'm not ready for this."

"I *know* that! I'm not asking for anything—"

"Yes, you are."

"Great sex, maybe," she said on a laugh, "but other than that—"

"I'm not kidding, Liza. You're getting something out of this relationship even if you don't see it."

"Okay, Dr. Freud," she said, folding up her long legs to watch him stand and get dressed. "What am I getting from you?"

Cliff slid into his jeans, frowning and struggling to put his feelings into words. He owed her that much. But he couldn't manage.

Maybe it's easier just to break things off now.

"I'm not a strong man," Cliff said at last, turning away from Liza and starting to pace in hopes of ordering his thoughts.

"You're stronger than you think."

"I'm not the kind of guy most girls are looking for—unless you're a girl who's got something to prove."

"Something to prove?" Liza repeated carefully.

"Or something you wish you could fix."

"I don't get it," she said, but her tone had grown dangerous. She folded her arms over her chest. "You think I'm trying to fix you?"

"I think you're trying to save me," Cliff said steadily, turning to face Liza from a safe distance, "the way you wish you could have saved your father."

Liza's blue eyes blazed, and for a split second Cliff wished he hadn't spoken. But then he could see he was right.

Liza's voice sank to a dangerous murmur. "That's a rotten theory, Forrester."

"Is it?" Braver, he said, "For years you've been angry with Alyssa for not saving your father from suicide."

"Don't talk about my father."

"Why not? Haven't you noticed the parallel?"

"What are you talking about?"

"I think you're hoping you can show your mother how she should have intervened in your dad's life. That's it, isn't it, Liza? That's why you've taken up with me."

Liza boiled to her feet. "That's not what I'm doing, and you know it!"

"No? What *are* you doing, then? Why have you come to the lodge except to rescue me from myself, Liza? Don't tell me you've come here hoping to go to bed with me. That's just the sideshow. You've bullied your way into my life hoping you can correct the past."

"I can't believe you'd say that!"

"It's the truth," Cliff said. "But I'm afraid you've come to save the wrong person. I'm not your father. I'm not the suicide type, Liza. If I was, I'd have done it long ago. You're wasting your time with me."

Liza stared at him coldly for a long minute. "Maybe I am."

CHAPTER THIRTEEN

LIZA WANTED to throw something at Cliff. Didn't he see how much she cared about him—not the past or anything else but *him?*

"What about last night?" she asked quietly, seething inside.

"It was a mistake," Cliff said at once, stiff and deadly calm. "I'm sorry. I shouldn't have let it happen."

"You didn't have any control over what happened last night," Liza argued. "For once, you let your guard down."

"And made a mistake," Cliff finished, still damnably composed. "I should have realized why you stayed around. I should have seen that your problems with your father's death were your real reason for—"

"You think I was here to play Florence Nightingale to a ghost? You think I made love to you because you're like my *father?*"

"That's not what I mean, and you know it. Can you honestly deny that you were trying to help me last night?"

"Maybe—maybe I was," Liza sputtered. "But, blast you, I'm not your nurse or your shrink or a doctor! Nobody can help you but yourself, Forrester! I know that better than you know it yourself!"

His face remained impassive. "Then what was last night about?"

"You idiot, it was about sexual attraction!" Liza exploded desperately. "We're two people who felt the sparks fly from the moment we met! We've had a hard time keeping our hands off each other as long as we did! And whether you'll admit it or not, last night was about love!"

"No, it wasn't," Cliff said sternly. "The sex part I can believe, perhaps, but as for...as for love, as you call it—"

Liza couldn't stop her voice from rising bitterly. "Oh, what do you know about love? You're even afraid to say the word! You've been hiding from it for years—afraid to test how much your family loves you, afraid to try for yourself—"

"Liza..."

"Maybe you're just incapable of loving someone! Maybe *you're* the one with the problem! Did you ever think of that?"

"I *know* I've got problems! That's why I warned you off from the start. But you wouldn't listen and now things are out of hand and somebody's going to get hurt."

"Well, damn you, it's not going to be me!" Liza snatched one of the cushions from the floor and slammed it onto the sofa.

"Where are you going?"

"I'm leaving, you heartless, blind bastard!"

"Liza—"

He caught her arm as she stormed past, but Liza flung him off and whirled on him in a rage. "You don't need to get mushy at this late date, Forrester.

You wanted me to hit the road ever since I set foot in this drafty old barn!"

"You don't have to leave like this. Not angry and—"

"Oh, I'm not angry! I'm *furious!* And if you don't get out of my way, I'm going to punch your lights out!"

"Liza, I want you to understand me."

"I understand everything, Forrester. It's you who's got to come to a few important conclusions. And it's obvious you're going to have to do that all by yourself. I'm leaving! And when you come to your senses, you'll have to find me."

"What?"

"Someday you're going to realize that I don't make love with just anybody. I may be reckless and foolish, but I'm not stupid! I don't get mixed up with a man unless I really care about him—the way I care about you!" Suddenly half-blinded by the tears that threatened to choke her, Liza cried, "I *love* you, Cliff Forrester! I'm not sure why, but I do! And if you decide you can love me back, you're going to have to come looking for me, because I'm not coming back here without a hand-delivered invitation!"

Liza rushed away from him and hurried upstairs. She threw her few meager belongings into a paper sack, and as an afterthought grabbed the items they'd found in the attic before she ran down the stairs again. The hell with her sketch pad and anything else she'd left at the lodge. She found herself panting from the effort of keeping her emotions in check.

Cliff had disappeared. He didn't have the guts to say goodbye.

Outside, Liza started the convertible with a roar and backed up without looking in the rearview mirror. The car thumped over the branches that had been knocked down by last night's storm, but Liza didn't stop to assess the damage to the T-bird. She tore out of the driveway in a spray of gravel and didn't look back.

By the time she reached the highway, she was weeping. As she gripped the steering wheel and cried a bucket of hot, stinging tears, she told herself they were tears of rage. But a niggling voice in the back of her head said something else. *You're sorry this is happening. You're making a mistake.*

But Liza ignored the little voice. Instead, she sped into Tyler with the wind whipping her hair into a tangle and her brain in a raging turmoil.

Without thinking, she drove to the Victorian mansion on the most familiar shady street in Tyler. It wasn't until she'd hastily parked the convertible with two wheels on the lawn, climbed out and slammed the door that she realized where she'd run to.

"Liza!" her mother called, stepping out onto the sun-dappled porch and lifting her hand to shield her eyes. "Is that you?"

Liza took a deep breath and held it, wondering if she had the strength to face her mother on this of all mornings. Hastily, she dried the tears from her face and tried not to sniffle as Alyssa came down the slate sidewalk toward her.

Alyssa wore another sleek pair of pastel trousers and a loosely elegant blouse. No jewelry except a set of gold earrings adorned her, but she looked as carefully coiffed as a magazine photo. She smiled brilliantly.

"Liza, I'm so glad to see you here!"

Numbly, Liza allowed herself to be hugged. But when her mother's arms enfolded her so eagerly, she felt more uncontrollable emotions boil up from inside herself. She tried to hug her mother back, but the hug turned into a desperate embrace and a flood of fresh tears.

Alarmed, Alyssa cried, "Honey, what's wrong?"

"Oh, Mom," Liza was able to say miserably, but she could explain no further.

Alyssa held her shoulders tightly. "Are you hurt?"

"It's not that. I just—I can't—He isn't—"

Gently, Alyssa slid her arm around Liza's quivering back and turned her toward the house. "It's okay, Liza," she soothed. "Come inside and tell me about it."

The porch hadn't changed, nor had the colorful pots of geraniums and the spanking white pillows on the wicker swing. The tall front door still squeaked when it swung on its hinges, and the cool air in the front hallway smelled like the same breakfast Liza had taken every day for the first eighteen years of her life— oatmeal and wheat toast and a fragrant Chinese tea with oranges.

It smelled like home, and Liza needed a home again, she realized. Since she'd left Tyler, she'd never felt so homesick as she did standing in the hallway of that familiar house with her mother holding her.

"I need you, Mom," Liza said.

"I'm here, honey."

"I've been a dope and I wish—I wish you could fix things for me."

"What's happened?"

Liza hiccuped and said, "It's Cliff."

"What about Cliff?"

"I—I'm falling in love with him, Mom."

Alyssa said not a word, but guided Liza down the hallway and into the kitchen. She poured two cups of tea from the cherry-red teapot and carried them through the dining room filled with mahogany antiques to the gaily painted sun porch on the back of the house. There, she pressed Liza into the white wicker love seat and perched herself on the matching footstool.

"Drink up," Alyssa ordered kindly. "Then we'll talk."

The tea tasted good, and Liza was surprised to find herself calming down once she'd taken a few swallows.

She smiled ruefully at Alyssa. "It's funny, isn't it? Me coming here with troubles in my love life."

"That's what mothers are for, you know, to help their children with their love lives."

Liza shook her head firmly. "But I never needed help before. I'd have drunk poison before I'd tell you anything personal..."

"Well, you've grown up a little," Alyssa said softly, and she squeezed Liza's knee. "What's the problem with Cliff? Did you mean what you said? That you were falling in love with him?"

"I know it's happened too quickly. But I think it's the real thing. I think about him all the time, and I want to be good to him."

"That's one of the first signs, all right."

"But I— Maybe I'm doing all the wrong things."

"He's very vulnerable," Alyssa murmured. "You can't make too many demands on him, I'm afraid."

Liza hung her head. "I told him I wouldn't go back—that he'd have to come get me. But he can't do that. I know he won't leave the lodge unless it's life or death. He's got some kind of phobia, I think."

"I've suspected that myself. It's not surprising. After all he's been through, he's finally found a place that's safe and he doesn't want to leave it."

"So I shouldn't have made that ultimatum."

"You could go back to him. Or is your pride at stake?"

Alyssa smiled to take the sting from her words, and Liza found herself smiling wryly, too. "My pride will be my downfall," she admitted. "But this time...well, Cliff said some things that really hurt."

"What things?"

"About Dad."

Alyssa's smile faltered.

Liza hastened to continue, saying, "I know I threw some pretty terrible accusations at you the other day—about not helping Dad before he died. I've always been angry about that, I guess, but Cliff said..."

"What did Cliff say?"

"He thinks I'm trying to save him the way I wished I could have saved Daddy."

Alyssa sat back, her gaze filled with pain. "We all wish we could have done something to save your father, Liza. His friends, his family—all of us. But we couldn't. He kept his secrets until the end. He didn't want our help."

"Asking for help was so bad?"

Alyssa nodded. "I think so. He had to admit terrible failure. He let down so many people, and he couldn't stand it."

"Cliff's trouble is different. There's nobody depending on him."

"Except you."

Surprised, Liza exclaimed, "I'm not depending on him! I just want to love him."

"Which means he's got to love you back. Maybe he's not strong enough to do that."

Liza sighed. "Well, I know he's not strong enough to come for me. He's afraid to leave the lodge for anything. You should have seen him at the Dairy King last night. He almost flipped out."

It was Alyssa's turn to look startled. "You got Cliff into the Dairy King? I didn't think he went anywhere but the grocery and the hardware store once in a blue moon. You must be doing something right."

"Well, it all blew up in my face this morning," Liza murmured. "I pushed too hard, I think. He panicked and wanted to get rid of me, so he picked the one subject he knew would get me furious enough to leave."

"What subject?"

Liza licked her dry lips before answering. "Dad."

Alyssa winced as if she'd been struck.

"Listen, Mom," Liza said, "I know it's hard for you to talk about him. It's hard for me, too. My feelings are all over the spectrum."

"Mine, too," Alyssa said softly. "You can't imagine. I feel so guilty sometimes, Liza. If only I'd known. If only I had done something. *If only!* I can't live by those words. I can't go back and do things differently."

"What would you do if you could?"

"I'd be more like you," her mother admitted. "I'd force him to talk to me."

"Mom—"

Alyssa shook her head, cutting off Liza's words. "I hope you'll never make a mistake like mine, Liza. It's an awful way to lose your innocence."

For the first time in her life, Liza could see how deeply her father's suicide had affected Alyssa Baron, and she felt very guilty. How could she have been so blind? Had she been too caught up in her own suffering to see her mother's pain? Suddenly Alyssa looked her age. The lines in her face deepened, and her complexion seemed to gray as she stared at the wedding ring on her hand—the ring she hadn't yet removed, even though Ronald Baron had been dead for years.

With a terrible quaver in her voice, Alyssa said fiercely, "Oh, Liza, hang on to love while it's in your grasp. Hang on to it with all your strength!"

Liza thought of Cliff.

"I wish I could hang on to him. But he won't let me get a hold, Mother. Sometimes he looks at me as if I'm a monster who's going to tear him limb from limb. I can see that I frighten him sometimes."

Alyssa smiled tremulously. "You're a forceful person, Liza."

"He needs some forcing, I think. He *should* be forced. I made him go up to the attic, for example. He's been haunted by noises up there, so I took him up. It seemed to help."

"You went into the attic at Timberlake?"

"Yes." Remembering their find, she said, "We came across a lot of things that belonged to Margaret, by the way."

Alyssa paled. "What things?"

"Mostly clothes. A few papers and some photos—that sort of thing. And her diary. I almost forgot that. It was hidden in a drawer with some nightgowns."

Alyssa's voice dropped to a strained whisper. "You found my mother's diary?"

"Yes, we thought we might learn more about her if we looked through her things."

Alyssa's hand trembled so violently that she dropped her teacup with a clatter. It shattered on the tile floor, shockingly loud on such a quiet summer morning. But Alyssa seemed not to hear. Her voice cracked. "What are you trying to find out?"

"Mom, are you okay?" Liza bent to pick up the broken pieces of the fine china cup. "What's wrong?"

"What are you trying to find out about my mother?"

Liza sat back, cupping the broken bits of china and staring at her shaken mother. "Take it easy, Mom."

Alyssa fought to compose herself. "I'm sorry. I just…it felt odd to see the lodge the other day, and I—I've been thinking about my mother ever since. Now this…"

Liza narrowed her gaze on Alyssa. "What's going on, Mom? Both you and Granddad reacted in such a weird way—"

"I'm never weird," Alyssa shot back, attempting to laugh.

"Mother, what do you know about Margaret that nobody else in town knows?"

The bald question threw Alyssa off balance completely. She stared at Liza, and her mouth opened, but no sound came out. Her beautiful features whitened so dangerously that Liza suddenly feared her mother was about to faint. Swiftly, she put out her hand to steady Alyssa on the footstool.

Alyssa looked away quickly, but Liza had time to catch a glimpse of the fear in her mother's eyes.

"What's wrong, Mom?" she pressed when Alyssa did not speak. "What's the secret of Margaret Ingalls? Is it so terrible?"

"You know as much as I do," Alyssa whispered harshly, withdrawing her hand from Liza's grip. "She disappeared."

"Do you believe that?" Liza demanded.

"Of course I do! What else could have happened to her?"

"Exactly the question I was going to ask," Liza murmured, studying her mother. For years, their family had kept secrets from one another. To avoid pain and confrontation, they swept important questions under the rug. But Liza wanted answers now. She thought she'd burst into flames if she didn't know the truth.

She decided to be blunt. "Did Margaret disappear, Mom, or did something else happen to her?"

"I—I don't know. I was only a child...."

"Seven years old, right? That's old enough to notice a few things." Fiercely, Liza asked, "Do you remember the night Margaret ran away?"

"No." Alyssa shook her head and hugged her own arms as if suddenly very cold. "I can't remember a thing...."

"But you remember other events that happened when you were even younger. Why, you used to tell me about the fancy dances they held at the lodge and—"

"I can't remember that night!" Abruptly, Alyssa buried her face in her hands. Her muffled voice quavered with emotion. "I know something bad happened—something terrible, but I—"

"Mom?"

"I've blocked it out, I guess," Alyssa said softly, lifting her head to stare at nothing. The emptiness in her expression frightened Liza, who had never seen her mother lose control. Gradually her blue eyes fixed on Liza, and she said softly, "I'm not strong like you, Liza. I can't cope with everything that comes my way."

Liza leaned forward and clamped her hand over Alyssa's wrist. It was time for answers, no matter how frightening. Steadily, she said, "Mom, Granddad came out to the lodge yesterday after Joe Santori dug up the body by the lake. He said some things that scared me."

Alyssa looked fearful. "What things?"

"He didn't make any sense—not exactly. He talked about Margaret, though, and asked for forgiveness."

"He loved her," Alyssa said suddenly. "He loved her very much. I remember that."

"Mom," Liza said firmly, determined to learn the truth, "did Margaret disappear? Or did she die?"

Alyssa began to weep silently. Tears formed in her eyes and ran unchecked down her cheeks as she stared mutely at her daughter.

Liza clenched her mother's hand and said bluntly, "Did Granddad kill Margaret?"

A harsh sob escaped Alyssa's throat. "Oh, God."

"Is that what happened, Mother? Did Granddad kill his wife and pretend she disappeared? Did he bury her by the lake?"

Alyssa shook her head frantically. "I don't know, I don't know! I can't remember! What does it matter now?"

"Mother, we've found a body. The police are involved...."

"It can't matter after all these years! Can't we just forget—"

"The police aren't going to forget."

"Liza," Alyssa said, trembling, "whatever happened—it was a long time ago. We can only break up the family by digging into the past. And you're home now—we could be a real family again! Please, don't start—"

"Mom, listen to me!" Liza snapped. "It's out of our hands. If the police decide the body *is* Margaret's, they're going to want to learn how she died. And if Granddad—"

"Judson didn't kill anyone!"

"How do you know?"

"I don't!" Alyssa admitted. "I just—it can't be possible!"

Liza frowned. Perhaps she was jumping to conclusions. Perhaps the body they'd found by the lake wasn't Margaret's at all.

But something told her otherwise. She knew in her heart that Margaret Ingalls hadn't quietly slipped away from Judson forty years ago and run off with one of her lovers. She'd have tried to contact the family at least once in all those years. No, Liza felt sure her grandmother had died.

But how? Had someone murdered the flighty, reckless Margaret Ingalls and buried her in a secret grave? Who would have done such a thing? And why hadn't Judson Ingalls tried to locate his wife in forty years?

"We have to find out the truth before the authorities do," Liza said at last. "If Granddad's guilty, we've got to protect him."

Alyssa was too upset to talk anymore. Liza made her mother comfortable in a wicker chair and left her alone. Although she felt more frightened than she ever had before, Liza knew she had things to do. She intended to find her grandfather and ask him some direct questions.

CHAPTER FOURTEEN

WHEN LIZA STORMED out of Timberlake, Cliff hoped to feel relief. He was afraid of her—of how she forced him to talk and think and feel again. He should have been delighted when she left.

But the crushing weight that burdened his chest when he heard the Thunderbird go tearing down the driveway wasn't relief. It was too painful.

"I should be *glad* you're gone," he snapped, leaning his forehead against the cool, cloudy glass of the boathouse window and watching the convertible disappear into the trees. "You were a pain in the neck from the moment you appeared in my life!"

Cliff spun away from the window and paced the length of the musty boathouse, where he'd taken refuge from Liza. He hadn't wanted to face another scene with her. He'd managed to send her on her way with a few well-chosen words, and he didn't trust himself to speak with her again.

Why not? Afraid you might change your mind?

"Shut up," Cliff muttered to himself—to the voice of reason in the back of his head. "I'm better off without her. That woman was nothing but trouble!"

But, she's very beautiful trouble. Beautiful and smart and funny. And sensitive. Observant, too.

Liza had made Cliff see a lot of things he'd managed to forget about himself. She'd dragged him into the light and forced him to take a long, hard look at himself. He hadn't liked what he'd seen.

But oddly enough, he didn't despise himself anymore.

And Liza hadn't despised him, either. She hadn't feared him or hated him.

She's in love with you, you idiot! Doesn't that mean anything? You didn't have to throw her out of your life!

"What if something went wrong?" Cliff asked aloud, slamming his fist down on the upturned hull of an old rowboat. "What if I lost my head and hurt her?"

You didn't lose your head last night. And you had plenty of chances. You made love to her without holding back anything. And nothing terrible happened. It was terrific, in fact. What are you really afraid of?

"I don't know," Cliff said softly. "Maybe I can't love her back. Not the way she ought to be loved."

She could teach you. She's taught you a lot of other things in the past few days, you moron.

Cliff jerked open the boathouse door and walked into the sunlight. The grass was still wet from last night's rain, and the air was fresh and aromatic. The lake was hushed, but brilliantly blue. Stopping on the dock, Cliff looked up at the lodge, and for a moment he marveled at its beauty. The sunlight shimmered on the roof, and the surrounding trees played dappled patterns on the walls. Cliff's heart contracted. Timberlake had been his haven for a long time. It had been his fortress, his hiding place. It was the only place he'd felt at home.

So stay here, taunted the voice in his head. *You're happy here, right? Safe and sound, all alone—that's you. No big deal. Waste your life, Forrester. Let her go.*

To the voice, Cliff said, "She deserves something better than living here with a recluse."

Right, answered the voice.

Cliff climbed the hillside and went into the lodge, conscious of how his footsteps echoed. He had only himself to contend with now. It should have felt good.

But in the hallway, he was faced by an immediate reminder of Liza. She'd ripped out the wall and left a tremendous mess behind. Bits of broken plaster mingled with lengths of old board and a scattering of dust so thick that her bare footprints were clearly visible.

"Trust that idiot to drive in her bare feet," Cliff muttered.

He found a broom and got a wheelbarrow from the garden shed to clean up the remains of Liza's expansion project. He'd carried a couple of loads out onto a burn pile behind the lodge when he heard a car engine in the driveway again.

It wasn't Liza, a sixth sense told him. Her car sounded different. Cliff edged his way to the door and looked out in time to see Joe Santori climb out of his truck. Cliff hesitated. Usually, he stayed out of sight when someone came calling at the lodge. He didn't like talking with people.

But Joe wasn't just people, Cliff reasoned. With the broom in hand, he pushed out through the door and greeted Joe on the veranda.

"'Morning," Joe called cheerily, striding up the porch steps. "You two live through the storm last night?"

"Barely," Cliff said.

Joe laughed. "It was a real downpour, wasn't it? Say, I thought I saw your truck down by the highway. Have some trouble with it?"

"Dead battery," Cliff supplied, relieved that he could come up with an explanation for having left the truck so he could make love to Liza.

Joe peeled off his cap and nodded, leaning comfortably against the porch railing as if ready for a long, pleasant conversation. "That'll happen now and then," he said. "Specially in wet weather. I'll run you down later and give you a jump start. I've got a set of jumper cables under the front seat."

"Thanks."

Joe seemed not to notice that Cliff couldn't manage more than a word or two at a time. Taking a pack of chewing gum out of his shirt pocket, he offered Cliff a stick. When he declined, Joe took one for himself and launched into a rambling story about an old truck he'd once owned but could never trust. The thing only started about half the time, and he couldn't keep the tires inflated. Finally he'd sold the truck to an old man, who painted it bright red and used the vehicle for years to collect trash in the neighboring countryside. Cliff didn't follow the thread of the story, but he must have smiled bleakly at the appropriate moments, because Joe laughed and clapped him on the shoulder.

"Just goes to show," Joe added. "You can't judge a truck by its color."

"Uh-uh," said Cliff.

"Where's Liza?" Joe asked suddenly.

"Liza?"

"She still in bed?" Joe asked with a grin and a suggestive wink. "The rain keep her awake last night?"

"No," said Cliff. "She's gone."

"Gone where? Into town?"

Cliff realized he couldn't guess where Liza might have gone. Perhaps to Tyler to see her mother. Or maybe back to Chicago. For all he knew, she might have decided to hightail it to California by now. She was likely to make that kind of snap decision about life. She was reckless and wild. And his heart ached, knowing she was gone.

Watching Cliff's face, Joe sobered and said, "Well, I thought I'd come out and see if she still wanted to go through with the improvements we talked about yesterday. After digging up that body by the lake, I wondered.... Discoveries like that have a way of changing things. You have any idea what her plans are now?"

Cliff shook his head. "I can't imagine."

"Well," Joe said, looking at Cliff strangely, "you tell her that I'm still interested, okay? I'd like to try my hand at fixing this place up. I'd hate to see it fall apart. There's a lot of history in a lodge like this."

"Yes," said Cliff.

"A lot of people around town used to say this place was haunted. I don't go for that nonsense, of course, but there used to be some pretty great parties up here, and some of the finest families in the state visited Timberlake. We ought to preserve it, don't you think?"

"Yes."

Joe laughed. "You're not the talkative type, but I like you, Forrester! A man of few words." He stood up and clapped his hat back on his head. "Well, how about it? Let's go start your truck."

Cliff hesitated. He didn't want to get into Joe's pickup and drive down to the highway. He didn't want to have to make conversation or struggle to appear normal for Joe's benefit.

But you are normal! shouted the voice in his head. *You don't have to pretend. Joe doesn't care if you're a little quiet. Just go get the truck, for crying out loud! See if you can leave the lodge with somebody besides Liza.*

"What do you say?" Joe prodded.

If you've learned anything from Liza, it's that you're not as crazy as you thought. Go with Joe. I dare you.

"Come on."

"Okay," Cliff said, almost giddy with adrenaline. "Okay, let's go."

It wasn't until he was standing beside Joe's pickup that he realized he was gripping the broom handle as if it were a life buoy. He left it propped against a tree and got into Joe's truck without a word. Joe started the engine and gabbed about nothing special as they drove down the drive through the trees.

When they reached the highway, Cliff realized he hadn't driven on that stretch of road with anyone but Liza in the ten years he'd lived at Timberlake. He concentrated on breathing evenly as Joe made the left turn and headed toward town.

Cliff didn't want to break down. He didn't want to go crazy in Joe's truck. He didn't want to hurt Joe.

Joe can take care of himself, said his inner voice. *Liza took care of herself and showed you you had more control over yourself than you thought you did.*

"You know," Joe said as he rolled down his window and let a blast of morning air rush into the cab, "I used to think you were a little weird, Forrester."

Cliff's throat was too tight to answer.

"But you're okay," Joe went on comfortably. "Not exactly a barrel of laughs, if you know what I mean, but you're a good egg. From what I hear about Liza Baron, you're probably the best thing that ever happened to her."

"What do you mean?"

"Oh, you know." Joe shrugged amiably. "A girl like that needs an anchor. She's got wild ways, but she can't get anything done until somebody gets a bridle on her. She needs gentling down from a guy like you."

"Gentling down," Cliff repeated, amused by Joe's choice of words. "You don't know how funny that is."

"Why? You're about as gentle as they come, right? No offense," Joe added quickly. "Some women really go for that teddy bear stuff, right? Treat 'em quiet and they're as sweet as pie. Get rough, and they leave you flat."

Had he been too rough on Liza? The remarks about her father's suicide had been meant to drive her away, all right. Cliff shouldn't have used such a painful weapon on her. Liza's feelings about her father's death were still very raw indeed. He had poured salt in her wounds by suggesting she was trying to change the past by working on him.

"It's not like I've had the best luck with women," Joe continued. "I'm still looking for the right one, mind you. But I'd say you're using the right technique with Liza. Give her room to be creative, but keep her within the bounds of reason. She's probably eating out of your pocket, right?"

"Not exactly," said Cliff.

"What's the matter?" Joe asked. "You don't go for her?"

"Sure," he said. "I go for her, all right."

"She's a beauty." Joe sighed. "And sexy enough to fry eggs on—well, she's sexy, that's all. I hope you don't mind my saying so."

"I don't mind," Cliff said. "I appreciate any help you can give me."

"Was Liza upset about the body we dug up?"

"Yes," Cliff replied. "She's afraid it's going to stir up trouble."

"It's already stirred up some excitement," Joe said, driving the truck along an open stretch of highway. "The whole town's been talking about it."

Cliff couldn't imagine Judson or Alyssa spreading the story around Tyler. He said, "I'm sure the family won't be happy to hear that."

Joe nodded. "I know what you mean. Chief Schmidt has a big mouth. I hope his gossip doesn't upset Liza and Alyssa too much."

Me, too, Cliff thought.

He listened awhile longer, as Joe talked about his philosophy of the fairer sex. They reached the stranded pickup truck shortly, however, and Joe grabbed a coil of jumper cables out from under the seat. Together, they worked at getting the pickup started, and when the old engine caught and roared at last, Joe gave Cliff a jaunty wave.

"Good luck with that pretty lady of yours!"

When Joe drove off, Cliff sat behind the wheel of the idling pickup for several minutes, trying to decide what to do next. The need to see Liza again pulled at him like a magnet. He wanted to hold her in his arms and feel her weight against his body. The scent of her hair seemed to float on the breeze.

And he could almost hear her soft whisper as she bit gently into his earlobe and told him how much she loved the way he touched her. His insides tightened at the memory of her smooth flesh and lithe limbs.

But he couldn't turn the truck toward Tyler and seek her out. It was too risky. Already he had ventured too far beyond his self-imposed safety point. And he needed time to think of the right words to say to her.

He reached Timberlake in a few minutes and retrieved the broom from the tree where he'd left it. Back inside the lodge, he began to finish cleaning up the mess when he noticed a puddle of water on the floor beside the stairs.

"Where did that come from?"

A quick glance upward told Cliff that Liza's tampering with the lodge's inner structure must have changed things they couldn't see. Clearly, the roof no longer leaked just into the attic, but also into the lower floors. The puddle at Cliff's feet must have come as a result of last night's rain.

He dropped the broom and headed for Margaret's room and the secret staircase to the attic. To make sure the leak hadn't caused any permanent damage, he found his way up the stairs and into the gloomy storage room that was piled high with Margaret Ingalls's belongings. It felt odd to be among those things without Liza—as if he were intruding on the privacy of a living woman. But he brushed aside the sensation and went looking for a leak in the roof.

The floorboards creaked under his feet as Cliff edged along in the attic's half-light.

"I should have brought a flashlight," he muttered. "Or brought Joe up here. I don't know what I'm looking for."

He whacked his head against a wooden truss and cursed loudly. Then he laughed.

"Serves you right, Forrester," he told himself. "Somebody has to knock some sense into you. Oh, hell!"

The groaning floorboards gave way, and Cliff's foot plunged through the rotten wood.

"I guess I found the place that leaks," he said, trying to pull his shoe free. "Where am I? Probably right over the wall Liza tore out single-handedly. She'd probably laugh her heart out to see me stranded up here in the dark."

But he wasn't stranded much longer. Cliff heard a loud, tearing groan of weakening wood, and then the whole world shifted around him. He lunged for a solid handhold, but his leg lurched deeper into the hole in the floorboards. He gave a strangled yell, and then everything gave way. In a huge rush of choking dust and screaming timbers, the roof caved in and the floor swallowed him up.

The last thing Cliff remembered was hurtling through darkness, the weight of the lodge roof crashing down on his head.

LIZA WENT LOOKING for her grandfather at his office at the Ingalls plant and at Marge's Diner. No one had seen him all day, she was told. And by the expression on Marge's face, Liza gathered that Judson Ingalls had never before missed a breakfast at the diner. "Where is your grandfather?" Marge asked. "I heard he was awfully upset about the body found up at the lake."

"We're all upset," Liza replied before leaving the diner.

Fearing the worst, Liza searched the town for her grandfather. But Judson seemed to have disappeared. Where could he have gone? She thought of asking Alyssa where he might have gone to find some privacy, but decided against pressuring her mother. Things seemed to be falling apart for the whole family.

Liza found herself turning the convertible toward the lodge and Cliff Forrester.

"He'll know what to do," she told herself, knowing she wasn't thinking clearly anymore. A terrible sense of foreboding had begun to fill Liza's mind. "At least, Cliff will calm my active imagination!"

Liza whipped the T-bird up the long driveway to the lodge and frantically tried to think of what she was going to say to Cliff. Should she apologize for going off half-cocked this morning? Should she demand an apology from him, perhaps? After all, he had a lot of gall talking about her family that way! But Liza couldn't think of the right words, the right combination of syllables that could communicate her complex feelings. She just wanted to see him, to feel his embrace. Then everything would be all right.

But it wasn't.

She rushed into the lodge and found the hallway looking like the site of a bomb blast.

"Oh, God!" Liza rocked to a stop at the sight. "Cliff!"

Rubble was piled at least eight feet in the air, and she could see daylight where the roof had once been. Stunned, Liza scrambled over the initial mess of fallen beams and cried, "Cliff! Cliff, are you in here?"

No sound. The mess of plaster and wood moved as if shaken by an earthquake beneath, and Liza grabbed the staircase banister to keep herself upright. The thought of Cliff being trapped underneath all that lumber was unbearable.

"Oh, my God, don't let him be stuck in here. Cliff!"

She began tearing away the splintered wood, her hands shaking with fear, her voice cracking with panic. "*Cliff!* You'd better answer me, you—Cliff! My God, this is blood!"

The sticky red stain on her hands was blood, indeed, Liza realized, staring in horror at the unmistakable evidence that her lover had been hurt.

"Oh, Cliff," she cried, trying not to weep. "Cliff, I—oh, damn you, if you're dead, I—I'm going to *kill* you!"

Feverishly, Liza ripped through the debris, but her frightened efforts were ineffectual, she realized at last. She was making things worse. She scrambled off the pile, sobbing with terror.

"I'll have to go for help," she gasped, hot tears streaming down her cheeks. "I can't do this alone. Can you hear me, Cliff? I'll be back as soon as I can!"

CHAPTER FIFTEEN

IT WAS A WONDER she didn't wrap the convertible around a tree. But Liza managed to negotiate the car down the winding drive without smashing into the woods, and when she reached the highway, she floored the accelerator and flew toward Tyler, counting the seconds and trying not to think of Cliff buried under all that junk, bleeding, and perhaps dying. Her heart pounded and she bit back sobs of terror.

In Tyler, she blasted through the red light at the first intersection and screeched around the corner. After years of living away from town, she wasn't sure she could find the fire station or the new police barracks, so she headed for home and the telephone.

She flew around the corner and there, parked in front of the house, was the pickup truck.

And standing by the hood was Cliff himself.

Liza hit the curb and ran the convertible straight into one of her mother's bridal wreath bushes.

"Liza!"

He ran across the lawn and yanked open the T-bird's door. "Are you all right?"

Liza nearly wept with relief. "Cliff, I thought...I was afraid—"

"Calm down. Take it easy."

Trembling, Liza rushed out of the car and wrapped her arms around his neck, breathing in gasps. "Oh, Cliff, I went to the lodge and saw the mess and I thought—I thought—"

"Easy, love," he murmured in her ear. His embrace felt like home, and his voice was deep and soothing. "I'm okay. Just a few scratches, see?"

Liza leaned back and took a good look at his face, touching his cheek with quivering fingertips. She saw a few scrapes on his forehead and one nasty slice in his cheek that oozed a little blood, but otherwise he looked healthy, indeed—just dusty and tired.

"I was so afraid you were dead. I couldn't stand it."

"I couldn't die," he said, his dark gaze full of emotion as he wiped at her tears with one bruised knuckle. "Not yet. I've got too much to live for."

Liza tightened her arms around him protectively. "What are you doing here?" she asked, realizing suddenly how difficult the trip into Tyler must have been for him. "You left the lodge!"

"I came looking for you."

"But—but—"

Softly, Cliff said, "You said I'd have to come after you, so I did."

"I'm sorry I said that. I know how hard it is for you."

"I'm here now," he said on a shaken laugh, "and relatively in one piece."

"But something must have happened. Something that would make you—"

He smoothed her hair, coaxing Liza to calm down. "Quiet down now, and I'll explain. I started cleaning up the mess you left at the lodge and realized the roof had leaked during last night's storm. When I went up to the attic to find the leak, the floor gave way. It was a hell of a fall, let me tell you—''

"You could have been killed!"

"That's what occurred to me as I climbed out from under the wreckage." Cliff smiled wryly. "I couldn't help remembering the day I woke up in the hospital in the Philippines. I was hurt worse then, and I was almost sorry to find myself alive. But this time—Liza, I realized how very much I wanted to live."

Suddenly Liza's throat was tight, and her eyes began to sting.

"I want to be with you," Cliff said, his voice rough. "I need you."

"Cliff—"

"I know I still have a lot of things to learn, a lot of things to change. I'll need your help."

"You've already taken the biggest step of all," Liza whispered hoarsely, joy overflowing in her heart. "And I love you for it."

Cliff pulled her snugly against his frame, pressing his rough cheek against her softer one.

His voice was raw. "I love you, too, Liza."

She stretched up and kissed him, her lips seeking to warm his the way his words warmed her heart. Cliff took charge of the kiss almost at once, his mouth communicating the one message Liza wanted to receive. He loved her. He poured his soul into hers, arms fastened tightly around her body. For an instant, Liza forgot the rest of the world and rejoiced.

How lucky she was! Coming to Tyler had been one of those reckless decisions she made in the middle of a bad situation. But this time she'd managed to find the one thing she felt as if she'd been looking for all her life. Of all the men in the world, she'd happened upon the one who needed her most, the one who had been created especially for her and no one else. She wanted to spend the rest of her life kissing him this way.

Reality swam into perspective in time, and Liza smiled up into his face. She took Cliff by the hand and drew him toward the house.

"Come inside," she said. "Let me take care of those scratches."

"No..."

"My mother will want to see you. You'll be okay."

If Cliff resisted any longer, it was only for a split second. Trustingly, he followed Liza up the walk, glad to hold her hand and feeling as if he'd never release it.

"You made peace with your mother?"

"For the moment," Liza said with a laugh. "Come on."

Cliff managed to keep his anxiety under control as he entered Alyssa Baron's house for the first time in his life. Alyssa looked pale and emotionally worn out, but she brightened when she saw him standing awkwardly in the hallway. When Liza and Alyssa pulled him happily into the living room, he couldn't feel nervous. He knew them both so well, and he trusted them both to understand him. He took no notice of the furnishings or the quick bite of pain as they daubed his scratches and applied bandages, but he managed to respond to the conversation when it was necessary.

But most of all Cliff wanted to be alone with Liza. She must have seen his true felings, for she terminated their visit within a few minutes after cleaning up his wounds. Then she hurried him outside again.

"Let's go back to the lodge," she whispered in his ear as they slid their arms around each other on the porch, under Alyssa's smiling eye. "I want to be alone with you."

SEVERAL NIGHTS LATER, with the chill of autumn in the air, Liza found herself drawn to the lakeside. She left Cliff in the lodge where he was starting a fire in the hearth, a fire that would warm them against the evening's cool breezes and perhaps ignite the fires of passion as well. With her heart full of warmth for the man who had become the center of her life, she walked down through the grass, pulled to the lake as if by another force, another love.

An eerie mist hovered over the lake, shrouding the old dock in a ghostly fog. Liza hesitated on the grass, torn for an instant. She could smell the fresh earth dug up by Joe Santori's backhoe, but she resisted the urge to walk to the graveside. Whoever had lain beside the lake for so many years was gone now. Instead, Liza turned her face toward the lake. She narrowed her eyes.

"Granddad?"

Squinting, Liza could see a tall figure standing stock-still at the end of the dock, and for an awful moment she believed she was seeing a ghost. But the set of his shoulders was unmistakable, and Liza realized Judson Ingalls had come back to the lodge. She started toward him, her sneakers making little sound on the boards of the dock as she hurried to her grandfather's side. She was happy for the first time in years, and she wanted to share her newfound joy.

"Granddad, is that you? I didn't hear your car! What are you doing here? You should have joined us for supper."

He did not answer, and Liza faltered suddenly, pleasure dying in her chest. Judson did not move, but stared at the lake as if hypnotized.

Somehow, Liza knew she had intruded.

Leaning forward, she caught a glimpse of his profile, saw the sheen of tears on her grandfather's otherwise stern face. "Oh, Granddad, what's wrong?" She took his arm tentatively between her hands. "Granddad?"

The ever-strong Judson Ingalls, a man of vision, a leader of men, a champion of industry in a town that needed men of his talent and ambition, heaved a painful, shuddering sigh and said, "Oh, Margaret, what have I done?"

"Granddad?"

Perhaps he did not even realize Liza was with him. He stood woodenly in the mist, staring out onto the still surface of the lake with tears etching his handsome face. Maybe he was remembering the past. Or perhaps he had begun to fear the future. It was impossible for Liza to guess.

Suddenly he bowed his head. Softly he said, "It's all my fault."

Liza released his arm and stepped back. In a matter of days, her life seemed to have become a shining world of happiness and hope. Cliff Forrester was more than she'd ever imagined possible for herself. And having him was within her grasp.

But could she be truly happy? Somehow a lurking danger seemed to hang over Timberlake. A mystery remained unsolved. And it was a mystery, Liza feared, that might shatter her family completely.

"Granddad, can you tell me? Can you tell me what happened?"

He shook his head. "I can't. I only wish it had never happened."

"WHERE SHALL WE GO?" Liza asked the next day, handing Cliff the picnic basket she'd prepared and folding the blanket over her arm.

"I know a place," Cliff replied.

He led her outside into the sunlight and up the hillside behind the lodge. Through the trees they walked hand in hand. Cliff's steps were silent, but a little unsteady. They pressed through the fronds of greenery together, inhaling the fragrance of the forest without speaking. Liza was uncharacteristically quiet, still a little unnerved by her disturbing encounter with her grandfather the night before.

At last Cliff found the grassy hilltop that overlooked the farmlands surrounding Tyler. He heard Liza's sharp intake of breath as she absorbed the panorama below.

"It's lovely," she whispered. "Like the top of the world."

"I like to come here."

"It's beautiful, but it's very lonely."

"Not anymore," said Cliff.

Liza smiled and bent to spread the blanket on the grass. She knelt a moment later and pulled Cliff down beside her. "I don't want you to be alone ever again. I'm going to stick by you, Forrester."

"For the first time in a decade, I feel like I can put my life back together."

"And I feel as though I'm just getting started with mine." Liza opened the picnic basket. "Are you hungry?"

"For you."

She laughed and allowed him to tumble her across the blanket. As the sky revolved overhead, Cliff pressed Liza into the earth, feeling the pulse of life all around them. The sun alone watched as he peeled off her clothes.

He took his time, undressing Liza and kissing her all over as each limb came to light. As last she lay naked beside him, and he brushed her hair with his fingers, murmuring love words and listening to her musical replies. Her kisses set fire to the blood that beat fast in his veins. Her blue eyes seemed to fill with sunlight as he touched her, and the summer breeze lifted the tips of her wisping hair to caress his face. She had never looked so much like an angel.

Though still fully dressed himself, Cliff stroked her slender body and admired each subtle curve and feminine muscle. Her skin was pale as pearl and sensitive to the slightest brush of his fingers. She smiled into his eyes, completely relaxed and trusting as he explored. In time, Cliff found himself unfastening the devil earring from her lobe and holding the small black object in the palm of his hand.

"Don't you like it?" Liza asked, watching the slight frown twitch between his brows.

"It seems like part of your personality," Cliff admitted. "The wicked part."

"Throw it away," she murmured with a smile. "I want to be good for you from now on."

But the earring was too much of Liza's persona—a part of her wicked side that just made her goodness much more lovable. Cliff tucked the little devil into a pocket, then buried his face in Liza's luscious body. He nuzzled her long throat first and nibbled her collarbone, and when her breasts became too tempting to ignore, he found her nipples in his mouth and let the scent of her fill his head like an aphrodisiac.

"I love you," he said, reveling in the ease with which she lay beside him, trust glowing in her face. "I love your body and your spirit. I love the things you do to me and the things you make me think about. I love the way you make me feel."

She gave him a languorously sexy smile. "I can't promise we'll always have a peaceful relationship."

"And I can't promise this relationship will last forever," Cliff said, knowing he must tell the truth. "I'm still a wreck of a man, Liza."

"A very nice wreck," she murmured, tracing imaginary lines on his face. "I love everything about you. Your body. Your humor. The way you look at me when I do something stupid...."

"You're not stupid."

"But I need a keeper sometimes." She tilted a solemn look up into his face. "Don't lose patience with me, Cliff. I need you as much as you need me. Maybe more. You'll heal eventually. But me—I'll always be a pain in the neck."

"That's only your own perception of yourself. I see a talented woman."

"But you should know," she said softly, "that I'm not as tough as I appear to be."

Cliff smiled. "I know. Underneath that tough-talking exterior of yours is a center like marshmallow—sweet and soft."

"I don't let most people see that part of me, you know."

"I'm glad you chose to share it with me."

She bit her lower lip gently. "I—I think you can give me what I need, Cliff. I'm an artist at heart."

"And you need freedom. I understand that. I want to give you whatever you need to flourish and grow and be great."

Liza tugged Cliff down to kiss her on the mouth. "In that case," she murmured, with a knowing smile, "we may last forever."

And now,
an exciting preview of

Bright Hopes
by Pat Warren

the second installment in the
Tyler series

Former Olympic track star Pam Casals arrives in Tyler to coach the high school football team. Phys. Ed. instructor Patrick Kelsey is first resentful, then delighted. Rumors fly about the identity of the body discovered at the lodge.

CHAPTER ONE

"A WOMAN FOOTBALL COACH?" Patrick Kelsey laughed out loud. "Come on, Miss Mackie. You've got to be kidding!"

Josephine Mackie sat back in her desk chair, adjusted her round, rimless glasses on her long, thin nose and looked up at the tall gym teacher. "Why, Patrick, don't tell me you're a chauvinist. Not with that superachiever mother of yours and three charming sisters."

Patrick ran a hand through his short, dark hair. That was the one drawback to growing up and living in a small town like Tyler, Wisconsin. Everyone knew you, your family and most of your business. Miss Mackie had been principal of Tyler High School when he'd been a freshman twenty years ago. She wasn't meddlesome so much as knowledgeable—about everyone. He flashed her what he hoped was a disarming smile.

"Not me. It's just that...well, these are guys, Miss Mackie. Young men, really. There'll be problems, like the locker room for instance. They're going to hate having a female around when they're changing."

"I don't imagine she'll shower with the boys, do you?"

Patrick reached for patience, never his strong suit. "How about the game itself? I never heard of a woman who knows football inside and out."

"Really? Ever hear of Phyllis George, to name one? I thought she did a highly commendable job, and on national television at that. And now there's Pam Casals. Have you read her credentials?"

Patrick felt his irritation grow as he paced her small office. "I know she was a runner in the Olympics."

"A little more than a mere runner. She won a silver medal when she was seventeen, then returned and won a gold medal at twenty-one."

"Okay, so she can run. But does she know football?"

Disappointed in his reaction, Miss Mackie nevertheless continued unruffled. "She went on to become an exhibition performer, earned a degree in Phys Ed, was head coach at a college in the east and an Olympic coach for a year in Seoul. For a young woman who's just turned thirty, I would call that an impressive list of accomplishments."

Stopping in front of her desk, Patrick braced his hands on the edge and leaned forward. "I repeat, does she know football?"

"I would think so, having coached football at the college level. Surely she can manage high school boys." Josephine Mackie felt her gaze soften as she studied Patrick's stubborn features. She thought she knew exactly why he was so upset, and chose her words carefully.

"I realize that when I asked you to join our coaching staff ten years ago, Patrick, your dream was to one day be football coach here at your alma mater. I believe you took on coaching basketball temporarily, thinking that when Dale McCormick retired, you'd shift over to football. But you've done such a tremendous job—guiding the basketball team from Class B to Class A status and giving us a championship season the past two years. We don't want to lose you in that capacity.''

Patrick's blue eyes were serious as he straightened. He figured that's what she'd thought, and the rest of the town, too. But they were wrong.

He'd been a star quarterback during his years at Tyler, and at the small Midwestern college he'd attended while earning his teaching degree. Then there'd been problems—serious problems—and he'd had to rearrange his dreams. When he'd returned to his hometown, he'd been pleased to be asked to coach basketball and assist Coach McCormick occasionally in football. Even now, what he really wanted was what was best for the Tyler High boys. But he knew that changing the thinking of a whole group of people who had their minds made up wasn't something he could do without revealing more than he felt comfortable doing.

''Miss Mackie, I'm perfectly happy coaching basketball. You're aware, I'm sure, that many of the boys on the football team also play basketball. I know these guys, and they aren't going to accept a woman coach.''

She narrowed her pale gray eyes and zeroed in. ''They will if you encourage them to accept her.''

Settling into the old wooden chair facing her desk, Patrick scowled. "I don't know if I can do that, in good conscience."

Propping her elbows on her desk, Miss Mackie leaned forward. "Patrick, I don't have to tell you that this town gets greatly involved in our school athletics. And the football team's been on a long losing streak. Dale McCormick was a good coach once, back when you were playing for him. But for some time now, he's been merely coasting along, counting the days to retirement."

"I agree," Patrick admitted.

"The school board felt we needed new blood, someone to get the boys all stirred up. Of our six applicants, Pam Casals is by far the most qualified. I've talked with her on the phone and she's personable and intelligent. I've hired her on a one-season trial basis and she's arriving next week. Won't you open your mind and give her a chance?"

Miss Mackie was a good administrator, her judgment usually on target, Patrick felt. This time, though, she was wrong. "I have nothing against this particular woman, you understand. I just don't feel any woman can coach football. It's too rugged a game, too physical." He picked up Pam Casals's file and flipped it open, where her picture was clipped to the inside front cover. "See how small she looks? She could get hurt out there."

Josephine Mackie sighed. Patrick Kelsey was an instructor who seldom gave her problems. He was making up for lost time today. Glancing at her watch, she stood, realizing she could debate this issue with Patrick all day and neither would bend. "It's only the first of August. We have several weeks before classes start. During that time, we'll be observing Pam and her training and practice methods closely."

Grabbing her purse, she walked around the desk. The school was deserted; she'd come in to get a head start on some paperwork and had been somewhat surprised when Patrick cornered her. "Why don't you study her file a bit more and then leave it on my desk? I have an appointment."

The gentleman in him had Patrick rising and smiling at the slim principal. "I don't mean to give you a hard time. But you know what these guys mean to me."

She smiled back at him. "They mean a great deal to me, too."

Patrick nodded. "You off to a board meeting?"

Josephine found herself blushing as she patted her sparse gray hair. "No, actually I have an appointment at the Hair Affair."

He grinned at her. "Big date tonight, Miss Mackie?"

Girlishly, she pursed her lips, turned from him and opened the door, choosing to ignore his question. "Please lock up when you leave," she said, then hurried down the hallway.

Chuckling, Patrick sat back down, wondering why Miss Mackie had never married. Too wrapped up in her job, he supposed. Few women could juggle work and children, and still maintain a happy marriage. His mother, Anna Kelsey, was about the only one he knew of. But she was one of a kind.

He opened the file again. Pam Casals did not look like his idea of a football coach. From the picture, she looked to be of medium height and quite slender, with the muscular legs of a runner. Her shoulder-length brown hair, wind-tossed, framed an oval face and her large brown eyes gazed directly into the camera. She didn't appear aggressive or arrogant, but there was a hint of determination to the angle of her chin. Still, if this woman could handle that rowdy group of high school boys, then he was the Easter Bunny, Patrick thought with a frown.

Quickly he read through her file. Like millions of people, he was always drawn to watch the Olympics. He'd heard countless stories of the dedication, perseverance, sacrifices and sheer guts it took to win a medal. She was a winner, he'd give her that. But could she make the Tyler boys into winners?

Doubtful, he thought, closing the file. He knew these boys better than anyone, certainly better than an outsider. And a woman at that. He would give her a chance, but he would remain in the picture. He'd keep an eye on her, check out her methods, look out for his boys. He'd mention to a couple of the guys—Ricky and B.J. and Moose—that he'd be interested in knowing what Coach Casals did during her training sessions.

It wasn't really spying, Patrick told himself as he placed Pam's file on the principal's desk. It was protecting.

Digging in the pocket of his jeans for his keys, Patrick left the office whistling.

A RAINBOW. Pam Casals glanced to the right as she drove along the country road, and smiled. Slowing, she pulled to a stop by a wooden fence bordering pastureland. Shifting into park, she slid out of her sporty white convertible and went to lean on the weathered fence.

It had been raining that morning when she set out from Chicago, a light drizzling summer rain. Wisconsin being north of Illinois, it wasn't quite as warm. Fall would be along all too soon.

The rainbow shimmered in the sky, where the last of the clouds were moving off. Rainbows were a sign of good luck—Pam remembered reading that somewhere. She certainly hoped so. It was time for a bit of luck.

On an impulse, she made a wish. "I wish that I might find happiness in Tyler," she said aloud.

A small herd of cows grazing nearby, brown shapes on a field of still-damp green grass, didn't even glance her way. She breathed in deeply, air so fresh it almost hurt to inhale. No automobile fumes, no pollution or even smoke. On the drive she'd passed dairy farms, many with large wooden barns, as well as cornfields, orchards and several horse farms. She'd taken the scenic route instead of the highway, enjoying the twisting rural roads and the lakes tucked in among rolling green hills. The clean country atmosphere was a welcome change from the city she'd left behind.

She'd left a lot of things behind, or so she hoped. Pain and confusion and doubt. Frustration and anger and broken dreams. And a shattered love affair. A few good things, too, like her father, Julian Casals, still living in the family home in a suburb of Chicago. And her two married brothers, Don and Ramon, who'd taught her so much more than football.

Pam swung around, leaning her elbows on the fence. She was only a short distance from Tyler, and she hoped there were more two-lane roads like this one around. It was a perfect place to run—smooth blacktop, very little traffic. And run she must, while she could. For her health and her mental well-being and the sheer, physical pleasure of it.

A low-throated bark drew her attention to her car, and she grinned. Her old, white, long-haired English sheepdog sat in the back seat, his head cocked in her direction, his pink tongue hanging low. "All right, Samson," she said, slipping behind the wheel again. "I know you're impatient to get going." With another glance at the rainbow, Pam shifted into drive. "I'm anxious to check out our new home, too."

Flipping on the radio as she pulled away, she heard Willie Nelson's unmistakable voice ring out. "On the road again..."

Pam glanced back at Samson, whose ears were blowing in the breeze. "That's us, pal. On the road again." Laughing for no apparent reason except a sudden happy sense of anticipation, she headed for Tyler.

IT WAS EXACTLY two o'clock when she arrived in the town. There was a town square—an open grassy area with huge old oak trees and well-maintained flower beds. The downtown business section consisted of two-story brick buildings, predictably lining Main

Street. The small-town atmosphere pleased Pam as she pulled up in front of the post office. High on its pole, the flag rippled in the wind, but the building had a Saturday-afternoon-deserted look. Stretching, she got out of the car.

According to the map Rosemary Dusold had sent her, she was only a couple of blocks from her friend's house. But there was no time like the present to get oriented. Across the way, she spotted the Tyler library and the brick town hall. On the opposite corner was a beauty shop, the sign heralding it as the Hair Affair. Cute, Pam thought.

Around a corner, she saw a sign proclaiming Marge's Diner. She patted Samson's shaggy head. "I'll be right back, fella," she said as she headed for the square.

A bank on another corner featured a tower clock. The usual array of grocery store, drugstore, cleaners and so on filled out that side of the block. She walked on.

A couple of older ladies seated on a park bench smiled up at Pam as she approached, giving her a feeling of friendly welcome. A handful of youngsters were playing tag on the far side. In the center of the green, she spotted several adults involved in a loosely organized game of touch football. Her interest heightened, Pam stepped closer.

Watching took her back in time to her early teens, when she and her father and two brothers would spend many an autumn afternoon tossing the pigskin. Soon, playing catch hadn't been enough for Pam, so she'd organized a group of neighbors and divided them into two teams. Then she'd mapped out strategies for her

side, trying to make up for her size by outwitting the
opponents. Much to her brothers' surprise, her ma-
neuvers worked more often than they failed. Their respect had spurred her on to try even harder.

She'd already been running then, her dreams fo-
cusing on the future Olympics. But her love of football had never died. She'd learned the game first by
playing, then by watching the college teams on television, as well as the pros. Fun times, Pam thought.
Times that had bonded their small family closer after
the devastation of her mother's early death. Shoving
her hands into the pockets of her white slacks, she
leaned against a tree.

There was one big guy, a solid wall of muscle, who
wasn't much on speed but nearly impossible to get past
due to his size. She noticed a woman about her age
with dark hair, a tall, rugged outdoor-type man with
black curly hair and, to Pam's surprise, her friend and
new roommate, Rosemary Dusold, leaping high to
catch a pass, her blond ponytail bobbing. Smiling,
Pam stepped out of the shade, hoping Rosemary
would notice her.

As she stood on the edge of the green, she saw a wild
throw coming her way. No player was out this far.
Forgetting herself, she ran a few steps, jumped up and
caught the ball. Acting instinctively, Pam began to run
toward the makeshift goal line, hotly pursued by two
or three players she heard running behind her.

Exhilarated, the ball tucked close to her body, she
picked up speed. *Almost there,* she thought. Then she
felt the hit. Strong arms settled around her waist,
sliding lower to her knees, taking her down. Her tack-

ler rolled, cushioning the fall with his lean, hard body, letting her land on him rather than on the unforgiving ground.

"Touchdown!" called out a voice from behind as thundering feet arrived.

"She fell short," yelled a dissident.

Still clutching the ball, Pam eased from the grip that held her and scrambled to her feet. Her opponent rose, too, and she found herself looking up into the bluest eyes she'd ever seen. Unexpectedly, her heart missed a beat and she found herself swallowing on a dry throat.

He was several inches over six feet, with curly black hair falling onto a lean face etched with laugh lines at the corners of those incredible eyes. He smiled then, his features softening as he reached out to brush leaves and grass from her shoulder. Pam's reaction to his light touch was on a parallel with the way she'd felt when her gaze had locked with his. Dizzying. She took a step backward.

"I hope I didn't hurt you," he said. She was lovely, with warm brown eyes and skin the color of a pale peach. Who was she? Patrick wondered.

"No, I'm fine."

She had on baggy white slacks and a comfortably faded green-and-white Jets football jersey with the number 12 on the back. "I see you're a Joe Namath fan."

"I was." She couldn't seem to stop staring into his eyes.

Strangers in Tyler—especially strangers who joined in impromptu games—were uncommon. There was something familiar about her, Patrick thought, but he couldn't put his finger on what it was. "That was a great catch."

"Thanks," Pam said, giving him the football.

"I'm Patrick Kelsey." He offered his hand.

Politely she slid her own hand into his grip, feeling the calluses on his roughened skin—and the warmth. "Hello," she replied. Before she could say more, Rosemary came alongside.

"Pam," Rosemary greeted her. "Glad you're here at last."

Pam withdrew her hand and turned to smile at her friend. "Me, too."

"Hey, everyone," Rosemary went on, "this is Pam Casals, a friend of mine from Chicago who's come to stay with me for a while. Pam, this is Kathleen Kelsey and Terry Williams and Al Broderick. The big guy's Brick Bauer. Watch out for him—he's going to be our next police chief. That's Nick over there and you've already met Patrick."

Patrick frowned. "You're Pam Casals?"

As Pam nodded, Rosemary chimed in again. "She's going to be working at Tyler High with you, Patrick. Pam's the new football coach."

"So I've heard. Welcome to Tyler."

Though his words were welcoming, his tone had cooled considerably. Pam couldn't help wondering why. "Thanks. Are you one of the teachers?"

"Gym teacher. Also basketball coach." Glancing at his watch, he tossed the ball to Rosemary. "Sorry to break this up, but I've got to run. See you all later."

"Nice to meet you, Patrick," Pam called to his retreating back.

"Yeah, you, too," he said over his shoulder.

"Don't let Patrick worry you," Kathleen said as she smiled at Pam. "He's my brother and I know he's a little moody, but he's a great guy. Glad you're with us, Pam."

"Thanks," Pam said quietly. So she would have the pleasure of working with the moody Patrick Kelsey. Terrific.

Calling their goodbyes, the others left to go their separate ways. Rosemary fell into step with Pam. "Come on. My place is only a couple of blocks from here," she said. Impulsively, she slid an arm around Pam's shoulders and squeezed. "I think you're going to like Tyler."

Pam heard the squeal of tires and looked toward Main Street as Patrick's truck zoomed out of sight. "I hope so," she answered.

THE WHITE FRAME HOUSE was on Morgan Street, two stories high with a wrap-around porch and green shuttered windows. There was a Victorian elegance to the old building, Pam thought as she parked her car in the side drive. She watched Rosemary hurry out of the car. Five foot-eight, Rosemary was bigger than Pam and incredibly strong, yet she moved with a style and grace that Pam envied.

"You want to put old slobbering Samson in the backyard for now?" Rosemary asked with an affectionate pat on the dog's head.

Pam nodded, slipped on the dog's leash and opened the car door. Settling Samson inside the fenced enclosure, she returned to the front and climbed the wooden steps with Rosemary. A swing, painted red, hung from two chains at the far end of the porch. Very inviting, she thought.

"About five years ago," Rosemary said, opening the screen door for her, "after the owner died, the heirs renovated the house, turning it into four apartments. They're all very roomy and comfortable. Mrs. Tibbs, a sweet but somewhat nosy widow, lives on the right, a young married couple upstairs on one side and a piano teacher across the hall from them. Mine's this one on the lower left." She paused in the neat hallway, glancing at mail spread on a small mahogany table. "Nothing for me." Pulling out a key, she unlocked the door.

Charming was the word, Pam thought as she looked about. A rich carved mantle above a huge stone fireplace, highly polished floors with gently faded area rugs in floral designs, and furniture you could no longer buy. Running a hand along an overstuffed rose couch, Pam smiled. "Are these your things?"

"No, not a single piece. I arrived with only my clothes." Rosemary went through the arch into the dining room and past into the spacious kitchen. "It even came with dishes and pots. Don't you just love it?"

Strolling past the drop-leaf table and an antique Singer sewing machine, Pam agreed. "Who owns this place now?"

Rosemary poured lemonade into two glasses tinted pale gold. "I don't know. Relatives of one of the original families of Tyler, I think. When you get to meeting people around here, you'll learn that half the town's related in some way to the other half." Handing Pam her drink, she tilted up her own glass and drank thirstily.

Sipping, Pam wandered back into the living room. Lace curtains billowed at the front bay window, dancing in a lively late-afternoon breeze. A large maple tree just outside shaded the whole front yard. She saw a squirrel with bulging cheeks scamper busily up into thick limbs and get lost in the leafy top. Turning, she sat down on the comfortably sagging sofa with starched doilies pinned to each armrest and sighed.

"It's like time has stood still in this house. I feel like I walked into a fifties movie."

Rosemary flung herself into the chair opposite Pam. "Maybe the forties, even. I was lucky to find this apartment."

"Are you sure you don't mind my moving in with you?" Pam asked with a worried look.

"I told you back in Chicago that I'd love the company. There're two large bedrooms and a big bath with this marvelous claw-footed tub. And I'm not even here much, what with working at Tyler General Hospital, my commitment to the Davis Rehab Center in Chicago and my backpacking trips."

"I'll pay half the rent, of course. I can't believe how low it is compared to Chicago apartments."

"Isn't it great?" Rosemary finished her drink and set the glass aside. "So tell me, how are you feeling?"

"Fine."

"Honestly? No pain, no numbness, no tingling. Don't lie to me now. I'm your therapist, remember."

"I remember. I truly feel great. No symptoms at all. I think I'm solidly in remission."

"Good." Rosemary nodded. "If you have any problems—I mean *any*—let me know. Therapy works best if we catch the problem early. You know how sneaky MS is. One day you notice a little blurry vision, next day your big toe goes numb and the third day you try to stand and you can't feel anything from the knees down."

Pam stared into the cloudy remains of her drink. "I know. Believe me, I don't want that happening. I'll tell you at the first sign."

"This job at the school, do you think you'll have a lot of stress with it? Stress can aggravate your condition, you know."

Pam shrugged. "No more than anyone else starting in a new position in a new town." She looked up, remembering the man who'd tackled her, the warm way he'd looked at her, then the way his eyes had frosted over when he learned who she was. "What do you know about Patrick Kelsey?"

Rosemary swung both legs over the arm of the easy chair, scrunching down comfortably. "His family goes way back. He's a descendant of one of the first families. His parents own and operate Kelsey Boardinghouse on Gunther Street not far from here. Plus his father works at the Ingalls plant and his mother is receptionist for Dr. Phelps. Anna's real personable. I want you to meet George Phelps, too. He's a good man in case you need a doctor."

This wasn't what Pam wanted to hear. "Why would Patrick have turned so moody back there in the square, when before he heard my name, he was smiling?"

"Maybe he wanted the job you got. He teaches gym and coaches varsity basketball. He's some kind of hero around here, dating back to his high school football days."

"Sounds like the people of Tyler take high school sports seriously—and have long memories."

"You got that right. Fierce loyalty around here. They give newcomers a hearty welcome, then sit back and wait for them to prove themselves. They accepted me, so don't worry."

"But you've been here three years. It seems I was here three minutes and managed to offend one of their favorite sons."

"Patrick will come around. He's really a great guy, always helping people, very family-oriented. I've often wondered why he's never married." Rosemary eyed Pam as she slipped out of her running shoes. "Maybe he's been waiting for the right woman to come along."

Pam shook her head. "Don't look at me. Besides, he seems a bit touchy. If he's lived here all his life, it can't be my fault I got the job and he didn't. Or is it a woman coach he's against, possibly?"

"I don't know. I wouldn't worry about it. Don't add to your own stress level."

"Good idea." Pam stretched and yawned. "I should unpack, go get some groceries and turn in early tonight. I want to look around tomorrow, and Monday morning I meet with the principal."

"Oh, she's nice. Everyone likes Miss Mackie. And she'll understand about your limitations with MS."

Pam leaned forward, her eyes serious. "I don't plan to tell Miss Mackie or anyone else that I have multiple sclerosis. And I don't want you to say anything, either."

Slowly, Rosemary raised a questioning brow. "Do you think that's wise?"

"I don't know. I do know I need to prove myself, and I can't do that if everyone's waiting for me to fall over from fatigue or show up one day in a wheelchair."

"But if they know, they can—"

"No. Please, Rosemary." She had to make her friend see. "This is my life and my decision. When we first started working out together at the rehab center, I was going through the aftermath of depression, really feeling sorry for myself. Well, I've spent all the time doing that that I plan to. You're the one who challenged me to learn to live with MS, and I'm honestly trying to. I realize that remissions are temporary, but I feel good and I don't want constant reminders that I could slip back again any day."

"Remission periods can last for months, even years."

"I'm hopeful that's the case with me. But I want no quarter given because I've got a problem here. I want to earn their respect, not their pity. Listen as my friend, Rosemary, not my therapist, and try to understand."

Gracefully Rosemary untangled herself from the chair and walked over to Pam, hugging her as she sat down on the couch. "I do understand. I just don't want to see you hurt. Over the past two years, I've grown to care about you a lot."

Pam blinked back a quick rush of emotion. "Me, too. I just have to do this my way, okay?"

"Sure." Rosemary stood. "Now, let me get your bag, so you can unpack while I start dinner. You can shop tomorrow. Tonight, I'm cooking my specialty. Chicken chow mein."

"Sounds great." Pam searched for her keys. "I hope you'll make enough so Samson can have dinner, too. He loves Chinese."

"Not dog food?"

Pam grinned at her friend's surprised look. "He never touches the stuff. And he likes a wedge of lemon in his water dish."

"Of course he does." Rosemary smiled at her friend. "I'm really glad you're here." Glancing down, she pointed. "Grass stains. I hope they come out of your slacks."

Pam considered the green stain on her pants. "Think I could get Patrick Kelsey to clean them for me?"

"You really should get acquainted with him. He knows the boys at Tyler High better than anyone else. They trust him."

Pam tossed her keys in the air and caught them in her fist. "Then I guess it'll be my job to get them to trust me. Why haven't you gotten to know him better, since you think he's so swell?''

Rosemary shook her head. ''I've been divorced five years and I intend to stay that way. Once burned is twice shy.'' She sobered, studying Pam's face. ''Do you ever hear from Bob?''

''No, never. It's best this way, really. When something's over, it should stay over.''

''Amen,'' Rosemary agreed.